CW01642646

# DISCOVERY

DAVID EVANS

*"With this third book, David Evans delivers another captivating instalment in the Tendring Series. It showcases his signature blend of meticulous research and vivid storytelling - with a dash of humour.*
*In this book, we are reunited with DS Cyril Clayton and DI Dick Barton. The detectives are entangled in two investigations from WW2 to the seventies and share chilling similarities. As always, Evans keeps us on our toes with unexpected twists that make it hard to put the book down.*
*A recommended read."*
Glynis Peters, International Best Selling Author

*"Another wonderful read from David Evans. With believable characters, seamless plotting and effortless time shifts, the reader is easily drawn in, and as the story unfolds we discover some surprising secrets. Highly recommended.*
Julie-Ann Corrigan, Thriller Writer

**ORCHARD**
**VIEW**
**PUBLICATIONS**



ISBN-13: 978 1 9996106 8 5

## ABOUT THE AUTHOR

Born and brought up in and around Edinburgh, David Evans graduated from Manchester University and had a successful career as a professional in the construction industry before turning to crime … fiction that is and writing thereof.

*DISCOVERY* is the third novel in The Tendring Series, set around north Essex in the late 1970s. The second, DISTRESSED, was published in 2021 and the first, *DISPOSAL,* was published in 2018.

His Internationally Best Selling Wakefield Series is also available and consists of:
*TROPHIES,* the first in the series
*TORMENT*, the second, was shortlisted in 2013 for the CWA Debut Dagger Award.
*TALISMAN* is the third
*TAINTED* is book four
All are available in ebook and paperback formats.

Find out more by visiting David's website at
www.davidevanswriter.co.uk
or follow him on Facebook at
www.facebook.com/davidevanswriter
and Twitter @DavidEwriter

# ACKNOWLEDGMENTS

I have been privileged to meet some amazing people, without whose help, encouragement, support and above all friendship got me through some occasions when it would have been easier to walk away and do something else with my time.

First and foremost, I have to say a huge thank-you to Sally Spedding who was the first in the publishing industry to take my writing seriously. I owe her a great debt for all her continued support and encouragement.

I am also fortunate to have a great little band of writing friends and I would like to thank Sarah Wagstaff, Jan Beresford, Julie-Ann Corrigan, Manda Hughes, Glynis Smy and Linda Farrow, all of whom are talented writers in their own right and have made some significant contributions.

I am deeply grateful for the input of Colin Steele, ex-Detective Superintendent of the Essex Murder Squad and Steve Eastwood, ex-DCI of the City of London Police who began his career in Clacton. Also Tom Harper, ex-Principal Crime Scene Coordinator for the Kent & Essex Serious Crime Directorate. Both have given their time and guidance generously. Any residual errors here, are all mine.

Finally, a huge thank-you to the various bloggers and readers who have supported both of my crime series over the past few years. Without readers, there would be no reason to write.

*For Jude,*
*I couldn't have done this without you*

# DISCOVERY

**David Evans**

# 1

## Clacton-on-Sea
## Thursday 30th January 1947

"You're not going out in this, are you?" Vera asked.

"It's stopped now." Cecil was peering out of the window. He pulled the curtain to and turned to face his wife. "Besides, Maisie's tetchy. She needs a walk."

Vera looked down at the big black Labrador who had just given one thump of her tail and risen to her feet, looking expectantly at her master. "But it's been snowing all day and it's gone nine," she persisted. "They said on the radio there's no let-up in sight."

"She likes it, Vera." Cecil headed for the hall. "Just as well she's not a Dachshund." He paused at the doorway and smiled. "We'll not be long."

Despite the blazing coal fire in the grate, Maisie followed Cecil out into the hallway, eager to get outside. She waited patiently, nose against the door while her master pulled on his boots. Cecil wrapped a scarf around his neck, thrust himself into a heavy overcoat and plunged his hands into a pair of woollen gloves. Then he took down his homburg from the shelf, placed it carefully on his head and checked himself in the mirror, subconsciously emulating Anthony Eden. Finally, he reached for the lead.

Once outside, the dog pushed her nose into the three inches of fresh snow that had fallen that afternoon, licked her lips and pulled on the lead, keen to reach the first lamp post. She sniffed for any fresh activity then squatted, turning the patch of white snow into a light yellow. There was a magical atmosphere outside, now that the snow had actually stopped falling. The sky had started to clear and moonlight reflected from the white covering which also enhanced the light from the dim street lamps.

About ten minutes later, the pair found themselves down on the beach, close by the pier. The moon had disappeared behind the next bank of snow-laden cloud. The tide was out and snow was lying on the sand where it had fallen since high-tide. This was looking bad, Cecil thought. It had been snowing every day for over a week, and if what Vera had said was correct, there really was no end to it in the forecasts, things would become really serious. He was glad he didn't have to travel into London any more, having retired last year. God alone knew what the trains would be like trying to cope with this.

Maisie was off the lead and thoroughly enjoying herself. Cecil was lost in his thoughts when the dog's barking suddenly alerted him to something that had aroused her interest. She had disappeared below the pier and it was difficult to make out the black dog in the darkness below the structure. "Maisie! Maisie! Come here!" he shouted to no avail.

He began to make his way over to where the dog was still barking excitedly and could just make out a shape on the sand. His first thoughts, or more to the point, fears, were that she had discovered some unexploded ordnance brought in on the last tide. There had been some instances of this since the end of the war. Finally, he caught up with Maisie and peered at what had caused her to fuss. His eyes were still adjusting to the low light level when he stopped in his tracks and took in the sight before him. The dog crept slowly back as he carefully approached what he thought was a bundle of rags that had been washed up onto the shore. As he got nearer, he saw the exposed leg on the far side. That's it, he thought, someone's dumped a shop dummy. He looked up to where the head was turned away from him and thought the hair was quite realistic for a mannequin. But when he walked round to the other side he finally saw her. He covered his mouth with his hand. The young female face stared up at him with sightless eyes.

# 2

## Clacton-on-Sea
## Thursday 2nd February 1978

The fever had begun to abate. It had started about five days before; flu, the doctor had diagnosed. It had begun with Cyril beginning to feel his joints ache. He'd put his thumb and forefinger to his eyes and they'd felt tender. His hands and feet had gone cold. An intermittent cough developed and a dull headache had formed. Once he'd taken himself off to bed, the odd sneeze woke him up. He'd called the doctor in the following day when he realised he wasn't shaking the symptoms off. Bed rest and aspirin or paracetamol was the answer; that and plenty to drink.

He turned over in bed to look at the clock; just gone a quarter-past-five. The bedside lamp was lit and the curtains were pulled. It seemed dark outside, so was it early morning or afternoon? He wasn't sure. Pulling the bedclothes to one side, he swung his legs over the side of the bed and sat up. His head was thudding dully but he wasn't feeling as woozy as he had done previously. Risking it, he got to his feet and walked over to the window, catching his image in the dressing table mirror. God, he looked dreadful; four days growth on his face threatening to join forces with the thin moustache he'd had since his war-time RAF days. Reaching beyond, he put his hand on the curtain, pulled it slightly to one side and looked out. Still a bit of light in the heavily overcast sky, so it must be afternoon. Thursday, if he wasn't mistaken. It was Saturday when he'd begun to feel ill and the days since had come and gone in a bit of a blur.

As a Detective Sergeant, part of the CID team based in Clacton-on-Sea, Cyril Claydon's recent workload had not been particularly heavy, and so he felt his absence shouldn't have too much of a detrimental effect on his colleagues. At various points over the past few days, he thought of his late wife, Maureen. She'd passed away in this very bed almost five years ago now, following a long fight against cancer. His sweating peaked whenever the thought struck him that he too might die alone, in the same bed. At times, he'd turned over to reach for her only to find an empty space.

About eighteen months ago, he was expecting to retire from the force as a uniformed sergeant. All that changed when he witnessed a light aircraft crashing into the sea at Clacton. That was at the end of the long hot summer of '76, a distant memory now. With that, he was drawn into a temporary role in CID where he had to work alongside DI Barton, a man with totally different attitudes to policing from his own. During that investigation, he realised that, at the age of forty-nine, he still had something to offer and the prospect of retirement wasn't appealing. The temporary role became permanent.

It was also at this point that his friendship with Cathy Rogers, a typist at the town's Jackson Road Police Station, had begun. He was reticent at first but they'd grown close over time. Since he'd fallen ill, she had called in to check on him several times, fetched him water and some Panadol which she thought would help. She'd invited him to come and stay with her but he'd declined. No point putting her and her sixteen-year-old son, Simon, at risk of catching anything.

His next-door neighbour, Doris, had also appeared a few times, he seemed to remember, trying to encourage him to eat. That had been the last thing on his mind earlier, although he thought he might be able to manage something small now.

Pulling the curtains together again, he made his way gingerly to the bathroom. Flushing the toilet and washing his hands, he heard the key in the lock of his front door and a greeting of, "Hello," from downstairs. It was Doris.

He hurried back to the bedroom, climbed into bed and waited for his neighbour to appear.

"Hello, Cyril. Are you awake?" she asked as she climbed the stairs.

"In here, Doris," he replied.

A few seconds later, her head bobbed round the bedroom door. "How are you feeling?"

"A bit better, thanks."

She took a step into the room and studied him from the doorway. "That's good. You certainly look a little better."

"I must have been pretty awful then."

She gave a laugh. "I brought you my morning paper." She walked forward and held out a copy of that day's Daily Mail that had been tucked under her arm. "I thought you might be interested in a read."

"Thanks," he said, taking hold of it.

"Now can I get you anything? Something to eat? A hot drink?"

"You know what," Cyril said, "I think I'll come down to the kitchen."

"That's good," she said. "I'll put the kettle on."

Doris had lived next door ever since he and Maureen had moved in. Already widowed, having lost her husband, Howard, at the end of the war in 1945, Doris was the best neighbour they could have wished for. She had spent many hours with Maureen as his wife grew weaker. This had allowed Cyril to continue working, which is what Maureen had insisted he do. Doris was seventy-seven now, but still fairly active. After Maureen died, she'd looked after his Golden Labrador, Charlie, from time to time, fed him when Cyril had to work late and generally loved him as if he belonged to her. She used to tell her friends that she looked after a police dog. She was with Charlie when the dog died last year and was as distressed as Cyril was.

Ten minutes later, Cyril, in a dressing gown with the cord pulled around him, sat at the kitchen table, Doris sitting opposite, both with a mug of tea. She'd also made him some buttered toast, which is exactly what he fancied.

"Is it okay for you?" she asked.

"Thanks, Doris. My throat's still a bit sore but I was feeling peckish." He opened out the newspaper. "Appreciate this too."

"You can have it, I've read it."

"I need to catch up as the past few days seem to have passed me by. Have I missed anything interesting?"

"That series of murders up in Yorkshire is continuing. They found another body in Huddersfield I think it was, yesterday, I believe."

"Really? All connected? I wonder how many that is?"

"Seems to be the same man," she said. "I think they said this is number seven now. Page four, if I remember correctly."

He turned the page and began to read.

"This is incredible," Cyril said, his toast held out in one hand as he read, absorbed in the latest horrific news.

"Apparently they've dubbed him *The Yorkshire Ripper*." Doris said before taking a sip of her tea.

He looked over at his neighbour. "Do you know," he said, "I've always reckoned that, at any one time in this country, there are at least two, maybe three serial killers out there." He bit into his toast and washed it down with a mouthful of tea before turning his attention back to the article.

Doris stared off into the distance. "I often wonder what happened to Elsie Smart."

He stopped reading and looked up from the newspaper. "Who's Elsie Smart?"

"Oh a tragic young girl. She was found murdered under the pier in Clacton in ... ooh, it must have been 1947." Doris looked back at Cyril. "They never found anyone for it."

"I don't remember anything about that. Then again, it was before I met Maureen. We only moved here in 1950."

"Oh, it was quite a sensation. There were all sorts of rumours but then it all seemed to fizzle out."

"So it's still unsolved?"

"As far as I know."

"Mind you," Cyril considered, "that's over thirty years ago. Whoever did it is probably dead."

"Not necessarily. There were some who thought she had a boyfriend at the time. If he was her age, he would probably still be alive."

"How did she die?"

"I'm not too sure on that, to be honest."

Cyril turned the paper over and began to read the back page. He quickly scanned the latest football news, West Brom's 3-2 win over Manchester United and the reports that John Toshack had taken the manager's job at Swansea were the leads.

"Will Cathy be round later?" Doris asked.

He folded up the newspaper. "I don't know. I can't remember what she said last."

"She was concerned for you."

"I know." He yawned. "Oh, I'm sorry ..."

Doris stood up. "No need to apologise," she said. "You get back to bed. It's just good to see you eat something."

"Thanks, I appreciate that. I feel exhausted; I think I'll go back up."

In bed once more, Cyril's mind turned over the brief conversation he'd had with his neighbour. He hated the thought of some unresolved murder case, the uncertainty for the family of not knowing what had happened to their nearest and dearest. Were the poor girl's parents still alive? Did she have any siblings? As he drifted in and out of sleep once again, all this melded into the images the newspaper report of the latest Yorkshire Ripper victim had seared into his mind. The victim running from her attacker, fear tearing through her, the arm poised to strike, and what was in the hand? Something heavy, he was sure. He turned sharply away to avoid the blow and then …

Cyril became aware of someone in the room and slowly opened his eyes to see a smiling Cathy looking at him.

"Now then, Rip van," she said. "You seem a bit restless."

"Oh God," he said, "I just had a … oh never mind." He felt drenched in sweat.

"I brought you some tasty soup. I heard you were getting your appetite back."

Cyril wiped his forehead with the sleeve of his pyjamas. "I had something earlier."

Cathy smiled at him. "I know. Doris phoned."

"You two should work for the Intelligence Services."

"She said you were looking better."

"And what do you think?"

She frowned, wobbled her head from side to side as she considered her answer before smiling again. "I can see some improvement."

He rubbed his face with both hands. "I could do with a shave."

"Never mind that for now. Come downstairs and I'll heat up your soup. And while you're having that, I'll change your bedding and get you some new pyjamas out. Do you want me to run you a bath?"

"I suppose you better had," he said. "No point putting a sweaty body back in a clean bed."

Ten minutes later, Cathy placed a bowl of hearty soup in front of Cyril at the kitchen table. "Right," she said, "While you have that, I'll sort out your room."

As he ate the soup, he heard the sounds from upstairs of Cathy walking around then water running in the bath.

He was still making progress with the soup when she reappeared.

"Bath's ready," she said.

He put his spoon down. "Listen Cathy, do you remember a murder case from just after the war in Clacton? A young woman by the name of Elsie Smart."

Cathy furrowed her brows. “Not off hand but the name rings a slight bell. Why?”

“Oh just Doris mentioned it. I’d never heard about it but, there again, it was before my time in Clacton.”

“Me too. George and I didn’t come here until 1964.” Cathy was referring to her ex-husband whom she’d divorced some eight years ago.

“Doris reckons it’s still unsolved.” He took a final spoonful of soup before asking, “Can you do me a favour tomorrow?”

“Sure, what is it?”

“Can you have a rummage around in the archives and see if you can dig out any files on the case?”

“Okay. But you get into that bath before the water goes cold.”

# 3
## Friday 3rd February 1978

Cyril had had quite a good war, he considered, especially in comparison to others. He'd joined the RAF and was trained as a mechanic as part of the squadron ground crew. He suffered nightmares from time to time, but in the past year or so, they had virtually disappeared. However, with the flu, he seemed to recall one or two instances over the past week. Doris knew of them over the years but he wasn't sure how much Cathy was aware of.

He'd had his first good night's sleep since coming down with the flu, waking with a clearer head and something like a normal temperature. He'd enjoyed the bath Cathy had run for him last night and certainly felt more comfortable in the clean sheets and pyjamas she'd provided for him. Last night's soup was tasty too. A glance at the clock told him he must have slept well as it was five to nine.

A visit to the bathroom and, after a wash and shave, he felt like some breakfast. But first he'd get dressed; he'd been in pyjamas constantly since Saturday night. Buttoning up his shirt he decided he'd leave a tie alone for now but, having looked outside, a sweater was a must.

Downstairs, he picked up the post from behind the front door and took it to the kitchen table where the accumulation for the week had been placed by Doris and Cathy. A sift through showed nothing requiring immediate attention, so his focus shifted to food.

About to get himself outside of two rashers of bacon, a fried egg and a sliced tomato he'd fried in the pan, the sound of a key in the lock and the front door opening interrupted him. “Morning, Doris,” he greeted from the kitchen.

“Oh, you’re up and about?” his neighbour replied. “I just thought I’d check and see how you were, but I’ll not disturb you.”

“Don’t be daft,” he said, “Come in and have a cup of tea. I’ve made a pot.”

“Well, if you don’t mind.” She came into the kitchen and made her way to the side of the sink and poured herself a cup from the pot. “That smells good,” she said as she added some milk. “You obviously feel better if your appetite’s back.”

“I think so,” he said, taking a sip of tea. “Sit yourself down.”

Doris sat at the table opposite him. “I hope you’re not thinking of going back to work too soon,” she said.

“I’ll give the station a call, but I don’t think there’s anything too pressing, otherwise they’d have rung me.”

“What about that DI of yours, Barton? Hasn’t he called you?”

“Cathy’s kept him up to speed.” He paused to take a mouthful of his breakfast. “I thought I’d have a walk down to the allotment, just to see how I feel.”

“Well just you be careful. You don’t want to overdo it and end up back in bed again.”

“No mum,” he said, a broad smile on his face. After a drink of his tea, he put his knife and fork down on the plate and looked over at his neighbour. “That story you mentioned last night …”

“What was that?”

“That murder back in 1947.”

“Oh, poor young Elsie Smart, you mean?”

“That’s it. What can you remember about it?”

Doris put her cup back in its saucer as she considered. “I seem to remember it was in the middle of the worst winter we’d ever had. I know they talk about ‘62/'63 but the early months of 1947 were atrocious.”

"You're right. It was snow for weeks. I was still in the RAF then, up in Norfolk and we were out every day helping to keep the roads clear."

"I seem to remember she worked in a shop on Pier Avenue. Some man walking his dog on the beach found her under the pier itself. The family were devastated. There was some talk of a boyfriend but I don't think they got anywhere with that."

Cyril gave the matter some thought. "So was the snow bad here? Sometimes the coast fares better."

"Oh, no, it was a foot deep at times. I can't remember exactly what it was like when she was found."

"I'm only thinking of footprints but … no, never mind."

"So, piqued your interest then, has it, Cyril?" She drained her tea cup.

"Oh, it's interesting." He rose to take his empty plate to the sink.

"I thought it might be." She gave a chuckle. "Anyway, I'il let you get on. I'm glad you're feeling better." She made her way to the door.

"Thanks Doris," he said before the front door closed behind her.

Cyril had taken the allotment on eight years ago now. It had provided some lovely produce over the years, mostly vegetables. As he walked towards the fenced off land, his thoughts drifted back to happy times, walking with Charlie, his old Golden Labrador. The dog was always ready for a stroll down here, especially if Cyril had bought some fish and chips. Charlie loved it when Cyril broke off a piece of batter from the fish and one or two chips. On sunny evenings, he would lie contented at Cyril's feet as he sat on his bench smoking his pipe. Other times, he'd just sit and watch as Cyril dug or hoed or raked.

When he reached the gate into the allotments, Cyril spotted old Frank Scowcroft sitting on the wooden bench outside his potting shed, two plots away from his own. "Now then Frank," Cyril greeted.

"Hello Cyril," the old man answered. "Haven't seen you down here for a bit."

"Not felt like it, Frank." Cyril joined the man and sat down beside him on his bench. "Just getting over a bit of flu at the moment."

"Can be a killer that, you know." Frank took out his tobacco pouch and a pipe from his pockets.

"Never usually get it but this year …"

Frank held out his pouch but Cyril put up a hand.

"Thanks Frank, but I couldn't at the moment. Still feel a bit rough, but you go ahead."

Frank packed some tobacco into his pipe bowl and lit up.

After a few seconds, Cyril spoke. "Wonder what sort of summer we'll have?"

"Nowhere near as warm as last year, Cyril," the old man responded. "The birds had all the berries early on and the snowdrops were late." A cloud of smoke partly obscured his face. "I reckon it'll be wet this year."

"You must have seen a few?"

Frank puffed out and smiled. "Years, you mean?"

Cyril gave a laugh. "Aye. Do you remember that bad winter?" he went on. "Not '63, but before that, 1947?"

"I certainly do," Frank said. "That was a hard one. Snowed every day for over two months." He looked at Cyril. "Flooded badly when it all melted but not a bad summer afterwards though, if I remember rightly."

Cyril folded his arms and took a deep breath. "That year, in the January or February … do you remember a murder here in Clacton?"

The old man considered a moment. "Aye, I do," he said. "Young girl, Elsie Smart." Frank puffed again. "Why do you ask?"

"Oh, nothing really … it's just someone mentioned it to me the other day and I hadn't heard about it. Before my time here."

"A complete mystery that, Cyril. Never found out who did it." The man studied his pipe in thought for a moment. "I worked with her dad a bit later."

"Oh?"

"Devastated he was. I mean, how can you get over that? Losing your only daughter, and in such a way."

"What way?"

"Strangled, she was." Frank lifted a thermos flask that had been behind his feet under the bench. "Would you like a drink?"

Cyril held up a palm again. "No thanks, Frank. I'll get myself a cup of tea when I get home." He shifted his seating position on the bench. "So what was the word back then? Were there any theories?"

"Some wondered if she'd had a boyfriend, but there was nothing definite. Her father, Joe, didn't think so at first. He thought it was a stranger, possibly some serviceman. There were a few around here after the war."

"You said, 'at first'. Later, did he think she'd had one?"

"I think he might have come round to that idea."

"Is he still around, do you know?"

"Joe? No, he died about ten years after Elsie. He was a broken man. People said he'd just given up."

"What about any other family?"

"I think Mrs Smart passed away a few years ago. There were two brothers though. I expect they're still alive, but they've probably moved away."

Cyril stood. "Well, good to see you, Frank. Take care."

"You too, Cyril."

The old man puffed on his pipe and raised a hand as Cyril walked away.

# 4

"Come in, Cathy," Cyril beckoned, having answered the door. It was just before six o'clock and the rain was falling steadily. "Why didn't you come straight in?"

"Didn't want to assume," she replied. "Doris said you were up and about and looking much better." She leaned forward, hugged him and kissed him on the cheek. "I think she's right." She released him and gave a cheeky grin as she walked off.

In the kitchen, she pulled some files from the carrier bag she'd brought with her.

"I had a rummage around at lunchtime and found these." She placed the old brown files on the kitchen table.

"Ah ... Stick the kettle on and I'll have a look."

"I won't be too long as Simon wants to go round to his mates, and I want to make sure he's eaten properly." She flicked on the kettle and put a teabag in each of two mugs.

"I wouldn't have thought you'd need to worry about him not eating," he said, "He can eat for England when he's hungry."

She stood leaning against the worktop watching Cyril sift through the files on the kitchen table. "I know, but it's just a mother's concern."

He looked up and smiled at her. "This is great, Cathy, thanks." He stacked the files into a neat pile. "I'll have a good look through these later."

The kettle flicked off and Cathy poured water into the two mugs.

"Anything interesting happening at the station?" Cyril asked.

"Seems fairly quiet. I haven't seen Mr Sanderson all week, much less Mr Viney," she said, referring to the DCI and the Detective Chief Superintendent. "Dick's been asking after you." 'Dick', being DI John Barton, Cyril's immediate boss. "I think his new woman has had a calming influence on him."

Cyril grinned at that. "Ah, the delightful next-door neighbour, Donna."

"The Flowerpot Men have been in and out," she went on, meaning DCs Bill Walker and Ben Miller, "and of course, your prodigy, Sam is still over in Oxfordshire on his course." Cathy squeezed out the tea bags and got a bottle of milk from the fridge.

"Sam will do well, I'm sure of it." Cyril took hold of the mug Cathy handed to him. "Thanks."

"So, are you feeling better?"

"I suppose so. Not back to full fitness, though. I probably ate too much at breakfast but I walked down to the allotments this afternoon. Mind you, I felt exhausted when I got back. I had to have a lie down."

"Old age."

"Hey."

Just before eight o'clock, Cyril sat at the kitchen table with the files Cathy had brought, spread out in front of him. They took him back to the evening of January 30th 1947.The first one he opened contained the post mortem report on Elsie Smart. He read the description; female aged sixteen, reasonably well-nourished, height five feet five inches, weight nine stones three pounds. No signs of recent sexual activity but she wasn't a virgin. Cause of death, strangulation.

Immediately, his thoughts went back to last year and the murder of Sharon Williams but, more poignantly, that of Ruby Clarke, who was just nineteen years old. Both women had been strangled. It rankled the detective team, particularly Cyril, as the perpetrator had made good his escape abroad. Despite their best efforts to trace him since, they had been frustrated by the lack of international agreements to track him down and obtain an arrest.

But back to Elsie Smart. The signature at the bottom of the report was a well-known pathologist who was sadly no longer with us. A pity, Cyril thought, as he would have liked to have had a conversation with him. There may have been additional information he might have been able to put forward.

The second file contained statements from the man who found the body along with the constable who was called to the scene. Ah, Cyril thought, there was a name he was familiar with. The first officer on site was a PC George Kidby, now Sergeant Kidby, if he wasn't mistaken, and close to retirement. In fact, it was George who had first met Ruby's mother when she came in to the station to report her daughter missing last year. He also planned to check out the Senior Investigating Officer and any other detectives involved in the original enquiry. One or two names from the files were familiar. George, a font of all knowledge, would, no doubt, be able to fill in the gaps.

After scanning through those, he took out another file with statements from Elsie's family. It would appear that she lived at home with her parents and two brothers, one older and one younger. From what Frank Scowcroft had said, Elsie's father had died in the late 1950s and her mother a few years ago. He'd check that, just to make sure. The brothers, Reginald, who was nineteen at the time and Edward who was fifteen, should both still be alive, so that would be another avenue to explore.

Finally, there was a statement from a Mrs Beatrice Palmer who was Elsie's supervisor at the shop where she worked. Nothing very controversial in her words, mostly praising Elsie for her timekeeping and her attitude to the customers. If she was still around, perhaps she could add something of use.

Cyril started when he realised his eyes had probably closed for the third or fourth time. He looked up at the clock. Twenty minutes to ten. Time to tidy up and get off to bed. He still wasn't back to normal but he felt better than he had for the past week.

# 5
# Saturday 4th February 1978

Cyril had slept through again until gone nine o'clock, a sign that he was still not back to normal health. Still in his pyjamas and dressing gown, he was enjoying a cup of tea and his second slice of toast when the doorbell rang. He sighed, put his toast down on the plate, walked up the hall and opened the door.

"Hello skip, just wondered how you were doing."

Cyril stared in surprise for a moment at Sam Woodbridge standing on the doorstep.

"Sam. I thought you were down in Oxfordshire, on that course at Eynsham Hall."

"Got a few days off."

"Come in, lad," Cyril said, "Come in out of the rain."

Cyril made Sam a mug of tea then sat down at the kitchen table to finish his toast after Sam had refused the offer of the same.

"What's happened to the hair then?" Cyril asked, looking at the young man's head.

"I've been scalped. Every week they make you cut it. It's ruined my credibility."

Cyril laughed. "You should have served in the war. It was the same then."

"But I tell you I've never been fitter, though."

"Plenty of PE? And the course itself is good?"

Woodbridge nodded. "Yeah, football on a Wednesday afternoon and the course is really interesting."

"When do you have to be back?"

"Monday. Exams next week and then I'm finished." Woodbridge was leaning against the sink and sipping his tea. "Anyway, how are you? Not been too well I hear."

"Jungle drums beating loud and clear then." Cyril drained his cup. "Just a bit of 'flu, nothing to worry about."

"You look okay."

"Thanks."

Sam cast a glance at the files on the table that Cyril had left out since last night. "What are you investigating?" he asked.

"When were you born Sam?"

"1951, why?"

"Ah, you're way too young."

"For what?"

"Just something someone mentioned to me and it aroused my interest," Cyril said.

"What's that then?"

"Apparently it's an old unsolved murder case from 1947."

"'47? That's going back a while." Woodbridge sat down at the table, opened the top file containing the post mortem report and began to read.

"A sixteen-year-old girl by the name of Elsie Smart," Cyril expanded.

"Strangled with her own stocking," Woodbridge responded, before closing the file. "So what got your nose going on this one, skip?"

Cyril smiled at the use of the term that uniformed constables used for their sergeants. Woodbridge had been on duty with Cyril that morning, back in August 1976, when they'd witnessed the light aircraft crashing into the sea at Clacton shortly after take-off. That incident had led directly to his return to CID. "It was something my neighbour said that got me thinking."

"Doris, you mean?"

"Yes. She remembered it happening but was still puzzled that no one had ever been caught. And then I thought about that bastard who murdered Ruby Clarke last year … and Sharon Williams." Cyril's expression was grim.

"We will get him," Woodbridge said, a determined expression on his face.

"If it takes me the rest of my life, I'll get him," Cyril promised. "I thought of Mrs Clarke and her not having justice for her daughter ... and that was the same for Elsie's parents, except I think they've both passed on now without that knowledge."

It was during the investigation into Ruby Clarke's murder that Woodbridge had been temporarily drafted into CID. He'd impressed his bosses and that led them to put him forward for the Detective's Course he was now nearing the end of.

Woodbridge tapped the files. "Any thoughts?"

"Early days, Sam. But listen, this is unofficial. I shouldn't really have these files here. Cathy only brought them round yesterday, and she'd get into trouble too if anyone knew."

"My lips are sealed."

Cyril nodded. "I'll need to make myself familiar with the contents and see who's still around from back then."

Woodbridge put his mug down and picked up another file. "Well, if you need any help, just let me know."

"Thanks, Sam, but you'll have your hands full on that course. You just make sure you pass."

"I will." He'd opened another folder and begun to read once more. "Got any paper?" he asked.

"There's a pad in the second drawer down." Cyril indicated one of the kitchen cupboards.

Woodbridge looked at him. "Are you not going to get dressed?"

Cyril was momentarily stunned. "Er, yes, okay boss."

"Go on then." Woodbridge grinned before standing up and turning to look in the drawer.

When Cyril returned, washed, shaved and fully dressed, he found Woodbridge poring over sheets of paper sellotaped together on the kitchen table.

"What are you up to, Sam?"

"Putting into practice some of what we've been learning about." He looked up from the paperwork. "It's easier to see if you put as many of the important points on one big sheet as you can."

Cyril came round to look over his shoulder.

Woodbridge pointed at what he'd written. "So here we have what we know about the victim; age, place of work, where she was found, how she died, etc. Down here, her nearest and dearest. What we could do with is some form of timeline to show where she'd been in the period leading up to when she was found."

Cyril nodded his appreciation. "I can see the logic, certainly."

"Then we'll need to see who's still around, friends, relatives, witnesses, even our own police officers," he continued.

"I had thought of that." Cyril looked as if Woodbridge was trying to teach him to suck eggs. But still, he didn't want to kill off any enthusiasm so soon. "George Kidby was a constable back then. He was actually first on the scene responding to the call from the man who found her."

"Sergeant Kidby?"

"Yep. I'll have a quiet word with him when I get back into the station."

"When are you going back to work?"

"Probably Monday, unless anything important has come up. I tell you Sam, this bout of flu has knocked me for six this week. I've never felt so ill, but I'm feeling a lot better now."

"Right, let's see what else we can add." Woodbridge opened another of the files.

Cyril was surprised, but secretly pleased. "Haven't you got anything better to do today? You usually like to go to football, don't you?"

"We've got Leeds at home but I think I'll give it a miss," he said, referring to Ipswich Town's match that afternoon. "I don't fancy standing on the terraces in this. It's like a monsoon out there."

Half an hour later, with sheets of paper filling up with more information gleaned from the files that Sam and

Cyril had worked through, the doorbell rang. Cyril broke off to answer it.

"Doris," Cyril greeted when he saw his neighbour on the doorstep. "Why didn't you come straight in?"

"Don't want to be presumptuous now you're back on your feet," she said.

"Don't be daft, come in." He held the door open. "Young Sam's here too."

"Well I won't keep you. I only wanted to tell you what I've just found out."

Cyril led his neighbour into the kitchen. "You remember Sam don't you?"

"Of course. How are you, Sam?" she asked.

"Very well, Mrs Appleby."

"No need to be so formal, you all know me as Doris."

"Cup of tea, Doris?" Cyril offered.

"Oh no thanks, Cyril. I can see you're busy. I just came to tell you something." She looked at the sheets of paper on the table. "It's about Elsie in a way."

"At least sit down a minute." Cyril pulled out a chair from the table.

Doris sat down and composed herself. "Well, since we started speaking about poor Elsie the other day, I mentioned it to Betty. You remember my friend Betty?"

"Of course, "Cyril said.

Woodbridge nodded. "She was the one who found Mrs Williams last year. I took her home afterwards."

"You did. Anyway, she mentioned Elsie Smart to one of our other friends who remembered a friend of hers who was the manageress at the shoe shop where Elsie worked."

Woodbridge bent down and pointed a finger onto one of the sheets he'd been working on. "Mrs Palmer, Beatrice Palmer," he said.

"That would be Miss Beatrice Palmer," Doris corrected. "Apparently, the old lady never married and she's still alive."

Cyril smiled at Doris's mention of an old lady, considering she was seventy-seven herself.

Doris continued, "This friend of Betty's tells us she's living in The Laurels Care Home over in Walton. It's supposed to be quite a nice place too."

"Do you know how Miss Palmer is?"

"Oh, she's pretty fit, sharp as a pin. I think this friend of Betty's visits her from time to time." Doris stood up. "Well, anyway, just thought you might be interested."

"That's great, Doris, thanks," Cyril said. "I'll try and nip over to see her at some point and see what she can remember."

"I think I saw her statement in the file," Woodbridge added.

"But you never know what someone might remember after the event when they've had time to consider," Doris said. "I know, thinking back about things that have happened in my life, there are certain things I've remembered long after they've occurred that I didn't particularly remember at the time."

"Absolutely," Cyril agreed.

"Well I'll let you boys get on," she said. "No need to see me out."

Cyril and Woodbridge exchanged knowing looks.

# 6
## Sunday 5th February 1978

Cyril had been looking forward to Sunday lunch ever since Cathy had phoned him the previous evening. He felt loads better and his appetite had definitely returned. Last night he and Sam had enjoyed fish and chips from Big Pete's. Pete was from Yorkshire and did the best fish and chips Cyril had tasted. And he was called Big Pete because he was only five feet five. He'd lived in Clacton since he was demobbed after the war but he still had a strong Yorkshire accent. Pete himself remembered the stories of Elsie Smart and the cloud of suspicion and sadness that hung over the town at that time. He also remembered it was in the middle of the big freeze that went on for several months. He promised to get in touch if he could remember anything useful but for the time being, there was nothing that he could add to what Cyril and Woodbridge had already gleaned from the files.

Cathy opened the front door to him and a tantalising aroma of freshly cooked food wafted out.

"Something smells good." He leaned forward and gave her a kiss.

She smiled at him. "Glad to see you looking much better. Go into the living room. Simon's in there. I've just got a few more things to do." She walked back into the kitchen.

Cyril opened the door to the front room and saw Simon on the settee studying the television.

"Hello Cyril," he said without turning round.

"Ah, The Big Match," Cyril said. "Who's on today?"

"Fulham and Spurs have just started. There were a lot of matches off yesterday with the weather."

He sat down next to the lad. "So I heard. Young Sam was going to go to Portman Road but thought better of it."

"Don't think he missed much. 1-0 wasn't it?"

"Not sure, mate."

They sat in silence for a few minutes watching the game.

"That just looks like trying to play on a ploughed field," Cyril commented.

Simon chuckled.

The first match highlights had just finished, Fulham had drawn 1-1 with Tottenham, when Cathy called them to eat.

After lunch, Cathy and Cyril sat on the settee in the living room. Simon had disappeared out to a friend's house which gave them some quality time.

"So how's your clandestine enquiry going?" Cathy asked, after placing two cups of coffee onto the low table in front of them.

"Making progress." Cyril picked up his cup and took a sip. "Sam Woodbridge called to see me yesterday and stayed all afternoon looking through the files."

"I thought he was still on his course."

"He is. Next week's his last with exams coming up at the end, then he'll be back the week after." He paused to put his cup down and take an After Eight chocolate from the box he'd brought for Cathy that she'd opened. "He was very useful, as it turned out."

Cathy took a chocolate too and lifted her coffee cup. "How so?" she asked, taking a bite of the chocolate and a sip of her drink.

"He's been learning all these new methods of presenting information, which I must admit, makes things easier to review, especially when there's a lot of information to assess."

Cathy finished the chocolate, put her cup back in its saucer and held up a finger as if she'd just remembered something. "Oh, I was talking to Jean, you know, one of the women who works in the canteen."

"I know. They let her work on past retirement. Nice old girl."

"Anyway, we were chatting yesterday and I gently dropped in the subject of Elsie Smart ..."

"You didn't tell her I was looking at the case again, did you?" Cyril interrupted.

Cathy looked taken aback. "Of course not. I know it's unofficial."

"Sorry, it's just ..."

"As I was saying, she was working in the canteen back then." Cathy broke off for a second. "God, that means she must have worked at Jackson Road for over thirty years. Imagine that?"

"I'm assuming she had something interesting to tell you," Cyril said, a smile breaking on his lips.

"Yeah, well, she was saying all the usual stuff about how awful the atmosphere was, the strain the officers were under and all that. And then how progress seemed to falter and the enquiry was closed down a bit quick, according to some. But she also mentioned that there was a young woman, Edith, who did what I do back then. She typed up a lot of the statements. She remembered Edith seemed quite affected by all she had to deal with. Anyway, she married some DC by the name of John Garland a year or two later then left. I just thought, if she's still around, she might be worth talking to. Some of the team working on the case might have said something that didn't find its way into writing. You know how it is."

"You're the second person to make that point to me, Cathy."

"Let me guess, Doris was the first."

"Quite right." Cyril stood, walked over to the window and stared out for a second. "I do remember John, though. He was here when I first joined. I think he died a few years ago; cancer, if I'm not mistaken." He turned round and walked back towards Cathy. "I don't suppose you've got any contact details for Edith?"

She also got to her feet. "You suppose right, Cyril Claydon," she said, grinning. "But I'll have to go through the personnel files for that. You know, sometimes I wonder if you're only after me for my inside knowledge rather than my body."

Cyril laughed, put his arms around her and pulled her close.

# 7
## Monday 6th February 1978

On his first day back at Jackson Road Police Station in over a week, Cyril hoped there was nothing too demanding waiting for him. He'd probably describe himself as ninety per cent back to full fitness, still a bit bunged up about the head and slightly lethargic but he hoped being back in the job would help add that extra ten per cent.

Climbing the stairs to the CID office, he was greeted by a few familiar faces. As he stepped into the room. DC Bill Walker looked up from his desk. "Sarge," he said, "Good to see you back."

Cyril liked Walker, he thought he would make a good detective. Twenty-five years old and in his second year in CID, he was keen to learn. "Thanks, Bill. Everything alright?" he asked, looking around the mostly empty room.

"Yeah, nothing much happening this morning. A couple of burglaries overnight. Ben's out there now but pretty quiet really. How are you doing?"

"I'm not too bad. Getting there." Cyril walked over to his desk and was about to sit down when he heard Barton's voice from the open door of his office.

"Cyril! You decided to get out of bed then?"

Cyril rolled his eyes and diverted towards Barton's office. "Morning, John. Not a lot going on I hear."

DI John Barton was sitting behind his desk sifting through some papers. Most of his colleagues called him 'Dick' after the radio and TV series character but Cyril didn't join in with that as a rule. "I don't like it, it's too quiet," Barton said.

"Sounds like a quote from a film."

Barton smiled. "Anyway, back fit and well?"

"Getting there," Cyril repeated.

"What do you have on this week?" Barton stubbed out his cigarette in a Guinness ashtray on his desk.

"I'm just going to check my desk but, from memory, there are a couple of court cases; shoplifting and that common assault. Apart from that, I'm hoping to catch up on some paperwork."

"Ease yourself back in, Cyril. Cathy tells me you had a bad bout." Barton smiled again. "She's obviously nursed you back to health."

"Miss lovely legs looking after you too," he quipped, referring to Barton's love interest, Donna.

"Man of your age shouldn't be looking."

Definitely mellowed, Cyril thought to himself as he struggled to conceal a smile.

Cyril had spent some time looking through the messages and pieces of paper that had been left on his desk in the week he'd been away before deciding that a mug of tea was what was needed.

It was just gone ten when he walked into the canteen. Scanning the tables, he caught Sergeant George Kidby's eye and waved a hand. Collecting a mug of tea from the counter he weaved his way round several tables before joining the man.

"Morning, Cyril, how are you doing?" Kidby asked. "Been poorly, I hear."

"That really knocked me for six last week, George." Cyril sat down in the chair opposite him. "But a lot better now, thanks."

"That's good."

"Anyway, I'm glad I spotted you, as I wanted to have a chat."

"Sounds intriguing."

Cyril took a sip of his tea and watched as Kidby pulled out a packet of cigarettes and lit one. Normally, that would prompt him to bring out his pipe but, this morning, after last week, he didn't fancy it. "Your memory's still pretty good, isn't it?" he began.

Kidby exhaled. "I might be only a few months off retirement but I'm not gaga yet."

Cyril smiled and leaned forward. "What do you remember about the Elsie Smart case?"

Kidby's eyes widened. "Now there's a name from the past. 1947 it was. Worst winter we've ever had, including …"

Cyril interrupted him. "Yes I know, George, 1963." This was becoming a recurring theme.

"Is it something you boys in CID are looking at again?"

Cyril looked round to see who might be at any nearby tables then lowered his voice. "This is unofficial at the moment. Just something that someone mentioned to me that got my attention."

"The family been talking to you? Although I think there's only Elsie's brothers left now."

"No, not the family. So what can you remember?"

"Have you sought the files?"

"I'm looking through them. Trouble is there's not many people left who were involved in the investigation but I know you were."

"Only insofar as I was the first on the scene. I took the statement from the bloke that found her." He took another drag on his cigarette and stared into the middle distance for a second. "What was his name now … Owers, Cyril … no, Cecil Owers. Lived up on Freeland Road at the back of the hospital. Walking his dog, he was."

"DCI Burns led the investigation, didn't he?"

"That's right, but he's been dead for over twenty years. I don't think there're any other detectives from the team that are still around. I can only think of one DC but, last I heard, he was in a home, and *he was* gaga."

"So what can *you* remember, George? What were the theories at the time?"

Kidby took a last drag of his cigarette, exhaled and stubbed it in the metal ashtray on the table. "Well, they discounted Mr Owers."

Cyril nodded. “Always look at who found the victim.”

“That’s right. The family were cleared, although I always thought the older brother was a bit weird. They thought she might have had a boyfriend she kept secret.” He leaned forward and spoke quietly. “You know she wasn’t a virgin?”

“That was mentioned in the PM report,” Cyril confirmed. “But was no boyfriend ever identified?”

“Not that they could establish. In the end, the investigation just fizzled out.”

Cyril finished his tea. “That must have been frustrating.”

“It was. There were a few who thought it was closed down a bit too soon.

Cyril glanced at his watch. “Look, I’ve got some paperwork to get on with, George. But I’d appreciate it if you could give a bit of thought to it. And listen, as I said, this is strictly under the radar at the moment.”

Kidby tapped his nose with a finger. “No problem, Cyril.”

On his way back up to the office, Cyril passed Detective Chief Superintendent Viney on the stairs. He thought the man had put weight on; at five feet eight he seemed squatter than before. His dark hair around a bald dome was beginning to be flecked with grey.

“Morning Cyril,” he greeted.

“Morning, Sir.”

“Laid low last week, I heard.”

“That’s right, Sir. Getting back to normal now, though.”

They started on their way again when Cyril suddenly thought of something. “Oh, Sir, I hear you’re looking to hang your boots up.”

Viney turned round and smiled. “That’s right, Cyril. Eight weeks, two days and …” he looked at his watch. “… about six hours. Not that I’m counting.”

# 8
## Tuesday 7th February 1978

Next morning, before eight o'clock, Cyril walked into the secretarial office with a carrier bag full of files. None of the secretaries had arrived for work yet. He was hoping Cathy would be the first. Through the back of the room was a door to the file archive. He carried the load through there and placed them on an empty shelf. He'd made copious notes that he had at home but it would still be useful to have copies to check through.

He heard the door open to the main office so he made his way back out. Cathy was taking off her coat and hanging it up behind the door when he appeared.

"Ah, good," he said. "I was hoping you'd be first in."

"What are you up to Cyril Claydon?" she asked, a smile playing on her lips.

"Quickly, before any of the others turn up. I've brought those files back." He waved towards the archive room. "I've just put them on one of the shelves."

She sat down at her desk and removed the cover from her typewriter. "So you want me to put them back where they came from?"

"Well, yes but ..." He moved closer. "You do know I shouldn't have had those files at home?"

"I did wonder."

"Anyway, I can see you have one of these Xerox machines in the office now." He nodded towards the new piece of equipment.

Cathy looked askance. "Well spotted, Mr Detective." She leaned back in her chair. "Why am I feeling some work coming up?"

Cyril smiled. "If you could copy the contents for me before you put them back, no one need know I've been looking at them."

Cathy frowned. "I'd have to do it bit at a time."

He reached across and put his hand on hers. "I knew you'd help me."

The door opened and he pulled away as one of Cathy's young colleagues entered.

"Thanks, Cathy. Morning Lizzie," he greeted the younger woman and walked from the room.

Later that afternoon, after a successful session in court where a serial burglar had been sentenced to eighteen months, Cyril walked back into Jackson Road Police Station. George Kidby was on the front desk.

"Fancy a pint later," Kidby asked.

"Sounds good, George. Next door?" Cyril was referring to the Medena, the pub next door to the station, popular with many officers for obvious reasons.

"I finish at five."

"See you then."

About a quarter to five, Cyril called into the secretaries' room. Cathy was on her own, her colleagues having already left for the day. He asked her if she wanted to come round this evening for something to eat. She agreed and they settled on half-past seven. That would give Cyril time for a quick catch up with George Kidby.

With not much else to deal with that afternoon, Cyril walked into the pub at just after ten past five. George was already sitting at a table with a half drunk pint in front of him. Cyril offered a refill by sign language and a few minutes later he sat down opposite the sergeant with fresh pints.

"Cheers, Cyril." Kidby took a sip from the new drink.

"Good health, George," Cyril responded.

"Successful day in court, I heard?"

"Only what he deserved. How long has that toe rag been an irritant on the population of Clacton?"

Kidby smiled. “Too long.” He took a cigarette from the packet he had lying on the table in front of him. Lighting up, he exhaled then continued, “Well, I’ve been thinking about our last conversation ...”

“I was hoping you had.”

“Not a lot has surfaced, I’m afraid.”

“I’m disappointed.” Cyril took a swig of his beer. “But I was wondering if you remembered a young typist who was here at the time, by the name of Edith? Apparently married …”

“John Garland,” Kidby interrupted, snapping his fingers as if a light bulb had been switched on. “Yes I do. A slim timid girl as I recall but John was smitten. I think they married around the time the enquiry was wound down.”

“Of course he’s passed on now.”

“Aye, very sad.” Kidby tapped ash from his cigarette into the metal ashtray. “He was a nice bloke was John.”

“But Edith is still around, is she not?”

“I would think so, Cyril. She’d only be, what, early fifties now?”

“Any idea where …?” Cyril put his pint to his lips.

“Last I heard she was still in the same house where they lived in Thorpe. But I don’t know what she could tell you.”

Cyril placed his glass down on the table and wiped some moisture from his thin moustache. “It’s just somebody mentioned to me she seemed greatly affected by what she had to do at that time. You never know, she might just remember some small detail that wasn’t recorded in the files.”

A grin appeared on Kidby’s face. “You’re not suggesting proper records weren’t kept.”

“Or even lost.”

Kidby grew serious. “DCI Burns …” he paused.

“Albert Burns?” Cyril looked round the pub then back to Kidby. “What are you saying, George?”

“There were whispers.”

“What sort of whispers?”

"Some of the team involved weren't too happy with how thorough the investigation was run. Word was some thought it was wound up too soon."

Cyril was thoughtful. "And of course there's no one around now who was personally involved."

"Except ..." Kirby seemed to recall something, "Burns had a favourite, acting as his sort of bag man. He was a DC then, of course. Put in a good word for him, apparently, and got him a promotion to DS in Hertfordshire, I think it was. I'd forgotten all about him."

"And who was that?"

"Oh, he came back a few years later ... after Burns had retired ... a bit further up the greasy pole."

"Who? Not DCI Sanderson?"

Kidby lowered his voice. "No. Detective Chief Superintendent Viney."

"Viney?"

"The very same." Kidby nodded as he drew on his cigarette. "Oh, I remembered her two brothers, by the way," he went on, "Edward the youngest was about fifteen, so he was still at school. The older one, Reg, he was about nineteen or twenty and doing some sort of engineering apprenticeship, I think."

"Was that the one you said was a bit weird?"

Kidby stubbed out his cigarette. "Yes. I just thought there was something not quite right about him. Couldn't put my finger on it but I wouldn't want him going out with one of my daughters."

"Of course, you've got two girls. How are they?

"Both married now, Cyril. Cost me a bleedin' fortune."

Cyril drained his pint.

"Another?" Kidby asked.

"I'd love to, George, but I'm cooking tonight."

"Oh, the lovely Cathy, is it?"

"We're just good friends," Cyril said, rising to his feet.

"Yeah, right." Kidby sounded doubtful.

Cyril wasn't going to rise to the bait. "I'll see you," he said, before leaning down, keeping his voice low. "Keep remembering whatever you can about 1947, George. But listen, I'm fitting it in where I can. It's just something that's got my interest, so this is just between us."

Kidby nodded his understanding. "Enjoy your evening, Cyril."

Since growing close to Cathy, Cyril had become more experimental in the kitchen. When Maureen was hale and hearty, she used to do most of the cooking but, as her health deteriorated, he'd taken up the mantle until her appetite had reduced so much that he began to lose interest in the activity as well.

Tonight, he was busy preparing a lasagne when the doorbell rang. Cathy stood on the doorstep, a carrier bag containing paperwork in one hand and a bottle of Chianti in the other. "I come bearing gifts," she said.

"Come in," he said. "Here let me take these for you."

"That's the first batch of files I managed to copy last off tonight." She handed over the bag. "And I thought this might suit whatever you're cooking up." She held up the wine bottle.

He studied the label. "Spot on," he said, leading the way down the hallway and into the kitchen.

"Whatever it is, it smells good." She shrugged her coat off and hung it on a peg in the hallway before following him into the kitchen.

"Just got to pop some crusty bread in the oven shortly, alongside the main dish and it should be ready in about fifteen minutes." He turned the oven temperature down.

"Turned into a real Fanny Craddock, haven't you?" Cathy joked, referring to one of the earliest television chefs.

"Not The Galloping Gourmet then?" he responded. "He was on the telly the other week."

"Not with that apron on."

He smiled and wiped his hands on the garment in question.

She looked round. "No paperwork then?"

"Tidied it away for tonight." He held up the bottle. "Shall I open it?"

"Of course. Let it breathe."

"Now who's an expert on wine?"

"Only what I've picked up."

He pulled the cork from the bottle before leading her into the sitting room.

As they both sat down on the sofa, she pulled out a slip of paper from her handbag. "By the way, I came across this address for Edith Garland."

Cyril looked at it and nodded. "I heard she might still be in Thorpe. Thanks for this." He put it down on the table in front of them.

When he sat back, she took hold of his hand. "I was just thinking," she began, "when Elsie left work that night, did she make it home?"

"No," Cyril replied. "Her parents called the station from a phone box at the bottom of the street about half-past ten. Initially, they wondered if she'd had trouble with the buses due to the snow. It's not clear how badly affected they were but that was the first time the alarm was raised."

Cathy was thoughtful. "Hmm, I'm not sure if it's any help but the old boy next door to me, Mr Cameron, he used to be a bus driver in the town back then. You might want to have a word with him; see what he can remember."

Cyril gave a laugh. "Sounds like we've got a full investigation team together now. There's you and me and young Sam; and then you can count Doris next door. Might need to get ourselves an office soon."

It was after Cathy had gone home when Cyril turned his attention to events that bitter January evening in 1947. From the cupboard he pulled out the sheets of paper that Sam had sellotaped together with various elements gleaned from the files. He thought Sam was right when he spoke about a timeline for this.

Elsie's body was discovered around nine-thirty. Her father reported her missing an hour or so later. It must have been a traumatic night for those involved; police and family. She hadn't returned home from work, which was unusual. So, where did she go when she left the shop where she worked? Did the murderer kill her below the pier and was his intention that her body be swept out on the next tide, hopefully never to be found? Cyril mulled thoughts around for a while before tiredness overcame him. Finally, he tidied the paperwork away once more and headed for bed.

# 9
## Wednesday 8th February 1978

"Cyril! In here!" Barton's voice boomed from the open door of his office.

Cyril looked round the CID room searching for a clue in the reaction of the others. Those that were in kept their heads down. He'd only just walked in, having been for a dental check-up first thing. Must be serious, he thought as he made his way over to Barton's office.

"Shut the door," Barton commanded, as Cyril appeared in the doorway.

Cyril turned and closed the door but not before he noticed the pile of familiar files sitting on Barton's desk.

"Sit down a minute," Barton said. He tapped the pile of paperwork. "Now what's going on?"

Cyril sat. "Ah."

"Exactly. Ah."

"Well it was just a name that was mentioned to me in passing and it just drew me in."

"Elsie Smart?"

"Yes."

"But you asked a secretary to copy confidential archive files for you. I could suspend you for that."

Cyril bristled but paused a moment then composed himself. "You remember last year; the Ruby Clarke murder? Of course you do. The same man was responsible for her murder and that of Sharon Williams. And you knew her personally, didn't you?"

"Don't you dare go there!"

"So can you imagine what Phyllis Clarke has been going through? Her daughter's murderer has escaped justice and fled abroad."

"We will get the bastard."

Cyril sat up straight. “Oh I know we will. If it’s the last thing I do.” He relaxed slightly and leant forward. “But imagine if someone had murdered her Ruby and we never found out who was responsible? That’s what Elsie Smart’s parents went through. And they took that pain with them to their graves. Someone out there was responsible and from what I can see, we just gave up.”

“But it isn’t your case. It’s over thirty years ago. It’s not an active case.”

“But it should be. They shouldn’t just be forgotten.”

“I agree but sometimes we just run out of avenues. We can’t keep all cases active. If we did, for how long? Fifty years? A hundred years?

Cyril shook his head. “Look, there’s something not quite right about this, I can feel it.”

“Drop it Cyril. And that’s an order.”

Cyril held Barton’s stare for a moment. “Can I just ask, who discovered this? Was it the DCI?”

Barton took a deep breath before replying. “Detective Chief Superintendent Viney walked in to the secretary’s office and found your Cathy on the Xerox machine. She tried to hide it but he saw what she was doing.”

Cyril shook his head. “It’s not her fault.”

“Probably not but she should know better.” Barton rubbed his face with a hand. “Was this the first time she’d copied files for you? I mean, you haven’t got anything else in your desk or … God forbid, back at your house?”

Cyril looked away.

“Fuck me, if you have, Cyril, you’d better destroy them.” Barton pushed his chair back. “Now Mr Viney wants to see you, so you’d best get up there sharpish. And don’t go upsetting him any more than you already have. He’s only got a few weeks until he retires.” He hesitated. “And I don’t need to lose you.”

Cyril walked back across the CID room and looked at the other officers at their desks. Nobody looked up or acknowledged him. He stopped at the door then walked out into the corridor and up the stairs to Detective Chief

Superintendent Viney's office. His knock on the door was answered by a terse, "Come."

Cyril opened the door and walked in. "You wanted to see me, sir."

Viney looked up from the single sheet of paper that was on his otherwise empty desk, swapped his reading glasses for his general dark-rimmed ones and studied Cyril for a moment. "Ah Cyril, take a seat will you."

Cyril closed the door and sat opposite the senior man.

"I presume DI Barton has spoken to you."

"Yes, sir."

"I can't say I'm not disappointed, Cyril. Mrs Rogers told me you had asked her to copy some files." He held up a hand to prevent a response. "She was reluctant to tell me why she was copying them. I did have to *persuade* her that it would be in her best interests."

Cyril stayed silent.

"So what is this all about?"

Cyril took a breath to gather his thoughts. "As you know, I was laid low last week and, as I was getting better, someone mentioned the Elsie Smart case to me and how, as far as they knew, no one had ever been brought to justice for it. I was also thinking about Ruby Clarke's mother and what she must be going through."

"And there's no news on our prime suspect?"

"No, sir. Last heard of in Thailand."

"He will surface. We will get him."

Cyril nodded. He wasn't going to affirm his determination again.

Viney lifted his glasses and rubbed his eyes with thumb and forefinger before he spoke again. "But the Elsie Smart enquiry was wound down thirty years ago. No new evidence has come to light. It was one of Mr Burns biggest disappointments," he said, referring to DCI Burns who led the enquiry in 1947.

"I'm sure it was, sir."

"In all probability, he considered the murder had been carried out by some itinerant ex-serviceman. There were many who passed through here at that time, just after the war. There was no hard evidence to place anyone in her company the night she was attacked. I know this because I worked the case with DCI Burns before I left for Hertfordshire."

"Don't you think it might warrant a review?"

"No I do not, DS Claydon, he snapped. "I'm sure you have other current investigations to carry out without trawling through archived files." He leaned back in his chair. "Good result on that burglar yesterday, by the way. We also appreciate what you did to help clear DI Barton's name last year and I'm sure he's made my instructions clear. So, let's have no more time wasted on this." Viney changed his spectacles once again, leaned forward and began to study the sheet of paper in front of him as if to reinforce that their conversation was at an end.

Cyril rose from his seat and made for the door. "Thank you, sir," he said as evenly as he could before leaving and closing the door behind him.

# 10

The atmosphere in the CID Room was tense when Cyril returned and sat down at his desk. Inside he was seething with anger. Why was he being warned off from any involvement in this case? Was there incompetence back then which could embarrass certain individuals, even now? But on that front, there seemed to be only George Kidby and DCS Viney who were still around. Could it affect the reputation of DCI Albert Burns, even after all these years? Even more than twenty years after his death? He also needed to see Cathy. After all, she was only doing what he'd asked her to do. She shouldn't have made those copies but he'd pressured her.

Before his thoughts could tumble around anymore, his phone rang.

"DS Claydon, CID," he answered.

*"Hello, skip, how's things?"* Sam Woodbridge's voice sounded cheerful down the line.

Cyril turned round in his seat to face away from his colleagues, lowering his voice. "Sam, what are you doing calling? Shouldn't you be studying for those exams?"

*"It's Wednesday and lectures have just finished. Football this afternoon."*

"So it is. Look, something's come up here. It's important that you mention nothing to anyone about what we were doing on Saturday."

*"Sounds a bit cloak and dagger."*

Cyril dropped his voice to almost a whisper. "It's vital for your own career that you do not mention any of this, especially not having seen any of those files at my house."

*"Er, yeah, okay, skip. You're starting to worry me now. But listen, I just wanted to let you know that if you need to*

*trace anybody … for any reason … my aunty Soph works in the Registrar's Office in Clacton."*

"That could be useful. What's her name?"

*"Sophie Robinson. But that's not all …"*

Cyril cut him off. "Okay, thanks for that. In the meantime, you just pass those exams."

*"Yes boss."*

He turned back round to his desk and replaced the receiver. To his relief, nobody seemed to have noticed his clandestine conversation.

For the first time since he'd recovered from the flu, he really fancied a smoke. He rose from his chair and put his hand in his jacket pocket to feel the comforting outline of his pipe and tobacco pouch. He also felt something else. He pulled out the piece of paper Cathy had given him last night with Edith Garland's address written on. He needed some time on his own, so he made his way out onto the corridor and down the stairs.

In the canteen, he sat himself down at a table in the corner with a mug of tea away from anyone else, not that it was busy – the lull before lunchtime. He puffed on his pipe and sipped his tea trying to make sense of this morning's events.

"You look lost in thought, Cyril," came the familiar voice of George Kidby.

Cyril looked up. "I'd be careful if I were you, George. You don't want to be seen talking to me."

Kidby looked puzzled.

"You've not heard?"

Kidby placed his mug on the table and sat down. "I'll risk it," he said. "And no I haven't."

Cyril put his pipe down on the ash tray. "I've been warned off, George."

"Warned off what?"

"Listen, if you're asked, we haven't spoken about the Elsie Smart case, all right?"

Kidby looked surprised. "Have you ruffled some feathers?"

"Apparently. Mr Viney caught Cathy copying some of the files for me this morning."

"Oh."

"He must have spoken to John," he said, referring to DI Barton, "who had words and I was told in no uncertain terms to drop my interest. Viney wanted a word too to reinforce the message."

Kidby gave a slow nod. "As I said to you, Cyril, he was DCI Burns pet poodle back then. Maybe he still feels he owes him something, despite him not being around."

Cyril took a swig of his tea. "Tell me about Albert Burns."

Kidby puffed out his cheeks. "Well, he married money. His father-in-law was worth a fortune from before the war. Made his money overseas initially, then in engineering, and with his political contacts, he earned some lucrative military contracts. Lived in some big pile over near Tiptree, I think. When he died ..." Kidby looked distant for a second. "... actually, I think that was the year before Elsie was found. Well when he died, his wife inherited the estate."

"That's interesting context," Cyril said.

"But Albert had a bit of a reputation. Thought he kept it quiet but, you know how gossip spreads in places like this."

"Reputation? What sort of reputation?"

Kidby looked round the canteen, as if the spirit of Albert Burns was still around. "Word was he liked the women, if you know what I mean."

"You mean he was prone to affairs?"

"Well there was one bint that was mentioned a few times. And if his good lady had ever found out then he would have lost everything."

"This 'bint', did she have a name?"

Kidby frowned. "Oh, now you're asking. I can't remember off the top of my head but I'll try and think about it."

"So as well as his police work, Mr Burns had his hands full ... probably literally ... juggling other things."

Kidby smiled. “That’s a lurid picture you paint, Cyril.”

He looked over Kidby’s shoulder and saw Cathy collect a hot drink from the counter. Kidby followed his gaze and stood up. “I’ll let you two talk in peace,” he said.

Cyril got to his feet as well. “Thanks, George.” He waved Cathy over.

She gave a wan smile to Kidby as they passed, her hands around a mug of coffee.

“Listen Cathy,” he said, as she sat down in the seat recently vacated by the sergeant, “I’m really sorry for putting you in a difficult position. I shouldn’t have asked you to do it.”

“Don’t worry about it. I knew it was risky.”

“But I put pressure on you, and I shouldn’t have. I should have copied them myself when I knew no one was around.”

“Well, it’s done now.” She studied his face. “What did Mr Viney say?”

He leaned forward, hands clasped on the table. “It’s obvious they don’t want me digging around on this one. And I can’t work out why.”

“Has he told you to stop?”

“Oh yes, in no uncertain terms. He briefed John Barton who laid it on the line then called me in to see him too.”

“And are you going to leave it be?”

“More to the point, what did he say to you?”

She looked down at her coffee mug. “I tried to hide what I was doing but he saw the file and picked it up. He looked … I don’t know … shocked, I suppose. He asked me what I was doing with it.” She looked up at him. “I had to tell him, Cyril.” She put a hand on his.

“I know you did. Don’t worry about it.”

“But I do.”

“He’ll forget about it soon, especially as you won’t be touching it any more. He retires in a month.”

“You didn’t answer my question.”

“What question was that?

“Are you going to leave it be?”

"No, you're right. I didn't answer the question."

Cyril tried to put the morning's events out of his mind and spent the afternoon sifting through the paperwork for his next court appearance the following day where he was a witness in an assault case. He needed to be on the ball for this as he knew the accused had a useful lawyer defending him. By a quarter to five, he felt as though he had refreshed himself of as much of the details as he could and decided he'd have an early finish.

On his way to his car he put his hand into his jacket pocket for the car keys and rediscovered the piece of paper with Edith Garland's details. On the spur of the moment, he decided to take a detour on his way home via Thorpe-Le-Soken.

Edith was a slim woman who, as George Kidby had said, appeared to be in her early fifties. She told him she'd been upset at the death of Elsie, mostly because, at the time, Elsie was the same age as one of her younger sisters. She'd also been aware of how the enquiry was proceeding, not only because of what she had to type but in conversations with John, the DC whom she later married. In summary, there wasn't anything of interest she could tell him that he hadn't already picked up from the files. When she spoke, it was obvious she still missed her husband who had died three years before after a battle with lung cancer. Cyril could relate to this and he felt saddened as he remembered not only John but his dear wife Maureen whom he'd lost to cancer five years ago now.

"What would you make of it all?" he asked the empty passenger seat on the drive back home. "Would you tell me to leave it be?"

There was no response.

# 11
## London's East End
## 10th May 1941

"I wish you weren't goin' out tonight, Glad."

"I have to, Alfie," Gladys answered. "We need the money."

Gladys Vaughan was studying herself in the mirror above the fireplace and applying some rouge to her cheeks. They were in the back room of the terraced house the family had occupied for the past fifteen years in a street just off the Mile End Road. She was an attractive young woman with blonde hair pinned up in asymmetric rolls like one of the latest film stars.

"Are we that strapped?" her younger brother, Alfie asked. He was actually Alfie Taylor, his sister having married Tommy Vaughan in 1939.

"What I get in the day from the shop doesn't cover much." She paused to pout, checking her lipstick. "Besides, I enjoy the company. The customers have been good to me since …" Her voice trailed off.

"I know, sis," Alfie said. "But how long has this bombin' been goin' on? We should have gone to Gramps in Clacton after …"

She turned around to interrupt him, a determined look on her face. "I promised Mum I'd keep the house going if anything ever happened to her."

Gladys slipped her coat on and bent down to kiss Patricia, her young daughter. "Be good for your Uncle Alfie," she said. Ruffling Alfie's hair, she told him to behave himself and keep an eye on Patricia. "And if the sirens go off …" she added.

"I know." Alfie rolled his eyes. "Take her to the underground station."

"If I'm not back, I'll come and join you there," she said before walking down the hall, out through the front door and into the street.

"Just you and me again, Trish," Alfie said. Gladys didn't like him shortening her daughter's name, so he only used that version when she wasn't around. Her full name was Patricia Margaret (after Gladys and Alfie's mother) Vaughan. Turning on the radio he waited for the crystals to warm up. It had been his father's pride and joy. "Let's see what's on."

Patricia looked up at the boy and gave a giggle and a smile. She was 16 months old, born just after Gladys's husband, Tommy, perished when the ship he was on as part of one of the North Atlantic Convoys was sunk by a German U-boat.

Alfie Taylor looked down on her and couldn't help smiling, then turned away, wondering how different things would have been if the family's luck hadn't turned so sour. It had begun with the passing of his father with consumption, five years ago now, in 1936. He was nine at the time. He thought hard to remember him. He'd worked in the docks but Alfie had one abiding memory of being taken to Upton Park one Saturday afternoon to see West Ham not long before his father became ill.

His mother struggled on, doing three jobs to keep food on the table and a roof over their heads before Gladys married Tommy when she was nineteen. Then tragedy struck again when their mum was knocked down by a bus not far from where they lived last year. Gladys vowed she'd keep the family together in the house they'd grown up in. It was a struggle but, so far, she'd managed by working her two jobs; the shop down the road and four nights a week behind the bar of the local pub at the bottom of their street. Alfie did his bit too. At fourteen, he worked early morning in a bakery before heading off to school. And then there was Mrs Bowman. She lived next door and looked after Patricia in the day. With four of her own, one more was no bother, she'd say.

The radio had come to life and Alfie began to read his comic and listen to some orchestral music. He glanced over to the clock on the mantelpiece. Half an hour yet before he could listen to Tommy Handley and ITMA.

It was just after eleven o'clock when the sirens started. Alfie was asleep with Patricia alongside in his bed. Freeing himself from the bedding, he picked Patricia up.

"Glad!" he shouted. "Glad, time to go!"

With no response, he ran into her room, the little girl in his arms wrapped in her blankets.

Gladys's bed was empty. He was puzzled. He'd taken himself off to bed about half past nine, along with Patricia, as he had to be up early for the bakery in the morning, but he hadn't heard his sister come home. She'd normally let him know she was in and take Patricia into her cot in her room.

The sirens grew insistent, so he pulled on his coat and set off for the shelter in the tube station, careful to lock the door behind him. Couldn't be too careful. Never mind all this goodwill spirit, there were looting gangs only too willing to take advantage.

Alfie and Patricia squeezed through the crowd at the tube station entrance and slowly made their way down to the platforms. When they got there, Alfie walked along past bodies huddled under blankets, trying to get some respite. He was searching for his big sister to no avail. Half way along, he heard a woman's voice call out, "Alfie, down here."

He spotted the familiar face of his next-door neighbour. "Hello, Mrs Bowman," he greeted.

"Here," she said. "Give Trish to me."

He passed the young girl down to the woman. "Have you seen our Gladys?"

"Was she not at home?"

"No. She was working at the Arms tonight and I've not seen her since she went out."

"She should have been back by now." Mrs Bowman gently rocked Patricia, settling her down. "Maybe she met a friend?"

"I don't think she'd do that without telling me," Alfie responded.

The woman looked along to her right and shouted to someone about four bodies down. "Here, Frank!"

A man in his sixties sat up and looked across. "What's up, Alice?"

"You were in the Arms tonight, weren't you?"

"What of it?"

"Did you see Gladys Taylor there?" Despite her being married, most people in the area still referred to her by her maiden name.

"Yeah, she was on behind the bar."

"Was she still there when you left?"

I think she was chatting to that bloke from the street behind … Woods, is it? Bit weird."

"Graham Woods, you mean, old Charlie and Dotty's lad?"

"That's him. I think he's back on a short leave to be with his mum after his dad died."

Before the conversation could go further, Alfie turned away. "Can you keep an eye on Trish for me, Mrs Bowman?"

"But where are you going?"

"I'll be back," he said, striding down the platform.

"Alfie! Alfie!" was all he heard as he made his way back to the exit.

He ran up the stairs and as he neared the top, he could feel the vibrations of some dull thuds, obviously bombs dropping on the docks some two miles away and the noise of a nearby ack-ack gun, the crew doing their best to intercept the German bombers. At street level, he was met by closed gates, patrolled by an armed Home Guard soldier and an ARP Warden.

"Where are you going, sonny?" the elderly Home Guard asked.

"I've got to find my sister. She was supposed to be at home then come down to the shelter with me and her daughter."

"You can't go out there now," the ARP warden said. "It's too dangerous. We can't let anyone out until we get the all clear."

"But I need to find her."

"Are you sure she meant this station? She might have gone to another station."

"But we always come here."

"I'm sorry, lad but we can't let you out."

As if on cue, a loud explosion rattled the street and a cloud of dust billowed into the entrance, the elderly man shielding Alfie.

It was gone five o'clock that morning before the all clear sounded and the people of the Mile End Road area began to emerge from the shelter of the underground station. Alfie had spent the past few hours huddled beneath a blanket next to the Bowman family alongside little Patricia. Sleep had passed him by. His mind was bouncing around in all directions, worrying about his sister.

"Look Alfie," Mrs Bowman said, "you get off to the bakery. I'll take care of Trish. I'll let you know when Gladys comes back."

He distractedly stroked his niece's cheek. "Thanks," he said, before hurriedly making his way back up to ground level.

Dawn had broken as he emerged onto the pavement and took in the damage caused by the Luftwaffe's night's work. About fifty yards away, soldiers and police were looking down a crater that had been blown into the middle of the road. Further on, towards the docks, several ruined buildings were still smoking, figures with hoses playing water into them. In the opposite direction towards the city, many fires burned. London had taken a pounding.

Alfie turned in the opposite direction and hurried towards Cunningham's Bakery.

Alfie hurried back from the bakery to his house at just after eight-thirty. He'd got fifteen minutes to give his face and hands a rinse and change his clothes, before walking the hundred yards or so to school. Fortunately, the house was sound after the night's activities but was deathly quiet when he opened the door.

"Glad! Glad, are you home?" he shouted.

With no answer, he checked his sister's room, then the scullery but there was no sign that she'd returned. Probably gone straight to her shop job, he thought. But then again, she would have changed her clothes from what she was wearing last night. It didn't add up. Something had happened, he was sure of that. He had to find her, school or no school.

Back outside on the street, people were walking by, conversations focused on another night's survival. Everyone he passed that he knew, he would ask if they'd seen his sister, but nobody had. At the bottom of the road, he stopped outside the pub where she had gone last night. Bracing himself, he knocked on the door. There was no answer, so he knocked again. About to turn away, an upstairs window opened and the publican, Mr Chapman, appeared. "Who the hell's there at this time?"

"Sorry, Mr Chapman," Alfie answered. "But I'm looking for my sister, Gladys. She didn't come home last night."

"Probably taken shelter somewhere with that raid again."

"She didn't turn up in the tube station where we normally go and she hasn't been home this morning."

"Who is it?" came a female voice from behind the man.

He turned back to the room. "It's Glad's brother, young Alfie. He says she hasn't come home."

The female voice said something else Alfie couldn't make out before Mr Chapman looked down at him. "Hang on lad, I'll come down."

The landlord opened the door and ushered Alfie inside. The smell of stale cigarettes and beer attacked

Alfie's senses. In a few minutes, Mrs Chapman had joined them, a dressing gown tied tightly around her waist.

"She would have come home to change before going to the shop," Alfie was saying.

The publican and his wife exchanged surreptitious glances. "We did a bit of after-hours last night," Mr Chapman said. "A few of the regulars and that. Gladys stayed to help but when the sirens went off, everybody set off for the shelters. At least I think they did."

"Did you see her leave?" Alfie asked.

"Well … no, not exactly. We were securing the till and … well, we had things to do."

"Old Mr Hargreaves said she was talking to that Woods bloke. He told me when I saw him in the shelter."

Mrs Chapman nodded. "That's right, he was chatting to her late on," she said.

"But you didn't see her leave?"

"Said so, didn't I?" Mr Chapman repeated. "She's probably taken shelter in the next station down and gone straight to work."

Alfie doubted that but he was getting no further information from these two. He thanked the couple and left.

In their street, there were two properties that had been damaged in previous raids last December. Anything of any value had been removed, either by the tenants or by looters. The houses had become playgrounds for the few children that had not been evacuated. At the first, he climbed in through the window and onto the pile of rubble that had been left behind. The first floor had been completely destroyed and he clambered over the bricks and timbers and out into what was the back yard. Ironically, the one thing that was intact was the outside lavatory. He pulled open the door and gasped.

# 12
## Thursday 9th February 1978

It had been a difficult morning in court but he felt he'd given a good account of the events leading to the arrest of a well-known local criminal. The defence lawyer had tried his best to trip him up but he'd held firm. The case would go on probably until tomorrow, so he could only hope the jurors came to what he considered the correct verdict.

Back at his desk, Cyril looked through the messages that had been left for him that morning. He hesitated when he saw one from Edith Garland. Could he please call, she had asked. Before he could act on it, his phone rang.

It was another half hour and two phone calls later before he picked up Edith's message again. He reflected on what Barton and Viney had said yesterday then decided he'd at least hear what the woman had to say. Picking the phone up once more, he dialled her number.

Edith was coming into Clacton that afternoon, she told him, and he arranged to meet her in a café not far from the police station.

"Thanks for agreeing to see me, Mr Claydon," she said, after the waitress had brought two coffees for them.

"No, thank you Edith. If you've remembered something since we spoke last night then that would be useful. And please, call me Cyril."

She smiled. "John always thought highly of you."

Cyril knew her husband well. "And me him."

Edith paused a moment, gathering her thoughts. "When you called round last night, you took me by surprise. I hadn't thought about Elsie Smart for years. The others were right, those who remembered me at Jackson

Road at the time. It wasn't just because Elsie was the same age as my younger sister, Janet. There was another memory it triggered; a nightmare, I suppose." She added some sugar to her coffee, stirred it and took a taste.

Cyril waited patiently for her to continue her story.

"My mum's still with us, thankfully."

Cyril wondered if that was relevant.

"We were brought up just off the Mile End Road in East London. We were bombed regularly during the Blitz but thankfully, remained relatively undamaged, not like a lot of our neighbours. There were six of us, except Dad was away in the army. Next door was a tragic family, the Taylors." Edith drank some more of her coffee before relating details of the Taylor family and the heartbreaks that had befallen them, culminating in the events of May 1941 when the last of the main German bombing spree took place. "Gladys was working behind the bar and her young brother Alfie was looking after her daughter, Patricia, when the sirens went off. Alfie took the little one down to the tube station where he met mum and us lot. But Gladys never appeared. Next morning, Alfie found her body in the outside toilet of one of the bombed-out houses. She'd been strangled with a stocking."

Cyril was surprised. "As was Elsie, of course," he said quietly. "And this event was brought back to you with the discovery of young Elsie?"

Edith nodded. "I couldn't help but wonder if the two events were connected. I spoke to Mum about it at the time of Elsie's death because she knew more about Gladys than I did."

Cyril finished his coffee. "And was anyone ever caught for Gladys's murder?"

"That's the thing," Edith said, "I don't think anyone has been. Mum would remember for sure."

Cyril was thoughtful. "You said your mother is still around?"

"That's right. She lives in Colchester now."

"Do you think she might be willing to talk to me; tell me all she can remember about what happened back then?"

"I should think so. She's as sharp as a pin."

"Maybe I could speak to her at some point? Along with yourself, of course."

"She's staying with my brother for a fortnight, up in Edinburgh but I'll give her a ring when she gets back. I'm sure she'd be more than happy to speak to you." Edith's face bore a look of concentration. "Can I ask you, Cyril, with all your renewed interest, is there some progress on finding out who killed Elsie?"

Cyril took a deep breath and sighed. "Honestly," he said, "I don't know."

When Cyril arrived home, he'd hardly had time to take his coat off before the doorbell rang. He turned and opened the front door again to see Doris on the doorstep.

"Hello, Doris," he said. "Come in. I've only just got home."

"I know," she said. "I've been watching from the window."

"Come through," he said, making his way to the kitchen. "You have me intrigued."

He filled the kettle and switched it on, offering his neighbour a hot drink.

"I don't want to take up too much of your time," she said, "but I was wondering if your investigations had thrown anything up."

Cyril took a second or two to answer. "You knew Maureen well, didn't you?"

Doris looked puzzled as she sat down at the table. "Surely not as good as yourself, Cyril," she said, "but ... yes, I believe I did. Those days we spent together when you were working ... well, I miss them."

"I know."

"What are you trying to say? Has something happened?"

He switched off the kettle and poured water into the teapot. When he turned round, it was obvious to his neighbour that he was struggling with a decision.

She sat without saying a word, waiting for Cyril to speak.

Finally, he did. "I'm being warned off for some reason, and I can't work out why. I was wondering … stupid, I know …"

"Go on," she encouraged.

"I was wondering what Maureen would say. I've tried … asking but …"

"And what you're wondering is, if I could suggest what her responses might be."

Over their tea, Cyril related the events of the previous morning, Doris listening carefully but making no comment.

"My dilemma," he concluded, "is whether to comply or carry on digging."

"And you've asked Maureen."

Cyril nodded, tears pricking his eyes. "I've asked out loud but I can't detect a response."

"I think," Doris began, "she would want you to follow your instinct. You're obviously feeling things aren't right. You like to have answers and you're not getting them. I think she'd tell you to carry on but be extremely discreet."

"You know what, Doris? That's exactly the word she'd have used."

# 13
## Friday 10th February 1978

After Doris had left the previous evening, Cyril had mulled over their conversation. He'd also given some deep thought to the exchanges he'd had with Barton and DCS Viney whilst studying the charts and notes he'd produced with Sam's help. More than once he'd spoken aloud to Maureen, asking what she thought he should do, and more than once he received no answer. But Doris had helped him to come to a decision.

When Cyril walked into the CID room that morning, DCI Sanderson was just leaving Barton's office. "Morning, Cyril," he greeted. "Fingers crossed for the right result this morning."

"I'll call back in later to see if they've reached a verdict, sir," he responded referring to the court case he'd given evidence in yesterday.

"Okay gentlemen," Sanderson said, looking round at those detectives who were in, "Carry on." With that, he left the room.

Cyril sat at his desk and as he checked the messages that had been left for him, it suddenly struck him that Mr Sanderson had not said a word to him about his interest in the Elsie Smart case. He wondered for a second if there was anything significant in that, before dismissing it from his mind as his phone rang.

By lunchtime, he'd heard from the prosecution team that the jury had returned a guilty verdict and the judge had sentenced the man to five years. Two successes in the week left Cyril feeling satisfied. But gnawing away in his thoughts were the events of January 1947. The room had all but cleared around one o'clock, most of his colleagues were in the canteen or next door in The

Medena. Remembering Doris's words, he picked up the phone and made a call.

The Laurels Care home had been converted from a large Victorian detached house some fifteen years ago. Set on the outskirts of the delightfully named Walton-on-the-Naze, the high laurel hedges that gave the property its name also gave it some shelter from the road.

The call Cyril had made earlier was to the manager, a Mrs Holcombe, who confirmed the resident he wished to see was indeed hale and hearty for her eighty-three years. He parked his car on the gravel behind the hedges and approached the impressive half-glazed polished front door. After he rang the doorbell, he saw a stout woman of around fifty appear from a rear room, plumping her hair then smoothing down her apron as she approached.

Opening the door, she greeted him, "Sergeant Claydon, is it?"

"Just plain old mister today," he said. "Mrs Holcombe, I presume?"

"That's correct. Call me Ivy," she added as she opened the door wider to allow him in.

"Cyril," he said.

She closed the door and began to lead the way down the hall. "The cook has called in sick, flu apparently, so I'm filling in, if you'll excuse me," she said, over her shoulder.

"There's a lot of it going around. I've just recovered from it myself."

She paused by a panelled door at the rear of the hallway. "Anyway, Miss Palmer was intrigued by your call."

"Yes I gather she never married."

"A spinster of the parish." Ivy smiled at him. "She's in the rear lounge, just through here."

The manager opened the door and walked into a large room with a coal fire burning in the grate giving the room a cosy glow. A small woman with white hair, wearing glasses and dressed in a skirt and thick cardigan, was seated at a dining table engrossed in a jigsaw puzzle. She looked up as the pair entered the room.

Ivy gestured with her hand as the old lady spoke, “Mr Claydon, how kind of you to visit.”

“Miss Palmer,” Cyril said, holding out his hand. “Miss Beatrice Palmer?”

“Oh, no need to be so formal,” she laughed. “Call me Beatty. Everyone else does.”

He shook her frail hand. “And I’m Cyril,” he responded.

“Now, can I get you some tea, Cyril?” Ivy asked.

“That would be lovely, thank you.”

“And I’ll fetch you some too, Beatty.”

“That’s very kind.”

Cyril walked over to one of the two windows in front of Beatty and looked out at the magnificent views over the large area of tidal marshland, grasslands, creeks, mud and sand flats, salt marshes, islands and beaches, collectively known as The Backwaters.

“Great views, don’t you think?” the old lady commented.

“I bet you never get tired of them,” Cyril agreed. He turned and looked down at the puzzle Beatty had been busily engaged on; a central London street scene with a red London bus, several taxis and buildings that looked like the Admiralty. It wasn’t far from completion.

“Have you been working on that long, Beatty?” he asked.

“Started yesterday morning just after breakfast. I like jigsaws.”

“I’m impressed.” He sat down in a dining chair opposite. “So how long have you been living at The Laurels?”

“Since 1974, nearly four years now.” She looked up from the puzzle. “I like it here,” she added, “especially the views.” Picking up another piece of the puzzle, she tried it in two locations before it fitted.

At that moment, Ivy Holcombe returned with a tray containing a tea pot, two cups and saucers with teaspoons, a milk jug, sugar bowl, two plates and a selection of biscuits.

"Oh, thank you, Ivy," Cyril said as she placed the tray on the table by the side of the jigsaw.

"If you need anything else, I'll be in the kitchen." The manageress turned and left the room again.

"Will you be mother?" Beatty said, with a glint in her eye.

Cyril smiled, he had a feeling he was going to enjoy this conversation. "Of course. How do you take it?"

"Milk in first and no sugar," the old lady responded.

Cyril stirred the tea in the pot, poured it into both cups, having added milk first to Beatty's, and placed hers by the side of the puzzle.

"Thank you." She looked across at him intently. "You're a policeman, I understand? Why do you want to talk to me?"

Cyril took a sip of his tea. "At the moment, this is unofficial," he said, "but I believe you knew a young lady by the name of Elsie Smart?"

Beatty put a hand to her mouth, as if shocked at the mention of her name. "Oh. Oh, yes, poor Elsie. I only knew her for a few months, maybe a year, when she worked in the shoe shop in Clacton. She died you know. Of course you do, how silly of me. That's why you're here. Have they caught him? Of course they haven't, otherwise this would be official."

Cyril offered Beatty a biscuit, which she accepted. "I was just wondering what you can remember of that time?"

The old lady paused and stared out of the window over Cyril's shoulder, as if conjuring up old memories. Finally, she began, "It was not long after the war. Elsie came for a job as she was leaving school in May the year before … before it happened. She seemed a nice girl, not the brightest but willing."

"Did she have any friends at all, do you remember?"

She held her tea cup in both hands and took a sip. "I think there were a couple of her school friends who called into the shop from time to time. Now what were their names?" She returned the cup to its saucer, giving herself time to think. "There was a Dorothy something. She was a bit blousy as I recall. She definitely seemed more worldly wise than Elsie. Then there was another girl, a slip of a thing ... Marjorie, Marjorie Duncan. I remember the surname because it reminded me of my uncle Duncan and I thought how confusing it must be to have a last name that could be mistaken for a Christian name, don't you think?"

Cyril smiled at the thought. "So these two girls, they used to come into the shop to see Elsie?"

"A couple of times, yes. I think Marjorie came a few times when Elsie was due to finish work and they were both going off to the cinema to see some film or other."

"And Dorothy?"

Her hands became animated. "Ooh now, I do remember she came in one time and she had an older man with her." She made a face. "I didn't like the look of him."

"When you say an older man, what are we talking about here?"

"Well she'd have been about the same age as Elsie, about sixteen, because they'd been classmates. But he seemed old enough to be her father, maybe early thirties."

"But he wasn't her father?"

Again, another disapproving expression passed over Beatty's face. "Not the way he was with her, no. He was ... what can you say, a bit too familiar. As I said, she always seemed to be a bit precocious to me."

"And you were a bit uncomfortable with this?"

"Not my business, but after that, I was a bit concerned for Elsie. I suggested she might want to be careful."

"How did she react?"

Beatty drained her cup and sat back in her chair. "She said she'd known Dorothy since she was six years old and she was good fun. The man she'd been with was just a friend." Beatty frowned. "I'm not sure she was aware of the dangers. Like I said, the poor girl could seem innocent."

Not that innocent, Cyril thought, remembering the notes from the post-mortem stating that Elsie wasn't a virgin.

"Can you remember the last time you saw Elsie?" Cyril asked.

"It was the night she was found. The shop closed at five-thirty. We hadn't had many customers through the door. The weather was awful. This was the bad winter of 1947."

Cyril nodded.

"Much worse than 1963," Beatty continued. "Elsie lived in Holland with her family and she usually got a bus, so I suggested she get off home about five and I closed up at the normal time."

"How did she seem when she left?"

"Just as normal. She thanked me for letting her go. It meant she'd be able to get an earlier bus. The last thing she said to me was, 'See you tomorrow'."

"And there was no one waiting for her outside?"

Beatty shook her head. "I saw her leave through the glass door and turn left as she always did. I don't think there was anybody out and about that Thursday evening. Most sensible people were staying home."

# 14
## Saturday 11th February 1978

Donna Wilkins peeped through the bedroom curtains and looked up at the leaden sky. There seemed no promise of any brightness this morning. Across the garden, her attention was drawn to a window of the house on the parallel street.

"Strange," she said quietly.

"What is?" he asked.

She turned back and looked at the man lying in her bed.

John Barton leant on an elbow, head propped on his hand, looking admiringly at Donna's naked body.

Detective Inspector John Barton had moved in to the next door property in March last year. Donna had made an immediate impact on him, especially her legs. After several years of living in a one-bedroomed flat in town, indulging in some reckless behaviour, drinking and womanising following his divorce three years earlier, he had re-assessed his life. The shock of being embroiled in a murder enquiry as a suspect when he was unable to account for his movements had finally been the wake-up call he needed to do something about his lifestyle.

Donna Wilkins was thirty-six and had moved into her house five years ago following the death of her husband. She was attracted to her new neighbour when he'd moved in and their friendship had developed over the past few months. Now, they'd spend the odd night together which suited them both.

Donna smirked at him. "Like what you see?"

He lifted the bedclothes up on her side of the bed. "Get back in and I'll tell you."

She smiled and climbed back in.

He pulled her towards him but he could tell she still had her thoughts elsewhere. “What’s the matter?”

Her forehead creased. “I don’t know … It’s just …”

“Go on.” He kissed her nose prompting a chuckle.

“It’s just the light’s still on.”

“What light? Where?”

“The old boy in the house at the bottom of the garden.”

“What old boy?”

“Oh, Harrison, I think he’s called. You must have seen him; thinning grey hair and a bit stooped.”

Barton looked blank.

“The light on the stairs has been on for two days now,” she said.

“Probably forgot.”

“Hmm.”

“Maybe he’s gone down with the flu? I mean, old Cyril’s was off with it the other week.”

“No, he always seems to switch lights off. He’s of that generation, not wasting anything. He’ll only put lights on when he needs to.”

“You seem to be paying a lot of attention. You sure you’re not a peeping tom? Or have you been giving him a treat flashing that lovely body of yours?”

She pulled her pillow round and thumped him on the head prompting him to wrestle her onto her back and hold her wrists above her head.

“Ooh, you big strong boy,” she teased.

He kissed her and the next half an hour passed in a haze of lust and passion.

Donna linked her arm through Barton’s as they walked down the street parallel to the one on which they both lived.

“What number is it?” he asked.

“Twenty-seven, just up here.”

They stopped on the pavement where privet hedges, badly in need of a cut grew between two paths.

“It’s that one on the left,” Donna said. “The upstairs flat.”

Barton looked up at the building; four apartments, two on the first floor and two on the ground was the layout. Front doors to the ground floor units were in the middle of the façade facing the street and the upstairs flats were accessed from doors at the sides. Curtains were pulled to the windows of the first floor flat and the whole frontage looked in need of redecoration. The garden to the left was scruffy and overgrown, although the two central areas, gardens of the ground floor flats, looked reasonably well-cared for.

He set off up the path to the side and found the white painted front door that had six feature panes of obscure glass at the top. The numbers two and seven in black were set above a waist-high letterbox. But the detail that caught his eye was the two pints of milk on the doorstep. Barton said nothing but approached the front door and knocked loudly.

"There is a bell," Donna pointed out.

"Force of habit," he answered. "We never trust bells to work."

He knocked again. "Mr Harrison," he called through the door before trying the handle.

With no response, he stepped back and considered the elevation of the building but there were no windows. "Wait here a minute," he said before squeezing himself past a couple of dustbins and round to the back of the house and down the garden as far as he could. On the rear elevation, at first floor level, there was a window near to the side that had open curtains and an internal door opposite which obviously led to the top of the stairs. The light that Donna had observed from her house could be seen through this. Next to that were a small window with obscure glass, a bathroom perhaps, and two more windows, both with their curtains pulled shut. There certainly appeared to be no sign of life.

He made his way back to the main door of the flat where Donna was waiting.

"Anything?" she asked.

"All quiet," he replied. "Just that light visible in the window through the stairway door."

He knocked loudly on the front door once again before bending down to shout through the letterbox, "Mr Harrison! Are you there, Mr Harrison?"

No reply.

Before giving up, he decided to look through the letterbox. The stair went up to a half landing then turned back on itself to the upper level. On the first flight, he saw a discarded man's slipper. His eyes followed the stairs up, and then he saw it; what looked like a socked foot protruding through the spindles on the top flight.

"Mr Harrison! Can you hear me?"

Silence.

"Is everything alright?" Donna asked. "Can you see anything?"

He studied the door for a second and recognised the Chubb lock. "Stand back." He raised his elbow and broke the nearest glass pane above the lock. Reaching inside, he opened the door. Thankfully there was no security chain.

Pushing the door open, he took a step inside and approached the bottom of the stairs. Donna made to follow but he held up a hand. "Just stay there a minute," he said.

# 15

Cyril was sitting at the kitchen table, mug of tea and plate with two slices of toast and marmalade in front of him. After returning home from visiting Beatty Palmer last night, he'd pulled out the notes on the case. Looking through them again, he'd added the information she'd provided. But he took a deliberate decision to put them back in the cupboard and try and clear his thoughts by watching TV. Bodie and Doyle in The Professionals had provided some much needed distraction before he headed for bed.

This morning, he was contemplating a walk down to his allotment to review what work he could do to prepare the plot for the growing season and plan which crops he fancied this year. On the second slice of toast, the doorbell rang. Answering it, he found a beaming Sam Woodbridge standing there.

Cyril returned the young man's smile. "Now then, Sam, something tells me you have good news."

Sam held his arms wide. "I passed," he said.

"That's brilliant. Come in, come in." Cyril stood aside and allowed Sam to enter.

After Cyril made a pot of tea and had put some bread in the toaster, the pair sat at the kitchen table.

"You've got me worried, skip," Sam said. "All that subterfuge on the phone. Has something happened?"

Cyril fussed around pouring tea into two mugs before answering. "Look Sam, It might not be a good idea for you to continue ... let's say, offering your thoughts on what we were looking at last weekend." The toast popped up and he began to butter them.

"Elsie Smart? But we were only getting familiar with the files and the background to the case. My mum could remember it."

Cyril looked intense. "Good God man, you didn't tell her you'd been looking at the files, did you?"

Woodbridge was puzzled. "I only asked her if she remembered it as someone had mentioned it to me. I didn't say we'd been studying the paperwork, no."

"Glad to hear it. Now, you never mention that to anyone, d'you hear? I told you at the time that I really shouldn't have had those files out of the station. It would seriously impact your career if anyone discovered you'd been looking at them too. And your career has hardly begun."

"Something's happened. Did someone find out what you've been doing? Have you been warned off?"

"Exactly that." They both sat at the kitchen table as Cyril outlined the events of last Wednesday and his conversations with DI Barton and DCS Viney.

"So why would they do that?" Woodbridge pondered.

"That's not the issue, Sam. The fact is, I can't be seen to be sticking my nose in anymore."

Woodbridge nodded thoughtfully. "But you will though, right?"

Cyril looked sternly at the young constable. "You do not mention any of this to anyone. Is that understood?"

Sam grinned. "So what have you got?"

Cyril shook his head. "Remember last Saturday when. you were here and Doris came round? She was talking about Beatrice Palmer who was Elsie's manager in the shoe shop where she worked."

"That's right; in a care home in Walton, she said."

"Well I visited her yesterday."

"Anything interesting?"

Cyril summarised his conversation with the old lady and all she'd mentioned to him about Elsie.

"Look, I said to you on the phone, my aunt can help you trace people. And the other thing I tried to mention to you before you closed down the conversation was that my sister works in the council rates records office, so I might get some useful info there too. But it sounds like Elsie's school friends would be the next logical step. They'd have been much closer to Elsie than anyone else, especially her parents and brothers. I mean I doubt if a young girl would share confidences with them, but she would with school mates."

"You're right, Sam, but I don't want you involved in this. The next step for you is to find an opening in CID. And that might not mean here in Clacton. But you need to keep your nose clean, because a whiff of anything ..."

"I know and I appreciate it, skip."

"When are you back on duty?"

"I'm on an early shift on Monday morning." Woodbridge got to his feet. "Look, I'll let you get on."

"All right, Sam. Thanks for calling round with your news. I'll see you on Monday, no doubt. Enjoy your weekend. And well done again."

With that, Cyril showed Woodbridge out. It was certainly a thought to try and contact Elsie's school friends but, for now, he'd stick to his original plan for today and have a wander down to his allotment.

# 16

Barton pulled the front door shut once again. He'd sent Donna back home after telling her Mr Harrison was dead.

"Was it an accident?" she had asked. He'd given a fairly non-committal response and that he would have to inform the authorities and hang around for a while.

Calling the station from the phone box nearby, he'd organised for forensics officers to come from Colchester. DCI Sanderson had been informed and DCs Bill Walker and Ben Miller were on their way. Inside, he'd walked up the first flight of stairs and could see the body of Harrison lying on the second flight, head down with his left foot through the banisters. He'd spotted that through the letterbox. The head faced the wall but, from the angle at which it lay, the neck looked broken and the man was obviously dead. He was dressed in dark trousers, the legs of which had ridden up, revealing grey socks. A slipper was still on the right foot but the other one had dropped through to the first flight of steps. His shirt was partly opened, some of the buttons having been tugged off. The left sleeve had been pulled up to reveal a dark brown oval-shaped birth mark just below the elbow. He'd chosen not to go any further up the stairs, his gut instinct telling him that something didn't look right here. And of course, all the while, this was assuming the body was that of Mr Harrison.

Whilst waiting for the others to arrive, he decided to knock on a few doors, beginning with the flat immediately below.

A small white-haired woman, probably in her seventies answered the door apprehensively. "Yes?" she said.

"I'm sorry to bother you, Mrs … er," he began.

"What do you want?"

"I'm a police officer." He held up his identification.

Her brows furrowed. "You don't look like a policeman to me."

"I'm a detective," he responded. "Detective Inspector Barton from Clacton CID."

The woman took hold of his warrant, pulled a pair of reading glasses from the pocket of her woollen cardigan and studied it. "I must say, it looks alright. What is it that you want?"

"Very shortly Mrs …er …"

"White," she offered this time. "Mrs White."

"Well, Mrs White, there will be some more of my colleagues down here shortly because, I'm afraid to say, that your neighbour upstairs has had an accident."

She looked surprised. "Mr Harrison, you mean? An accident?"

"I'm afraid I had to break in just now and I've just found him on the stairs."

"Have you called an ambulance? Is he alright?"

"I'm afraid it's too late for that."

She looked down for a second. "Oh, I am sorry to hear that."

"I just wondered if there was anything you could tell me about your neighbour?"

The woman seemed flustered. "Well … I don't know. He was very quiet, kept himself to himself most of the time."

That overused phrase again, Barton thought. "Can you remember the last time you saw him?"

She frowned as she gave the question some thought. "I normally see him in the mornings on his way past going down to the shop about half-past nine. He usually gets a paper and a bit of shopping but …" She appeared to be in thought for a moment. "I didn't see him yesterday, so it would have been Thursday morning I last saw him."

"So not since?"

She shook her head. "No."

Just then, the patrol car arrived and Barton turned to see Ben Miller step out of the front passenger door, cigarette in hand.

"Well thanks just now, Mrs White. One of my colleagues will want to speak to you again and get a statement."

"So he'd want to know about the noises I heard from the flat on Thursday night then?" she said.

Barton turned back. "Noises?"

"Yes. There seemed to be a lot of noise from upstairs; stomping around and thumping, raised voices too."

"The voices, were they male, female?"

"Hard to say. Male probably. I just turned the telly up to drown it out."

Barton nodded. "Thanks Mrs White. I'll probably be speaking to you again."

The arrival of the patrol car had raised some attention from the locals, a few had slowly wandered past, puzzled looks on their faces, no doubt on their way to the shop for a paper or some bread or milk, others walking dogs. And now one or two were standing watching all that was happening.

Miller approached Barton as he walked back down Mrs White's path. "What's occurring?" he asked. "All we got was a message to attend, something about a suspicious death."

"Quite correct, Ben," Barton replied. "Now, can you make sure we avoid any incursions. This may be a crime scene."

"I'll get Phil and Don to keep them moving," Miller said.

Barton stifled a laugh. Every time he heard reference to the two constables who had accompanied his DCs, he thought of the American duo, The Everly Brothers. "But first I'd like you and Bill to have a chat with the locals and see what you can find out about the man who lives here."

Miller took a drag on his cigarette and nodded. "Sure."

Just then the duty doctor turned up.

Barton greeted him grimly. "Sorry to spoil your Saturday, doc," he said.

"No you're not," the medical man replied. "So what have we got?"

Barton explained his find, led the doctor round to Harrison's front door and leaned in through the broken pane to let them in. He stepped aside to let the doctor climb to the second flight of stairs and study the body.

After a few minutes, the doctor looked over to him. "Well, I can safely certify life extinct, but I assume you've notified the coroner and the pathologist?"

"Of course," Barton nodded. "However, what can you tell me in the meantime?"

The doctor puffed up his cheeks. "Well, as you can probably tell, the poor man has broken his neck," Barton gave a nod. He could see that from first view of the body and the acute angle of the head. "Whether that was due to tumbling down the stairs or beforehand," the doctor continued, "that's a job for the pathologist. Whether that was the cause of death though, again we'll have to wait and see."

"What gives you doubt?"

"You're the detective but it would appear he's had his shirt ripped open, sleeve pulled up, some ante-mortem bruising, so he may have been subject to assault beforehand, pushed down the stairs maybe. Like I say, you might want to see what the PM shows."

Cheeky bastard, Barton thought. "Any idea on time of death?"

"Should know better than to ask that."

"Come on, doc, just something to work with."

The doctor paused and considered for a moment. "Again, you'll get more from the PM but, at a guess, I would say he's been dead between twenty-four and forty-eight hours."

"Thanks, doc. Hope I didn't drag you away from anything important."

The man made a point of studying his watch. "I should still be able to get nine holes in, hopefully." With that, the man walked back down the stairs and strode out through the front door.

Barton stepped up onto the half landing and looked at the body once again. The doc was right, he'd be surprised if the man had ripped open his own shirt, although if he'd had a heart attack, maybe. There again, he could see the signs of bruising and that could indicate some third party involvement. A familiar voice broke his train of thought.

"Dick, are you there?" DCI Sanderson shouted.

"Up here, guv." Barton took a few steps down towards the front door.

Despite it being a Saturday, Sanderson was, as always, smartly dressed, scarf around his neck and hands deep in his Crombie overcoat pockets. Forty-eight years old and with a full head of salt and pepper hair, he climbed up the stairs and stood looking at the victim. "You got some suspicions, Dick?"

"Initially, I didn't think it felt quite right. Anyway, the duty doctor's just gone. He declared life extinct, reckoned he's been dead for a couple of days maybe, which ties in with the last known sightings. He also pointed out some bruising, which you can see on the arms and the chest, but we'll see what the PM throws up."

Sanderson bent down to look more closely at the deceased. "No SOCOs yet?"

"On their way, sir." Barton checked his watch. "Should be here any time.

"Yes it does look as though he could have been roughed up before he died?" Sanderson thought out loud.

"Definitely something not right," Barton agreed.

Sanderson walked back down to the door and pulled out his radio before making contact with the station to chase up the scenes of crime team. "Just tell them we need them down here now," he concluded.

"No doubt another one on the golf course," Barton remarked as he followed the DCI out into the daylight.

Sanderson looked round at the scruffy gardens. "Who found him?"

"Me, guv."

"How did that happen? I mean, how come you were here?"

"I only live over the back." He waved an arm in the general direction of his road. "But it was Donna, my next-door neighbour."

"Oh yes." Sanderson gave a knowing look.

"She noticed the stair light had been on for a couple of days."

"We'll need a statement, obviously."

"Obviously."

"So, things been too quiet for you? You need to go out and find crimes to give yourself some work," Sanderson commented.

"Something like that."

"So what do you know?"

Over the next few minutes Barton brought his boss up to speed with the downstairs neighbour's comments. Sanderson considered what he was being told. "We've got Miller and Walker down here and a couple of uniforms," the DCI said. "That should be enough for the moment. We'll leave Cyril out of it for now. He'll be keen to get his teeth into this if it proves sinister, I'm sure."

A white van drew to a halt behind the patrol car.

Sanderson nodded to the street. "Looks like your SOCOs are here, Dick."

# 17

With the body on its way to the mortuary at Essex County Hospital, Barton and Sanderson were standing in the lobby at the top of the stairs. The Scenes of Crime officers were busy on the staircase itself, along the hallway in the living room and in the bedroom.

DC Bill Walker walked into the house and looked up to where Barton and Sanderson were standing on the top landing. "Sir, I've had a word with the old lady downstairs," he began.

"Mrs White, yes," Barton said. "I spoke to her earlier."

"She reckons she heard raised voices and thumping around on Thursday night. Thought it might have been the telly as she reckons Mr Harrison is a bit hard of hearing. Nothing wrong with hers though, she heard Ben giving some kids a bit of stick out on the street when I was talking to her on the doorstep." He smiled at his reference to DC Ben Miller. "She also says she last saw him come home about four o'clock that afternoon and hadn't seen him since."

"That ties in with the doc's first estimation of time of death," Barton said, looking at Sanderson. "He reckons he's been dead between twenty-four and forty-eight hours."

"Not to mention the lights being left on," Sanderson said, raising his eyebrows.

Barton ignored the comment. "No sign of forced entry," he said, "so he either knew his attacker and let him in ..."

"Or whoever they were had keys," Sanderson completed.

"Where's Ben now?" Barton asked Walker.

"House to house with the uniforms."

"Good. Why don't you give him a hand?"

"Yes guv."

As Walker left the house, Barton turned to walk down the hallway to the living room. "Let's see if they've discovered anything interesting in here." Sanderson followed him.

As they entered the room, Barton could see an open door to the left leading to a small kitchen. In the living room itself, a two-seater settee and two matching armchairs that had seen better days faced a fireplace that contained an old gas fire. A television set was placed on a small table in the far corner by the side of the window and another small table stood in front of the window with a plant in a pot which appeared dead. Net curtains that looked as if they'd not been washed in years obscured much of the view out into the street. The only other significant item of furniture was a sideboard set against the wall behind the door. Here, a SOCO was thumbing through documents from a drawer.

"Anything interesting?" Barton asked.

"Just a couple of bank statements, electric and gas bills made out to Mr Trevor Harrison at this address," the officer responded. "Nothing particularly untoward. But there's also a marriage certificate. Seems our Mr Harrison was married to a Helen Margaret Chalmers." He held out a sheet of paper for Barton to see.

Barton looked at the certificate. "I wonder where she is now? There's been no mention of a woman living here. But that's useful." He showed the paperwork to the DCI.

"She could be dead, of course, but let's see if we can track her down," Sanderson said. "Right, I'm heading off. You can handle things from here, Dick."

"Oh, righto," Barton responded, not without a hint of irony, as his boss left the room and headed for the stairs.

The SOCO and Barton exchanged looks. "I'll just check with your colleague in the bedroom," he said.

Barton left the living room and walked into the bedroom which was situated to the rear of the property behind the kitchen and looked out over the rear garden towards his own house. The other Scenes of Crime officer was sifting through items that lay on a bedside cabinet.

"Hello, it's Cliff, isn't it?" Barton said as he walked in, recognising the man.

"That's right, sir," the officer responded. "It's Mr Barton, right?"

"Spot on. Anything of interest?" Barton looked at the unmade double bed that stood against the wall. Some clothes were scattered on top.

"Not really, sir," the officer replied, "Apart from these." He held up a packet of Durex prophylactics.

Barton raised his eyebrows. "Would have thought he was too old to need those."

Cliff smiled. "You'd be surprised. My wife's a nurse and during her training she had to look after a married couple in their eighties who'd been brought in for observation overnight. They'd fallen out of bed while having it off."

"Jesus," Barton responded. "Imagine having sex with an eighty-year-old woman."

"Might be just the thing when you're eighty yourself."

Barton considered for a moment. "Fair point."

In front of the window was a dressing table with a triple angle mirror as part of the unit. A few toiletries lay on top. There was a top drawer with two cupboard doors on either side. Barton took a step towards it.

"I'm just going to check the dressing table now," Cliff said.

Barton stood aside to let him approach.

The man opened one of the side cupboards and pulled out a couple of porn magazines. "Interesting," he said.

"They look pretty tame to me," Barton responded glimpsing the titles.

"No, I mean these." The SOCO produced three packs of ladies stockings, holding them up so Barton could see. "A pair of fishnets and two pairs of seamed," he announced.

"I can think of a pair of legs they'd look good on."

"But not our victim," Cliff said, raising his eyebrows.

A further search of the cupboard produced more. "There are some single ones in here too. Quite a fetish." The officer examined them before announcing, "In fact, these look quite old."

There was nothing of any interest in the other side cupboard so Cliff opened the top drawer. There, he found a cardboard box with a name and number on it, addressed to another location in Clacton. Inside were a collection of six medals from World War Two. Also in the drawer were a few war-time photographs of soldiers. One of them was a group of men dressed in shorts and smiling for the camera.

Barton took it from Cliff and, looking on the reverse, he read the names that someone had written there. He quickly spotted the name Private Trevor Harrison, the fourth from the left. Turning it over he picked out the man himself, smiling for the photographer. Next to him was a comrade with a stern expression on his face contrasting with the happy smiling expressions the rest wore.

Barton rummaged in his coat pocket and pulled out an envelope, opened it out and placed the medal box and photograph into it. "If you log these, I'll take them back to the station and have a closer look there," he said. "Looks like that might be a previous address for our victim." He scanned the room again before asking, "Have you been in the bathroom yet?"

"Not unless my colleague has, no, not yet," Cliff responded.

"I'll just have a quick look and let you get on."

* * *

It was dark when Barton returned home. A search of Harrison's bathroom had revealed a substantial amount of prescription drugs. The SOCOs were wrapping things up and a uniform would secure the house, so he'd left them to it. He was in the kitchen wondering what he could have for his evening meal when the doorbell rang.

"Just saw you pull up," Donna said as she stood smiling at Barton standing on his doorstep. Her coat collar was pulled up around her ears in an effort to keep out the drizzle that had fallen for most of the day. "I've got a bottle of Chianti," she pouted. "Thought we could ..."

"You thought we could what?" he teased.

"You know, relax and unwind."

"Best come in then." Barton opened the door wider.

She stepped into the warm hallway.

He closed the door and turned to ask, "So how was your ..?" His question was cut short by Donna taking hold of his face and kissing him full on.

"That good, eh?" he said, as she turned and walked into the kitchen. His mind immediately returned to the find of ladies stockings in Harrison's bedroom as he studied her legs.

"Where's the corkscrew?" she asked as he followed her in.

Bottle uncorked and a glass of red wine in their hands, he toasted her.

"Are you hungry? I'm starving," he said.

He cobbled together a quick meal of sausages and egg which was about all his pantry would allow. Afterwards, they sat in mellow contemplation snuggled together on his settee in the front room.

"So what's happened to the old bloke then?" she asked, sipping the last of her wine.

"Fell down the stairs apparently but we're still investigating."

"I've seen him around a few times. Uses the newsagent at the end of the road. Oh, and I've seen him a couple of times in the pharmacy next-door, collecting a prescription."

"That fits. He seemed to be on a lot of medication."

After a pause, she looked up at him. "So you won't be going in to work tomorrow then?"

"I've called a briefing first thing, why?"

She looked surprised. "I thought you said he'd just fallen down the stairs? Taken a tumble?"

"At first glance, yes but the lads will have made other enquiries. Why do you want to know?"

She turned back round into a comfortable position. "Oh it's only I fancied going to see Star Wars tomorrow."

"In the evening?"

"Could do, if you fancy it. Although it's on in the afternoon too." She pouted. "And you know how depressing a wet miserable Sunday afternoon can be."

"I could think of something else to take your mind off things in the afternoon." He took the glass from her hand.

# 18
## Sunday 12th February 1978

Barton had called together a group of detectives and some uniformed officers to brief them on the death of Trevor Harrison. Bill Walker and Ben Miller were at their desks looking through paperwork and the uniformed sergeant Alan Morris plus the Everly Brothers, Phil and Don who were on scene yesterday stood around in the CID room. Also there was one of the SOCOs who had attended yesterday. For now, Barton had decided not to call Cyril Claydon in.

"Gentlemen," Barton began, "thanks for coming in today. I know some of you were on your days off."

A general grumbling was the response.

Barton began by introducing the SOCO. "For those of you who don't know," he said, "This is Cliff Wood who enjoys poking about at crime scenes." Some groans broke out before he continued, "What, if anything of interest did you find?"

Wood listed the items of interest found in the house. Some whoops went up at the mention of the condoms, porn mags and the ladies' stockings."

"He wasn't wearing any at the time, was he, guv?" Miller asked, a smirk on his face.

"No he bloody well wasn't, Ben," Barton replied.

"Perhaps he has a lady friend," Walker suggested.

"Anyone hear anything like that on your house to house?"

Shaking of heads and mumblings of 'no' greeted that question.

"Sorry for the interruption, Cliff," Barton said, "Please carry on."

The SOCO then mentioned the other items; the marriage certificate, the medals and the army photograph.

"But this might just be an accidental fall, guv," Miller said. "We didn't find anything to indicate foul play, did we?"

"Just call it intuition, Ben," Barton responded. "Something just doesn't seem quite right to me. Plus there were the bruises the doc pointed out. I'll make a decision after the PM." He turned his attention to DC Walker. "Bill, can you trace the wife? She might be dead, of course, but it would be useful to find someone to identify the body officially."

DC Walker nodded. "On it, guv."

"We'll also try and get some background from the medals and photograph."

"One for Win..." DC Miller hesitated for a moment when he saw Barton's expression as he realised he was about to refer to Cyril Claydon as *Winco*, which some officers called him behind his back. Cyril had been a mechanic as part of the ground crew to a squadron during the war and some thought it a humorous nickname. It irked Cyril. "I mean Sgt Claydon, guv."

Barton decided to ignore the slip. "He might be able to add something useful, I suppose."

A few stifled laughs.

"What *did* we get from house to house?" Barton asked.

Walker reiterated what the downstairs neighbour had told him, confirming what she'd told Barton earlier.

"What about others on the street?"

"Nothing very much," Walker replied. "Used to be seen walking up and down to the shops on the main road. Nobody had much conversation with him from what we can find."

"What about the shops? They're always a font of knowledge," Barton said.

"Didn't get that far, guv," Miller responded.

"Well get back out there when we've finished and see what the word is. I'm told he visited the newsagents regularly." Barton looked round the room. "The other thing was the amount of prescribed medication found in the bathroom cabinet. You bagged that up, didn't you, Cliff?"

The SOCO nodded and indicated the evidence bags he'd brought with him. "It would seem he wasn't a particularly healthy individual. Medication for heart problems, blood pressure and diabetes."

"So, Ben, check out the pharmacist and see who his doctor was and get access to his medical records."

"Guv," Miller acknowledged.

"Okay," Barton said, "Work your way through those house to house reports we have and anything else we can find out about our Mr Harrison. The PM's scheduled for tomorrow at eight at Essex County Hospital, so I'll attend." He glanced at his watch. "Right let's give it an hour, see what you can find out, then bugger off. Back on it tomorrow." His thoughts were already moving towards Star Wars and Donna; but not necessarily in that order.

# 19
## Monday 13th February 1978

Cyril walked into Jackson Road Police Station in a good mood. Not even the steady rain could dampen his spirits. He'd taken Cathy out for a drink on Saturday night and had a productive day on Sunday, clearing about a third of his allotment ready for planting potatoes. Seed varieties should be in the garden centre and he wanted to obtain Wilja, his favourites.

George Kidby was on desk duties as he passed. "Morning, Cyril," he greeted.

"Hello George. Have you seen young Sam this morning?"

"I certainly have. Smile as wide as the Thames at Southend. Should be back for refs about ten."

"I'll try and catch up with him then."

Before Cyril could disappear into the building, Kidby thought of something else. "Oh," he said, lowering his voice. "That 'bint' we spoke of the other day ..." he passed over a folded piece of paper.

Cyril quickly put it in his coat pocket. "Thanks, George."

In the CID room, DC Ben Miller looked up as Cyril entered. "Dodged one at the weekend, Sarge." He flicked ash from his cigarette into the tray by the side of his typewriter before continuing with his one finger typing.

Cyril was puzzled. "What have I missed?"

Bill Walker quickly brought Cyril up to speed with the events of Saturday and the subsequent briefing on Sunday.

"So there was no real evidence of foul play?" Cyril concluded.

"Only the guv's instinct," Walker replied. "We'll know more when he gets back from the PM this morning."

Cyril had read through the statements that had been given by Trevor Harrison's neighbours and was studying the photos taken at the scene when Barton strode into the CID room. All eyes turned towards the DI.

"All right," he said, removing his coat. "Listen up everybody – we still don't know if we have a murder case on our hands or not." He spotted Cyril. "Ah, you're in. Good. A word, Cyril." Heading into his office, he addressed the rest of the team. "Ten minutes. Briefing, okay."

"Close the door," Barton said once they'd entered his office.

Cyril did as instructed.

Barton placed a manila folder on his desk and looked over at Cyril. "The others told you about the weekend's activities?"

"Bill filled in some of the details. But why didn't you call me in?"

Barton pulled a Piccadilly cigarette from a packet in his jacket pocket along with a lighter. "Thought you'd appreciate an uninterrupted weekend." He lit up, blew out some smoke and put the packet down on his desk

"Nothing to do with Mr Viney's instructions then?"

Barton gave him a cynical look but let the comment go.

"So what's developed?" Cyril asked.

Barton indicated for Cyril to sit opposite. "Have you got yourself up to speed with the case?"

Cyril sat down. "I've read the statements and seen the photographs."

"Good. Have a read of this." He tapped the folder on his desk. "Results of the PM."

Cyril picked up the file and read through the report. When he got to page three, he looked across at Barton. "That's interesting."

"You reached the part about the marks on the buttocks?"

Cyril nodded. "Not immediate injuries though. But overall, the findings are inconclusive then?" He closed the file once he'd completed reading.

"They're running some more tests."

"And when will you get the results?"

"In a few days, I suppose."

"In the meantime, what's your plan?"

Barton took a drag on his cigarette and exhaled before answering. "I think we need to run with this a bit longer."

"Why are you so keen to dig into this, John?" Cyril very rarely, if ever, used Barton's nickname.

He pointed at Cyril. "What makes you want to look into the case of Elsie Smart?"

"Different situation," Cyril replied. "This case is current. Elsie's is thirty years old. Besides, I'm not sure we should be talking about that one."

Barton leaned back in his chair. "Come on, you can't tell me you've left it alone since we spoke. If you have ..."

"Back to my original question." Cyril attempted to re-focus the conversation. "What do you sense about this one?"

"From the moment I saw the body, I just thought there was something not quite right. The bruising ... and now the state of his arse. I mean, what was he into?"

"More to the point, was that relevant to his death?" Cyril wondered.

"It's certainly unusual." Barton leaned forward onto his desk. "What we need to find out is who our victim really was. We have the same old bollocks from the neighbours, *'kept himself to himself,' 'harmless old man.'* The usual stuff. But he was in the army in the last lot, so I reckon you might be the man to get an inside track."

"You want me to check his army records?"

"We found medals and a photograph amongst his things."

"It's possible somebody didn't like him. But it's not cut and dried. Are you going to share all this with the others?"

"I'll be out in a minute," Barton said as he lifted the telephone receiver. "I just need to let the DCI know."

Five minutes later, Barton addressed the assembled officers. DCI Martin Sanderson had joined them in the CID room. Barton repeated the points raised at Sunday's briefing, the discovery of the body, the items of interest found in the flat before outlining the details of the post-mortem report.

"So it still looks like it was probably a heart attack?" Miller said.

"Only we have some suspect bruising," Barton countered.

Miller sniggered. "Especially on his arse."

Sanderson shook his head. "Just remind me again, when did you leave school, Ben?"

Miller looked contrite. "Sorry, sir."

Barton looked across at Walker. "Bill, any joy on tracking down Mrs Harrison?"

"I've got enquiries out with a couple of departments and just waiting to hear back, guv."

"Let me know, soon as." Barton turned to Miller. "What have you found out about all that medication in the bathroom cupboard, Ben?"

"It came from a pharmacy not far from where he lived and I've got his GP address and number. I'm about to call round later to get a look at his records."

"Good. If you get anybody blocking that, let me know and we'll get it sorted," Barton said. "The amount of medication he seems to have been on ties in with another aspect of the PM's findings - the number of puncture marks on his arms, probably the subject of various blood tests as well as insulin for diabetes."

He picked up the evidence bags containing the medal box and photograph found in the dressing table cupboard. "Cyril, can you have a look at this and see if you can get some background on the victim." To the rest of the assembly, he instructed, "Now what we need is as much information as we can gather on Trevor Harrison. Has he got any living relatives, what did he do for a job after the army, how long has he lived there? Previous addresses, that sort of thing. Usual checks. Right, let's get to it."

With the briefing closed, Barton made his way back to his office, Sanderson following him.

* * *

It was after ten fifteen by the time Cyril made his way downstairs towards the canteen. Sam Woodbridge was just leaving as he got there.

"Ah Sam, I just wanted to congratulate you on last week's success," Cyril said.

A broad grin broke on Woodbridge's face once again. "Thanks. skip. I hear you're investigating a suspicious death?"

"The DI seems to think it's a bit more than natural causes so we're looking into the surroundings." Cyril seemed to have a thought. "Actually, you mentioned your aunt who works in the registrar's office ..."

"That's right. Why? Is there something she might be able to help with?"

"The deceased was a Trevor Harrison. She might be able to find out something about him, I'm not sure." Cyril gave Woodbridge the address which he noted in his pocketbook.

"Leave it with me, skip. I've got to go now, we're back on the beat."

"Sure. Take care ... and well done, lad."

# 20

Cyril decided the best use of his time was to visit Harrison's flat and get a feel for the scene; also see what his furniture and possessions could tell him.

He parked his car kerbside and looked up at the windows; could do with a good clean, he thought. Walking up the path he saw that Harrison was no gardener either. There again, the man was late sixties, possibly early seventies, according to what they knew. DC Miller was still trying to obtain his medical records for an exact age.

Just before he disappeared around the side of the building, heading for the flat's main door, a silvery grey head popped out from the door of the flat below.

"You won't find anyone in," the elderly woman said.

Cyril paused and walked towards her. "I know. I'm with the police." He opened up his warrant card to show her. She put on her glasses and studied it. "And I'm glad you take so much care of who visits. You must be Mrs White, if I'm not mistaken," he went on.

"That's right." She smiled. "Must have been a horrible accident."

"Well we're still looking into what happened."

The woman thought for a moment. "Would you like a cup of tea, sergeant?"

Cyril's sense was telling him this woman could be a good source of material and that it might be worth spending some time with her to see what she could tell him. "That would be very kind, thank you."

She led him down the hallway and into a kitchen at the far end. The window looked out over the garden which was mostly grass but did contain some clothes poles and a washing line.

She filled a kettle and switched it on. “Sit down a minute,” she said, indicating one of two chairs on either end of a narrow dining table that had the extendable flaps each side folded down.

“Thanks.” Cyril sat in the seat nearest the hallway door. “Have you lived here long, Mrs White?”

“Nearly ten years now. We moved in about a year before my husband passed on.”

“I’m sorry to hear that.”

“It was his heart, you see.”

Cyril nodded and looked around the room. “You keep the place very neat and tidy.”

“I’ve not got much else to do now.” She turned back to the sink as the kettle was now boiling, switched it off, and poured water into two mugs she’d already placed tea bags in. “These are a God send,” she said. “Much more convenient than loose tea, don’t you think? Milk and sugar?”

Cyril couldn’t help but smile that the woman had discovered the convenience of tea in bags. “Just milk for me,” he responded.

A few minutes later, she had joined him sitting at the table, a mug in front of them both and an impressive display of biscuits alongside.

“So how long has Mr Harrison lived upstairs?” Cyril asked, carefully dunking a Rich Tea biscuit in his drink.

“Must be a couple of years now. I heard he’d moved from somewhere in town.”

“Have you spoken to him much? I mean, does he have any regular visitors, family, friends, that sort of thing?” Cyril had eaten the Rich Tea.

“Have another.” Mrs White indicated the biscuits.

Cyril obliged.

“Not really. I have noticed that he’d developed a limp over the past few weeks though and he’s been getting regular visits from the district nurse, so I wondered if he’d injured his leg. But apart from that bit of activity, I only ever see him in the mornings going off for a paper and a few bits of shopping; and the odd trip out now and again.”

"And no friends that you could tell?"

An earnest expression passed across her face for a moment. "There was one visitor…"

"Yes?"

"About three weeks ago. Actually, it was just before he seemed to have injured his leg."

"Any idea who this visitor was?"

"No, but when the man left, he seemed … I don't know, sort of upset and angry at the same time; the man, I mean."

"So you saw him leave?"

"Oh yes, it was maybe about four o'clock one afternoon and I was sorting out some weeds in the garden. It was one of those bright days, so I wanted to tidy the front up a bit."

Cyril drew his notebook and pencil from his coat pocket. "So you got a good look at this man?"

"Pretty good, yes. I think he'd be about your height, fair hair, probably mid to late thirties and wearing a smart overcoat. He got into a fancy car, a big blue one, one of those with some sort of statue on the front."

He paused writing and looked up at the woman. "What, you mean like a Rolls-Royce?"

She shook her head and smiled. "Oh no, not that fancy."

"A Jaguar then?" Cyril suggested.

"Possibly. But I did notice the number."

"You did?"

"Yes. It reminded me of my late husband, Harold. It seemed to spell out his name."

"Can you remember the details?"

"Well, it started H A R but the rest … oh, I can't quite remember now."

Cyril jotted down a few more notes. "That's interesting, Mrs White. A R, that's a local Chelmsford registration, I think. And if you thought it spelt out your late husband's name, it might have ended 0 1 D," Cyril thought out loud.

"It might have done."

"But back to Mr Harrison, apart from this visit … and the nurse of course, did he have any lady friends?"

She gave a chuckle. "No dear, I never saw him with anyone that could be described as a lady friend. Always seemed to be a bit of a loner. When you've lived as long as I have, you get quite good at judging those things."

Cyril took another drink of his tea and moved the conversation on. "I understand you heard activity from upstairs last Thursday night?"

"That's right. I mentioned it to one of your colleagues."

"Could you describe it?"

She thought for a moment. "Well, there seemed to be a bit of thumping around … you know, heavy footsteps. At first I thought Mr Harrison might just be having difficulty getting around, what with his bad leg."

"But you also heard raised voices?"

"Not clearly. It sounded like his telly, or so I thought. So I turned mine up. It was only when I discovered what happened on Saturday that I thought a bit more about it."

Cyril motioned for another biscuit.

"Please, help yourself," she said.

Cyril dunked another in his tea and nibbled it. "So you wouldn't know if it was Mr Harrison and another male or female voice?"

"No, sorry, it wasn't that distinct."

"And how long did this disturbance last?"

"Difficult to tell. I left the volume up on mine for a bit, at least until the next break," she said, meaning the advert break. "I turned it back down then." She leaned in closer, conspiratorially, "You know they increase the volume for the ads?"

Cyril nodded. "Yes, I'd noticed that."

"Anyway, it had all gone quiet by then."

"And you didn't see anyone coming or going to Mr Harrison's flat on Thursday evening?"

"No, the curtains were pulled and I don't look out after dark."

Cyril drained his tea. "Well, Mrs White, thanks for the tea and biscuits. You've been very helpful." He stood up.

"But I haven't really told you anything." She seemed disappointed.

"No, you've given me some useful background."

Mrs White also got to her feet. "Oh, before you go, sergeant, you couldn't do me a little favour, could you?"

"If I can."

"It's my hall light. The bulb's gone and I don't like to get up on a chair to change it, especially when I'm on my own."

Five minutes later, hall light fully functioning, Cyril stepped onto the staircase of Trevor Harrison's first floor flat. He had to smile to himself at the thought that the old lady downstairs probably only invited him in for tea and biscuits so she could ask him to change her light bulb.

The staircase was familiar to him from the photographs, copies of which he'd brought with him for reference. He stood on the half-landing to study the upper flight where Trevor Harrison was discovered. He'd obviously toppled from the top floor landing and ended up with his left foot though the banisters, the slipper dropping onto the bottom flight. The man had been lying on his back which, to Cyril's mind, meant he'd been facing the hallway door, which was open, and tumbled backwards. The stairs were concrete with a painted finish; no carpeting was fitted. Up on the top landing, Cyril could see no evidence of scuff marks. As he made his way into the hallway his attention was caught by the door frame. About halfway up on the right hand frame, there were a couple of small paint chips. He stood with his back to the stairs and held out his right hand towards the frame. An idea was beginning to form.

Into the hallway, he looked for anything unusual. The floor was uncarpeted, bare floorboards. Along the hallway, there were a few scuff marks on the skirting boards on either side. Were they new, or had they been there a while? On into the kitchen. Plates and a couple of mugs along with some cutlery were still on the draining board by the sink. In the corner was a pantry. He opened the door and took in various tins and a cereal box on the shelves. Nothing out of the ordinary. There was a bin in the opposite corner. He lifted the lid. It looked as though a fresh carrier bag had been placed inside but, at the bottom were a couple of banana skins. Outside, he heard a familiar noise.

He turned and hurried his way along the hall, back down the stairs and out to the side path just as a council employee was walking towards him. The bin lorry had pulled up in the street. The man made to lift the lid from the bin and take it out to the street.

"Can you leave that for now," Cyril said.

"Sorry mate, I've got a job to do." The man made to carry on.

"And so have I," Cyril responded, producing his warrant.

The man stopped dead in his tracks. "Okay, fair enough," he said before walking back to the street to continue the round.

Cyril looked at the dustbin for a second then removed the lid.

# 21
## Tuesday 14th February 1978

At eight o'clock that morning, Barton left his office and walked into the CID room. DCI Sanderson who'd been with him in his office, followed.

"Okay, let's recap what we know," Barton began. "A lot has come to light since the body of Trevor Harrison was found on the stairs of his flat on Saturday. We believe he was attacked some time on Thursday night. Initial thoughts were he had had a heart attack and collapsed on the stairs. However, the PM threw up something unusual." Barton repeated the findings of Dr Maquire, specifically the marks on the buttocks, before asking Cyril to outline what he'd discovered in Harrison' dustbin.

"SOCOs found discarded syringes and needles below other waste items which we think were pushed down into the bin in an attempt at concealment," Cyril stated. "Those are in the lab now to check for blood and fingerprints. I'm expecting results sometime today."

"Okay, chase the lab up please, Cyril," Sanderson stated.

Barton turned to the uniformed sergeant who'd attended on Saturday morning. "Where are we with door to door, Alan?"

"All complete now, sir, and reports are with Ben."

"Going through the last of them now," Miller clarified.

"Also Ben, we need Harrison's medical records."

"I'll chase that again this morning," Miller said.

"Priority," Sanderson added.

As the briefing broke up, Barton and Sanderson left the room. Officers began phone calls or sifted through files. Cyril returned to his desk to check through his messages before picking up the phone. The lab was still waiting for any results from the syringes that had been found in Harrison's bin.

Suddenly, Bill Walker replaced his telephone receiver and let out an exclamation, "Yes!"

Miller raised his head at the next desk. "What have you done now? Got eight draws up?" he said, referring to the football pools.

"The ex-Mrs Harrison ..." Walker tore a sheet off the pad he'd just written details on. "She's now a Mrs Helen Hunter, married to a Dennis Hunter."

"Got an address?"

Walker stood and took his jacket off the chair back. "Just going over to the Town Hall. Should be able to find out." With that he slipped his jacket on and headed for the door, grabbing his coat on the way.

Cyril checked his watch and decided it was time for a drink, so he followed Walker out of the room and down the stairs to the canteen.

A little while later, Barton walked through the CID office heading for his own. "Where is everybody?"

"Bill's gone over to the Town Hall and I think Win ... I mean Cyril's gone for a tea."

"Looking for me?" Cyril said, appearing in the doorway and giving Miller a stern look.

Barton continued on into his office, removed his coat then returned to the doorway. "Any joy with background on our victim, Cyril?"

"Waiting for a call back," he replied.

"What about the lab?"

"I'll chase them up again now."

Barton turned his attention to Miller. "What about you, Ben? Where are you with Harrison's medical records?"

"Got copies here now, guv."

"Anything of interest?"

Miller held up some paperwork. "We've got a date of birth; 28$^{th}$ June 1907, so that makes him seventy. He'd also got a history of heart problems going back five or six years and he was diabetic but latterly, he was being treated for leg ulcers. Getting visits from the District Nurse, lucky bugger."

"Not that lucky," Barton remarked, "the bugger's dead."

Walker appeared at that point. "We have an address for the ex-Mrs Harrison," he said, taking off his coat.

"Local?" Barton asked.

"Great Bentley, guv."

"Well don't bother taking that off." Barton was already returning to his office to collect his coat. "Let's get over there and speak to her." Walking back through the CID room on his way to the stairs, he turned to Cyril. "Why don't you and Ben get over to the surgery and see if you can speak to the district nurse who treated him?"

Miller's face broke into a grin.

"And you can knock that attitude off," Barton added as he and Walker disappeared.

* * *

"I wonder if they still wear stockings?" Miller mused. He was sitting in the passenger seat of the pool car, a stupid grin on his face.

Cyril, driving to the surgery where Harrison was registered, was confused. "What?"

"District nurses," Miller clarified. "They used to. All that rustling under the uniforms."

"You need some help," Cyril said. "Just remember you're a police officer."

Miller caught Cyril's expression. "Sorry Sarge. Didn't mean anything by it. Just a bit of banter."

"But interesting you said his records showed he was diabetic."

Miller looked puzzled. "Why's that, Sarge?"

"Well it would explain all the syringes and needles we found." His conversation with the lab technician added nothing. Although the only blood traces on the needles were of Harrison's blood group, which was rare, there were no fingerprints on the syringes which is what you'd expect if the nurse was using gloves.

Cyril drew the car to a halt in the street outside the surgery and stepped out. He made his way inside, Miller following. The receptionist told him that Sister Gallagher had just left to begin her afternoon rounds. If they were quick, they might just catch her in the rear car park.

Cyril hurried back outside and spotted a brown Mini about to drive round the side of the building, a woman in an outdoor nurse uniform in the driving seat. Holding up his hand, she stopped. Sliding the window back she looked at him, a look of annoyance on her face. "Look, I'm late for my rounds already. You need to speak to reception."

Cyril discreetly showed his warrant. "I'm sorry to bother you. Sister Gallagher, is it?"

"That's right."

"I'm DS Claydon from Clacton police and this," he half turned as Miller appeared at his shoulder, "is DC Miller. I wondered if we could have a quick word about one of your patients; Trevor Harrison?"

"Ah, I've just heard," she said. "Let me pull back in and we can have a quick word in my office. But I can't be long, I'm late for my round already."

They stood back as she reversed into the space she had just left. Gathering her bag and locking up the car, she led the two officers through the back entrance and into a small room at the rear of the building.

Cyril saw the look of disappointment on Miller's face as he noticed Sister Gallagher's rotund shape and her obvious age; possibly in her fifties.

"Take a seat a minute, gentlemen," she said, as she sat in her chair behind the small desk.

"I don't know how much you're aware of Mr Harrison's death but for the moment we're just looking at all the background." Cyril was trying to be as circumspect as he could.

"All they told me this morning was that he'd been found dead on Saturday, on the stairs from a possible heart attack. But the PM will tell you more," the nurse replied.

"That wouldn't surprise you?"

"Well I know he had a heart condition and was on regular medication. Why? Is there a problem with his death?"

"With a sudden death, we look at all the circumstances. It's just routine, really."

Cyril didn't think she would be convinced but he didn't want to impart many details. This was an information gathering exercise after all. "Can you tell us why you regularly visited him?"

"He had developed leg ulcers which I was treating. That and regular general monitoring for his diabetes; BP, blood pressure that is, pulse rate and so on to keep an eye on his heart."

Cyril had a sudden thought. "Would you examine Mr Harrison thoroughly?"

The nurse looked puzzled. "I don't know what you mean."

"What I mean is would you carry out a full body examination at any time."

"That's a strange question. I would only examine those parts of Mr Harrison that I'd be treating. Is there something unusual about the death you're not telling me?"

"No, not at all." Cyril didn't want to alarm Sister Gallagher any further. It was obvious from her response that she was unaware of the marks on Harrison's buttocks. "Can you recall, when was the last time you called on Mr Harrison?"

"Ooh, let me see …" She opened a diary on her desk and flicked back through some pages. "Here," she said. "It would have been two weeks ago." She looked up at Cyril. "I've been off for over a week with flu. Came back last Friday."

Cyril smiled sympathetically. "There's been a lot of it around," he said. "So, Mr Harrison hadn't been seen by anyone for over a fortnight?"

"Ah, I didn't say that. I think Pat, she's the other district nurse attached to the practice, she would have seen him in between."

"And where is Pat now?"

"Sister Nelson will be out on her rounds. I expect you'll have to call back." She closed her diary and stood up. "Now, if you don't mind, I really need to be going. I've a list of house visits to do plus a primary school clinic to run."

# 22

The lights were on this time, which was promising. When Barton and Walker had visited that afternoon, no one was home.

"Some money here, guv," Walker had commented earlier in the day.

"Well just you keep those thoughts to yourself," Barton had retorted. "We're here for a purpose."

The pair strode up to the front door of the large detached house on Great Bentley's Green at just before nine o'clock. Great Bentley was reputed to have the second largest village green in England and the prime location to live was actually surrounding the green itself. Cricket was played here in the summer and football in the winter with loads of open space for everyone to enjoy. From experience, Barton mistrusted door bells so he ignored the bell push to the side and gave a loud rap on the ornate knocker in the middle of the white painted front door. In answer, the door was opened by a well-dressed man of around six feet tall who appeared to be in his late fifties or early sixties. His hair was of a distinguished salt and pepper grey.

"Mr Hunter?" Barton enquired, displaying his warrant card. "I'm Detective Inspector Barton, Clacton CID and this is ..."

"DC Walker, sir," his colleague said, also showing his warrant

The man looked puzzled. "How can I help, Inspector?"

"It's actually your wife who might be able to help us, sir," Barton expanded. "Is she Mrs Helen Hunter who was at one time married to a Mr Trevor Harrison?"

A sour expression came over him and again a guarded response, "Him? Used to be."

"May we come in? I think this is better dealt with inside."

"Oh, yes, sure. Come in." He stood aside to let the officers pass.

"Who is it?" came a female voice from somewhere inside.

"Some people to see you, dear," Mr Hunter responded.

The detectives entered the hallway and, as the man shut the front door behind them, Helen Hunter appeared from a room towards the rear of the house that was obviously a kitchen. About six inches shorter than her husband, she appeared to be in her mid-fifties with short fair hair. She finished drying her hands on a towel. "This looks serious. You best come in here," she said, opening a door to a large sitting room.

She switched on a couple of lamps. "Please, sit down. Would you like some tea?"

Before Walker could respond, Barton jumped in. "No thank you, Mrs Hunter, we're fine."

Barton and Walker sat side by side on a cream leather sofa whilst Mrs Hunter sat on a matching armchair with her husband perched on the chair arm, a protective arm around his wife.

"Exactly what's this about Inspector?" Mr Hunter asked.

"I'm afraid we have some bad news about your former husband, Mrs Hunter," Barton began.

"That shit," she spat, then realising what she'd said, "Sorry."

Barton was momentarily taken aback by her reaction. "That's okay, but I'm sorry to have to tell you Trevor Harrison was found dead at his home on Saturday morning."

"You brought some good news then," Mr Hunter responded.

"But what has this got to do with me?" the woman asked. "We've been divorced for years."

"We're trying to find some information about Mr Harrison," Barton explained. "I know you said you were divorced, but can you tell me when?"

Mr and Mrs Hunter exchanged looks before he stood up. "Are you sure you're real detectives?"

Barton was puzzled.

Mr Hunter went on, "Are you seriously trying to tell us you don't know?"

Barton held up a hand. "I'm sorry, Mr Hunter but is there something we *should* know."

"Damned right there is." The man had gone puce. "That piece of dog excrement was convicted on two counts of indecent assault on young women in 1956."

"That was when I divorced him, Inspector," Mrs Hunter clarified.

Barton looked across at Walker, struggling to contain a mixture of embarrassment and anger, then back to the Hunters. "Look," he said, "I'm sorry we're not up to speed with Mr Harrison's history. In fact we're struggling to find out anything about the man in general. We really would appreciate any help you can give us."

Mr Hunter seemed to have calmed. "I'm sorry too," he said, "but it's a real shock to have his name brought up again and then find that the police, of all people, are in blissful ignorance."

Mrs Hunter put a hand out towards her husband. "It's alright, Dennis, there must be a good reason for all this and I don't think this is helping."

"Thank you, Mrs Hunter," Barton said.

"Please, call me Helen," she offered.

"Thank you." Barton looked over to Walker. "We will of course make full enquiries regarding Mr Harrison's criminal record."

"So what exactly do you think we can provide that you shouldn't already know?" Dennis Hunter sat back down on the arm of the chair.

After a brief pause, Barton looked at Helen Hunter. "We're trying to locate any relatives Mr Harrison might have had. Can you help us shed any light on that?"

She shook her head slowly. "No. No, I think all his nearest and dearest were gone by the time we met. He never mentioned anyone."

"I know we'll probably have this on file but can you tell us anything about his history?"

"As far as I understand, he was born and brought up in Elephant and Castle in London in … oh, 1907, I think. He was older than me. He'd been called up into the army in 1939, the Tank Regiment, but by that time his parents were both dead and I don't think he had any brothers or sisters. He certainly never mentioned any."

"So how did you two meet?"

"It was at a dance in Chelmsford towards the end of 1950. I worked in an office in the town and he was working in a small engineering workshop near the railway station." She paused briefly as if thinking how best to continue. "After … what happened …and the divorce, I got myself a better job in London in an accountants' office and that's where I met Dennis." She smiled at her husband.

"I'm in finance," Dennis Hunter added. "We still work there, travel up every day." He looked down and returned wife's expression. "It can be tiring but we both love it, working in the City. And we moved out here after we married in 1960. The train service is good."

"So, since your divorce, you've had no contact with your former husband?"

"No. I hoped he'd still be rotting in prison."

"And you were unaware that he was living in Clacton?"

"God, of course not." She shuddered. "I dread to think what would have happened if I'd ever bumped into him …"

"What about friends? Did your ex-husband have any friends that you can remember?"

She gave the question some thought before answering, "No, not really. I remember his best man was from his old regiment. Bob something. I'll try and remember, but I don't think Trevor had much contact with him after that. I think the old engineering workshop has long closed too. We didn't really socialise much back then. Never seemed to have any money for that sort of thing. But I think, even if what happened hadn't happened, it would have ended in divorce sooner or later."

"It was Hewitt," Dennis said. "Bob Hewitt."

"That's right," Helen agreed.

Barton stood up, prompting Walker to follow suit. "Well, again, I do apologise for any unnecessary upset we may have caused you both. I appreciate your help."

Dennis and Helen both rose. "I'll show you out, "Dennis said.

Barton hesitated and turned to Helen. "Oh, if we need to speak to you again, Mrs Hunter ...?"

"The number's in the book," she replied.

The detectives walked back down the path in silence after the front door had closed behind them. Barton waited until they were both in the Rover before he exploded. "Fuck me, Bill, why didn't we know about Harrison's past?"

Walker shook his head but didn't respond.

"And to think I was considering asking Mrs Hunter to conduct a formal identification. Jesus, what a fucking mess!"

He turned the key in the ignition and fired up the engine. "Let's get out of here!"

# 23
## Wednesday 15th February 1978

DCI Sanderson had joined Cyril and Barton in the DI's office next morning. Barton had lit up a cigarette.

"Christ, Dick, why didn't you know about this?" Sanderson asked, after Barton had explained the revelations from the previous evening.

Why didn't you? Barton immediately thought. Instead, he blew out smoke sharply and said, "We don't hold the records here and the name wasn't familiar to us. He hadn't been flagged up on any probation list. At the end of the day, it was 1956, and it sounded like the offences didn't take place here. Anyway, we'll know more soon. I've requested the files to be biked over." He looked at his watch. "They should be here soon."

Sanderson turned to Cyril. "And the name meant nothing to you, either?"

"Like John says, the offences weren't on our patch." Cyril pulled out his pipe and prepared to light up.

Sanderson changed tack. "You saw the nurse that was visiting him regularly, didn't you, Cyril?"

He puffed his pipe into life before answering. "Ben and myself called at the surgery and spoke to Sister Gallagher who was his regular nurse but she was off last week and she thinks the other nurse in the practice would have visited him then. I'll be speaking to her later."

"Anything interesting to tell us?"

"Only what the medication told us – he had diabetes and a heart condition and had recently developed leg ulcers."

A knock on the door interrupted the conversation and Sgt George Kidby poked his head round the door and looked at Barton. "Excuse me, sir," he said, "but you've just had a delivery from Chelmsford I believe you've been waiting for."

"Bring it in George. You can put it on the other desk." He indicated the table in the corner he sometimes used for meetings.

Kidby brought in the package wrapped in brown paper and put it on the table then left.

Barton walked over and began to unwrap the parcel as the other two officers joined him. There were about a dozen manila files, all fairly full of paperwork.

"Let's take a few each and see what we've got," Sanderson suggested.

A few minutes later, all were engrossed reading the notes. Cyril was the first to speak. "Here we have statements from one young woman who was approached from behind by Harrison in Central Park in Chelmsford."

"And no wonder Helen Harrison, as she was then, was so angry," Sanderson said. "Looking at the statements here, they gave her a good grilling. How much did she know or suspect, that sort of thing."

Barton joined the discussion as he sifted through the files he had hold of. "So he was charged with sexually assaulting two women over the course of ..." He flicked through a few pages to check details. "... about six months. That is between October 1955 and March 1956. And the victims were aged nineteen and eighteen."

"But there were another two alleged attacks he was never charged with. The senior officer deeming not enough evidence," Cyril noted.

Barton was thoughtful. "Oh, have you had anything back from the lab on those syringes and needles found in Harrison's dustbin?"

"Ah, yes, I spoke to them yesterday after you'd gone to see Mrs Hunter," Cyril replied. "No prints on the syringes, they'd contained insulin, and on the needles traces of blood of the same type as Mr Harrison, so they don't really tell us anything."

"So looking at what we've got," Sanderson said. "It still only points to some old sex offender having had a heart attack which hardly warrants our time, does it Dick?"

Barton sighed. "I just feel there's something not quite right about this. And don't forget, we still have some more PM test results to come."

Sanderson stood and made for the door "Alright," he conceded, "we'll run with it until the end of the week, unless we have something more important to deal with, but that's it. Chief Superintendent Viney thinks we're wasting time."

Once the DCI had closed the door behind him, Cyril looked across at Barton, eyebrows raised. "So Mr Viney wants to close it."

"Don't go there, Cyril."

A short while later, back at his desk, Cyril had just completed a call when the phone rang again. His contact at army records had some information for him. From the service number attached to the medals, the name and the medals themselves, the man at the other end could confirm that the details were those attributed to a Private Trevor Harrison who had served in The Royal Tank Regiment during WW2 and was demobbed on 31st August 1945. The address they had coincided with the previous address they had for him in Clacton. Cyril was able to glean that he had been called up in October 1939 and had been wounded at Tobruk in 1941. Cyril thanked him and asked if he could provide any details, specifically an address, for another individual, Robert Hewitt, who he believed served in the same regiment alongside Harrison at the end of the War. The man promised to look into it and get back to him.

With all the activity regarding the death of Trevor Harrison and who he actually was, Cyril had not given the Smart case much thought over the past few days. Now though, as he made his way down to the canteen for something to eat, he reached into his jacket pockets to pull out his pipe and tobacco pouch. At the same time as his favourite tobacco appeared, the folded piece of paper that George Kidby had given him on Monday morning fluttered to the floor. He'd only given it a cursory glance then. He bent down to pick it up. Unfolding it, he looked at the name written there. It rang no bells. Putting it back in his pocket, he walked into the canteen and reviewed the culinary delights on offer. He'd only had one slice of toast this morning and was feeling hungry.

Settling on a cottage pie, carrots and peas, he took his plate and mug of tea to an empty table. After about ten minutes, Sam Woodbridge entered, spotted him and made his way over.

"How are things, skip," he greeted.

Cyril nodded as he swallowed a mouthful. "Got some things on the go. Are you eating?"

"I could eat Ghandi's loin cloth," Woodbridge remarked.

"Well get yourself something and come and sit down."

A few minutes later, Woodbridge sat at the table opposite Cyril with a plate of beans on toast and a mug of tea.

Cyril had finished, knife and fork parallel on his empty plate and wiped his moustache with a napkin. "Missed your breakfast then?"

Woodbridge grinned. "Something like that. How's your mysterious death?"

"Not sure to be honest. DI Barton has a 'gut instinct' that something doesn't add up. For the moment, I'm inclined to agree." Especially as Chief Superintendent Viney seems keen to wrap it up, Cyril thought but kept that to himself.

"And what about ... you know?" Woodbridge asked, shovelling a forkful of beans into his mouth.

"Actually, with your contacts, Sam, see what you can find out about this." Cyril pulled the piece of paper Kidby had given him the other day, unfolded it and held it flat on the table so Woodbridge could see the name.

"Who's she?"

"Just a name someone gave me."

“Is there any other information you’ve got? I mean, what do you want to know?”

Cyril folded the note again and put it in his pocket. “I would say you’re looking at someone aged between sixty and eighty perhaps, who lived in this area in 1947.”

Woodbridge slowly nodded. “Okay, leave it with me, skip. I’ll see what I can find out. I’m still on the case with your man Harrison.”

“Thanks. But listen,” Cyril warned, “don’t mention this to anyone else.”

# 24
## Clacton-on-Sea
## July 1941

Stan and Dolly Tanner had made the dreadful journey up to London two months earlier to collect Alfie Taylor and little Patricia. They were the children's only living relatives now that Gladys was dead. Alfie had been distraught, having been the one to discover his sister's body. Stan was especially concerned for the lad as he seemed to have become introverted and withdrawn. It was only when he was with Patricia that he appeared anything like a normal teenage boy. Stan tried to develop a relationship with Alfie; they'd come to stay several times before the war broke out, their daughter, Margaret - Alfie's mum, bringing him and his sister on the train. It was a convenient summer holiday option, especially after Alfie's father had passed. But Stan and Dolly were struggling too, not only with what had happened to Gladys but having lost Margaret, when she was killed by a bus crossing the Mile End Road last year. They had to remain strong for Alfie and Patricia now, but God, it was difficult. Dolly was heartbroken. Stan had to be stoic. This was a period in time where you didn't show emotion in public; but in private, behind closed doors, it was trying. Stan was sixty-five and still working as an electrician for a small local company. Dolly was two years younger and, apart from some part-time work earlier in her life, now classed herself as a housewife.

The letter had arrived that morning, addressed to Alfie. It was the first he'd had since he'd left the East End. Dolly watched him open the envelope and read the contents. It was from Mrs Bowman, his old next-door neighbour. As he read, his eyes became moist before he turned away and put the letter back in the envelope and tucked it into his trouser pocket.

"Everything okay, Alfie?" his grandmother asked.

The boy said nothing, just nodded before walking out of the kitchen and into the front room of his grandparent's bungalow situated not far from the sea front. Patricia was playing with a doll's tea set on the rug in front of the fireplace. Alfie sat down beside his eighteen month old niece and joined in, prompting a giggle from Patricia, who offered him a cup and saucer. Dolly, who had watched him, turned and went back to the kitchen to carry on mixing the contents of a cake.

Later that evening, after tea, Stan had suggested Alfie and he take a walk along the sea front. They'd made their way down to the pier before walking along the promenade.

"I hope they'll get that repaired and opened up again when all this lot's finished," Stan said, referring to the pier, damaged by a sea mine and part blown up by the ministry to thwart any potential German invasion. "It's been a real attraction over the years."

Alfie made no response. After a while, Stan guided the lad to sit with him on a bench. The sun was still warm and a few people were walking past, making the most of the fine weather.

"You know, Alfie," Stan began, "this is difficult for me and your gran too." Alfie remained silent. "She told me you got a letter this morning."

Alfie pulled the envelope from his trouser pocket and flattened it out before handing it over. Stan looked at the boy for a second, his eyes cast down, before he opened the letter and began to read.

*Dear Alfie,*
*I hope this finds you and little Trish well. I miss her and hope, when it's safe, you'll bring her back to see us.*
*I have been asking Constable Turner about progress on the enquiry but he tells me they*

*are no further forward. They have tried to make contact with Graham Woods but he's apparently away with his unit and can't be contacted. His mum says he was at home with her that night but we know what old Frank said about him still being in the bar till late.*

*Over here, things seem to be a bit quieter and we've had no more of those ruddy Germans since you left. People are a bit calmer and some work has been started to repair the damage.*

*Oh, I nearly forgot, a new family moved in to your old house next door. He works in the docks, just like your dad did and she looks after their two young sons. They seem quite nice.*

*Mr Cunningham from the bakery asked to be remembered to you. Anyway, I must get off now, give my love to your grandparents and look after yourselves.*

*Yours.*

*Alice Bowman*

*xxx*

Stan folded the letter into the envelope and handed it back to Alfie. "I like Mrs Bowman," he said. "She's a good sort."

"I know," Alfie said, still with his head down.

"Listen lad, we've gone through some difficult times over these past few years … all of us." He put his arm around the boy's shoulders. "I know things are hard right now. But we're here for you and little Patricia."

Finally, Alfie looked up. "I know, Gramps," he said, before bursting into tears and burying his head in Stan's shoulder.

Stan gave Alfie a minute or two to compose himself before picking up the conversation. "You know I won't be around forever, lad? At some point, you will have to step up. Patricia will need you."

Alfie was puzzled. "What do you mean?"

"I'm not a young man anymore. Your gran'll see me out. And who knows how long this will all last." Stan looked to the sky, referring to the war.

"You're not ill, are you?" Concern was etched on the boy's face.

"No, no, Alfie," Stan responded. "All I mean is that you need to be prepared to help out more."

"Of course, Gramps."

# 25
## Thursday 16th February 1978

It was a quiet street, in contrast to the nearby busy A12 that had been thick with traffic between Suffolk, north Essex and London. The houses were neat, semi-detached, two storey properties and the address was actually in Collier Row, technically a more salubrious part of Romford. Neat waist high hedges surrounded the front garden and edged the path to the front door of number thirty-four. This was the address that Cyril's army contact had provided in a telephone call that morning. Cyril chose to ring the bell rather than use the standard police procedure of rattling the knocker. He could hear it ring inside the house. A few seconds later a short, stocky man opened the door.

"Mr Hewitt?" Cyril asked.

"Depends who wants to know." The man eyed him with suspicion.

Cyril produced his warrant card. "I'm sorry to disturb you, but are you Mr Bob Hewitt who served in The Royal Tank Regiment?"

The man straightened. "That's right."

"I'm Detective Sergeant Cyril Claydon from Clacton Police. It's nothing to be concerned about but I wondered if I might have a word."

The man's demeanour altered. "Sure, come in," he said.

Cyril judged him to be in his mid-sixties; the bald pate and heavy jowls supporting that view. As he stepped past, Hewitt began to offer apologies.

"Sorry about my manner but we've had some suspicious door-to-door salesmen doing the rounds here. Go through to the lounge." He indicated the first door on the left of the hallway as he closed the front door behind him.

"You can't be too careful," Cyril said, as he took in the cosy front room. A velour settee and two armchairs were focussed on the lit gas fire, on a low setting. In the corner, on a unit, sat a television set. Against the wall as he came in was a modern radiogram, music gently playing.

As the man followed Cyril into the room, a small woman with tight grey curls appeared at the doorway, drying her hands on a towel. "Everything alright, Bob?" she asked.

"Ah, Joan, this is a policeman from Clacton," Hewitt explained. "Sergeant Claydon, this is my wife, Joan," he said to Cyril.

Cyril smiled. "Don't be alarmed, Mrs Hewitt, I only want to ask your husband a few questions about someone I believe he knew."

"I'm intrigued." Hewitt indicated Cyril to sit on the settee.

"So am I," his wife commented. "Can I get you a tea or coffee or anything?" she asked Cyril.

"Do you know, a tea would be lovely." He considered that, after the drive from Clacton through heavy traffic, that was exactly what he needed. "Just milk for me," he added.

"Go on, love," her husband said. "I'll have one too."

As Joan Hewitt left the room to make the drinks, Cyril introduced the reason for his visit. "I understand from your war-time experiences you knew a man by the name of Trevor Harrison."

Hewitt's eyes widened in surprise. "Now there's a name from the past. I haven't seen Trevor for … oh, must be over twenty years. I was his best man, you know."

"So I believe, Mr Hewitt."

"Please, call me Bob."

"Well Bob, I'm afraid I have some bad news for you. Trevor Harrison was found dead at his home in Clacton on Saturday morning."

Hewitt put a hand to his mouth. "Oh I am sorry to hear that. How … I mean …?"

"We're not too sure yet," Cyril replied. "But we're trying to get a picture of the man."

"Well I'm sure I've got some photographs somewhere …"

Cyril smiled. "No, I didn't mean that. We're trying to get some background on who he was and how he lived."

"Sorry, yes, I see what you mean. But Clacton, you say? When we knew him, he lived in Chelmsford. But what about his wife, Helen?"

"It was Helen who mentioned your name."

"I liked her," he said.

"They were divorced about five years into the marriage. She's since remarried."

Joan appeared at the door with a tray of refreshments, walked in and placed it on the coffee table in front of Cyril. "Who are you talking about, dear?" she asked her husband.

"Trevor Harrison. You remember him … and Helen, of course."

Cyril caught Joan making a face. "Of course, we were at their wedding. You were best man. I never really warmed to him," she said. "There was just something about him. She was lovely though. Too good for the likes of him, I always thought."

"Don't speak ill of the dead, Joan," Hewitt rebuked.

She looked up sharply from pouring the tea. "Who's dead?"

"Trevor."

"Oh." She looked relieved as she passed a cup of tea to Cyril, who thanked her, then one to her husband.

"Was there anything in particular about Trevor Harrison that you didn't like, Mrs Hewitt?" Cyril asked.

"Hard to say now. I suppose I always thought he was looking at me, you know? Just made me feel a bit uncomfortable."

Bob Hewitt laughed. "Come on, Joan, he was alright really. I think you're just a bit … sensitive, that's all."

"I told you how he brushed past me at the wedding … closer than he needed to. More than once. I know he was your friend but I was glad when we sort of lost touch."

"Well I wouldn't say he was my friend," the man said, almost under his breath.

Cyril was intrigued just listening to the conversation between the couple.

"So you met Mr Harrison during the war?" Cyril asked.

"That's right. In Italy in 1943. God that was some do. He joined our unit there."

Cyril took out the photograph of the group of soldiers that Barton had found in the drawer in Harrison's bedroom. "Do you recognise anyone on this?" he asked.

Hewitt produced a pair of glasses, put them on, then took the photo from Cyril and studied it. "Here. Here," he said. "This is Trevor." The man pointed to the soldier third from the left, the one wearing a stern expression.

"This one here?" Cyril clarified. "Third from the left?"

"Yes, that's him. That was how he looked when we first met. He always seemed a bit deep."

Cyril paused a moment to sample his tea but also give himself time to digest what he'd just heard. "You say Mr Harrison joined your unit in 1943 … where had he come from?"

"When we met up, he'd come from North Africa. I think he'd been wounded with his previous group in Tobruk, probably these other fellows. He was the only one to survive, apparently."

"You said you had other photographs of Mr Harrison?"

"That's right." He rose from his chair.

"There's the wedding snaps," Joan said. "In the cupboard below the stairs. The album is in there."

Bob Hewitt went out to find them.

"Is there something not quite right with his death, Sergeant?" Joan asked.

"It's just routine in the case of sudden death. And we're a bit limited in that he appears to have no living relatives."

Mr Hewitt returned with a silver coloured album in his hand. “Here it is,” he said, sitting down next to Cyril on the settee.

Cyril opened the book and saw the usual poses of bride and groom, on their own, then with best man and bridesmaids (two) and then the family groups.

“Were there any of Mr Harrison’s family here?” Cyril asked.

“No. They were all Helen’s lot. Trevor had no living relatives. His parents had both passed on before the war. Is there something suspicious here?” Hewitt asked.

“No, not at all, Bob. I was just saying to your wife that it’s standard procedure in the case of sudden death, especially as, when you’ve just said, there appears to be no living relatives.” Cyril turned back to the pages with the bride and groom on their own. “Could I borrow one of these? I’ll make sure you have it back.”

“Please,” Bob Hewitt replied. “If you think it’ll help.”

Having offered his thanks and said his goodbyes to the Hewitt’s, Cyril sat in his car for a few minutes and thought about what he’d learned. He looked at the photo of the soldiers and then of the bride and groom. The groom was certainly the soldier on the war-time snap identified by Bob Hewitt. Why then was the name on the back of that picture attributed to someone else?

# 26
## Friday 17th February 1978

Barton was thoughtful as he made his way to the Superintendent's office that morning. It was early and he'd just arrived at his desk when DCI Sanderson had called him to say Mr Viney wanted to see them both regarding the Harrison enquiry. With what had happened with Cyril last week, Barton wondered if his DS had actually discovered something interesting with regard to the old case that Viney would rather have kept hidden. Coupled with what Sanderson had said on Wednesday about wrapping this one up, he decided he'd hold his council for now and hear what his bosses had to say. After all, Cyril was a shrewd old bugger who'd been proven right on a number of occasions since they'd worked together and maybe he'd been onto something.

Barton knocked on the Superintendent's door and entered. Sanderson was already seated opposite the senior man.

"Ah, morning, John, thanks for coming," Viney said, a stickler for using his real name.

Like I had a choice, he thought, but "Sir," was all he said.

Viney was sitting in shirt sleeves with his jacket on the back of his chair. His reading glasses were on the desk in front of him. But what struck Barton was his complexion. It appeared ruddy and unhealthy. "I've been discussing this sudden death case of yours with Martin," the Superintendent began. "And I think if we've got no further evidence to suspect foul play, you need to conclude this and file it as natural causes, John."

"I've just got some last PM test results to get …"

"Don't let's waste any more time on this," Viney interrupted. "Thanks, John."

Barton hadn't been invited to sit and the Super's last comment was obviously a dismissal. "Sir," he said again.

Sanderson nodded to him and he turned and left the office.

Just after half-past-nine the phone rang on Barton's desk. It was Dr Maguire, the senior pathologist at Essex County Hospital. The conversation surprised Barton and when it concluded, he made a call to DI Sanderson.

Ten minutes later, Sanderson was sitting opposite him, the details of his conversation shared.

"So Maguire was clear?" Sanderson said. "There was a slightly raised level of potassium in Harrison's blood and puncture marks on the arm along with bruising likely to have been caused just before death?"

"That's about the size of it," Barton expanded. "Heart attack induced by higher than normal levels of potassium interfering with the electrical impulses of the heart."

Sanderson put both hands to his cheeks and rubbed his face. "Christ, Mr Viney's not going to like this."

Before the conversation could continue any further, there was a knock on the door.

Cyril was invited in to join them.

"Something puzzling you, Cyril?" Sanderson asked.

"I think there's something that doesn't quite add up, sir," Cyril responded.

The DCI indicated the other chair in the room and Cyril sat down.

Cyril began to explain what he'd learned from his visit to Bob Hewitt the day before. In conclusion, he produced the wartime photo they'd retrieved from Harrison's flat along with the wedding photo he'd borrowed from the Hewitt's. "This is definitely our victim." Cyril pointed to the bridegroom in the photo of the happy couple.

"And the bride is definitely Helen Hunter," Barton confirmed.

"But why is the man in the group of army colleagues labelled differently?" Cyril pondered.

Sanderson picked up the wartime picture showing six soldiers in uniform, studied it for a moment then turned it over. He flipped it over again. "Trevor Harrison is listed as this guy here, the fourth from the left. The one identified by the man who knew him is listed as Graham Woods."

Cyril looked from one to the other. "The third from the left. You see what I mean?"

"Here, let's have a look." Barton took the photos and studied them. After a few seconds, he handed them back to Cyril. "Maybe they just got confused when whoever wrote the names on the back."

"Maybe," Cyril conceded. "But I just ..."

"You're obviously not happy," Sanderson stated.

"When I was in the RAF," Cyril began, shooting a stern look at Barton who had made a face. "When I served, I took many a photo of the crews for them to keep as a record. I saw a lot of them after we had them developed and printed. Great care was taken when they noted who was who on the back, especially when they never knew if they'd return from a mission. I'm sure these lads would have done the same. Look, I'm not saying mistakes might not have happened but ..."

"How do we find out?"

"We could try Army Records but they probably won't have photographs of individual soldiers. And all the others on here are dead from what Bob Hewitt said, although this dates from before he knew Harrison ... or Woods, or whatever he's called."

"Maybe that's the first thing to do then, check that the others named on there died, and when," Sanderson said to Cyril, prodding the photo.

"In the meantime," Barton said, "what do we do about the Chief Super?"

Sanderson stood up. "Best leave that with me." He headed for the door.

# 27

"Cyril, this is Mr Cameron from next door," Cathy announced, ushering Cyril into her front room. She'd invited Cyril round for something to eat. Simon was upstairs in his room playing music on his new cassette player. "Mr Cameron drove buses in Clacton back in 1947," she continued.

"That's right." The man stood up from the settee. "Ended up as an inspector five years later." He had a soft Scottish accent and offered a hand which Cyril shook.

"I told Barney you might like to talk to him about the events of January 1947," Cathy explained, as Cameron sat back down.

"That was the year of the great snow." The man lifted a cup of tea from the coffee table in front of him.

Cyril smiled at the comment and sat in one of the easy chairs. "It certainly was," he agreed.

"I'll fetch you a tea, love," Cathy said before leaving the room.

"Thanks." Cyril studied Cameron for a moment; a full head of dark hair, no glasses and smartly dressed. "Have you actually retired, Barney?" He was unsure of how old the man would be.

"Last summer," he replied. "I loved the buses. I miss them but the wife is glad to have me around. I didn't think she would but she keeps me busy with all sorts of odd jobs. I like my garden too; more time for that."

"I've got an allotment," Cyril replied, "but it's a struggle finding time for that these days."

"Cathy says you're a detective … in CID, like."

"True. That's where we met."

Barney lowered his voice. "Lovely lady is Cathy. My wife thinks the world of her."

Cyril nodded.

"She tells me you're looking into the death of Elsie Smart," Cameron went on.

"It's unofficial at the moment, Barney." Cyril needed to keep things low key for the time being. "I understand you were driving buses out of Clacton the night she died?"

Cathy came back into the room with two mugs of tea and handed one to Cyril before sitting in the other armchair.

"That's right, although I didn't know it at the time. The news broke next morning." He looked to a point above the fireplace as if he'd actually travelled back in time in one of his beloved buses. "End of January. It was a difficult night for driving as I recall. More snowfall and we struggled for grip, but we persevered." An expression of pride passed over his face. "They'd stopped running beyond Holland. The road over the marshes to Great Clacton, Frinton and Walton was blocked."

"I'm assuming my colleagues at the time would have questioned you?" Cyril wondered.

"Not straight away." Cameron screwed up his face. "It was maybe a couple of days later when we had two young detectives call round to the garage."

"And what could you tell them?"

"As well as all the other crews that were on duty that night, they questioned me. But they never spoke to Molly Pearson; she was the clippie on with me that night. She'd have seen more of the passengers than me. For the most part, all I ever saw were bodies wrapped up in scarves, coats and hats, almost impossible to tell whether they were male or female." He gave a laugh. "It was a wild night."

"Do you know if Molly saw anything?"

Cameron looked into the middle distance again. "Ah, Molly was a real character. Sometimes she used to get the passengers singing along." He broke into a smile. "I think she started that during the war. Anyway, she was a good age then. Retired a few years after that. Passed away about twenty years ago. But in answer to your question, Cyril, she was off the day the detectives came. The next time we were on together, I mentioned the visit and asked her if she'd seen Elsie. She was really upset, Molly was. She knew Elsie from the times when she used to get on our bus going to or coming back after work, but not that night. She certainly never got on then. But Molly said she thought she'd seen Elsie in a doorway in town with a man."

Cyril sat up straight. "A man? Did she describe him?"

"She thought he looked a bit older. At first she thought it might have been her dad come to make sure she got home okay. It wasn't a night to be out. But then she thought there was something not quite right. The way they were together, I don't know. We'd been on the move, albeit slowly and as we passed, they sort of cuddled each other."

"Cuddled?"

"That was the word she used."

"And did she report this to the police?"

"Went over to Jackson Road on her next break. Spoke to one of the detectives that had called to see us earlier. They took some notes, she said, but she never heard another thing."

After Barney Cameron left, Cathy and Cyril sat down along with Simon to eat the meal she'd prepared for them. Later, when Simon had gone back upstairs to listen to more of his music, Cyril helped clear the plates away and they both washed up.

"It's strange, you know," Cyril said as he dried a plate.

"What is?" Cathy paused wiping the table.

"I've looked through all the files you brought me, copies of some that you made I still have, although that's purely between us ..."

"Is there something wrong?"

Cyril looked directly at Cathy. "It's just ... I don't remember any statement from a Molly Pearson. In fact there was nothing in the files detailing anything from any bus crews. I'll choose my time but I need to have another rummage through them at some point. I'll also check the copies I have when I get home."

"Home? Why don't you stay over tonight?"

Cyril put down the plate. "Ooh, Ms Rogers, what would the neighbours say?"

Cathy grinned at him. "Bugger the neighbours," she said, taking the tea towel from his hand.

# 28
## Saturday 18th February 1978

Cyril left Cathy's house early, before breakfast and drove in to Jackson Road Police Station. He needed to check a few things before anybody else appeared. Barton had called a briefing for eight, so he had two hours. He also established that DCS Viney was playing golf over in Maldon that morning and wasn't expected in.

In the archive room off the secretaries' office, he started with some of the Elsie Smart files he hadn't already obtained copies of. He knew there had been no mention of Molly Pearson's report to the police or any statements from bus crews in the copied files he had at home.

An hour in and he'd still found no mention of Molly Pearson in any of the files. He had, however, found statements from six members of the bus crews who had been spoken to by a DC Viney and another officer whose name Cyril didn't recognise. So Viney was involved in the investigation 'at the coal face', so to speak. None of the bus crews had seen Elsie Smart that evening.

Rather than risk copying the files, he'd taken notes in a notebook for future reference. He was just tidying one of the boxes away on the shelf when he heard the door to the secretaries' office open. Trying to make as little noise as possible until he was sure he could leave the archive store undetected, he turned to pick up his notebook. That was when his jacket caught on one of the cardboard boxes. It crashed to the floor. A second or two later, the door was snatched open and DI Barton stood looking down at Cyril as he lifted the errant box back onto its shelf.

"Christ, Cyril," Barton said. "I knew you couldn't leave it alone. What if I'd been the Chief Super?"

The box was back on the shelf and Cyril turned to face him. "It's Saturday and I have it on good authority he's playing golf."

"The DCI then?"

"Admittedly, that might have been a bit awkward."

"He'll be in for the briefing."

"Will you tell him?"

Barton sighed and gave a slight shake of the head. "You need to get out of there. Come on, we can have a chat upstairs before the others appear."

"What is it with you and this case?" Barton asked when they'd sat down in his office. "I know you're comparing the situation with the murders last year but … what is it that makes you want to return to it?"

Cyril had pulled his pipe and tobacco from his pockets and was lighting up. Several puffs and he wafted the smoke away with a hand. "We both had the same feeling on Wednesday when the DCI said we'd got until yesterday to find something or close the Harrison case down ... didn't we?"

"But the pathologist's findings changed that. You can't have any new evidence in your case."

"But, what makes me suspicious is Mr Viney's obvious … discomfort, shall we say, that someone is looking again at the files." He puffed on his pipe. "Now, I was speaking to someone who was around at that time and they tell me a colleague of theirs made a statement of what they'd witnessed the night Elsie Smart was found …"

Barton looked to the ceiling. "I knew you wouldn't do what you were told."

Cyril waved his pipe towards Barton to make his point. "But here's the thing, that statement doesn't appear in the files."

"Sometimes that happens. You know that, Cyril."

"But other statements from the bus crews that night do appear, some of them made to a certain DC by the name of Viney."

"Christ, you're not saying the Super tampered with evidence?"

Cyril blew out a cloud of smoke. "I'm not saying anything at the moment, I'm just looking at what's there ... or more to the point, what's not."

The assembled group in the CID room fell silent as DCI Sanderson began to speak. "Okay, gentlemen, as some of you are aware, certain findings from the tests carried out on the deceased have thrown up some questions."

Over the course of the next half hour, the team reviewed all the relevant facts discovered so far following the discovery of Trevor Harrison's body. The main focus to come out of the briefing was the need to revisit the neighbours to flush out any further information about activity at or near Harrison's flat. All available officers were detailed for that pursuit. At one point, Sanderson was called out to take a telephone call.

As the meeting broke up, Sanderson summoned Cyril and Barton to his office. Cyril wondered if word had somehow emerged of his activities earlier that morning.

"Take a seat, gents," Sanderson said as they entered the room, "And close the door."

Cyril and Barton sat down in the chairs opposite the DCI's desk, glanced at one another before focussing on the boss.

Sanderson seemed a little uncomfortable as he settled himself into his seat. "I'm afraid I've just had some bad news. Mr Viney has been taken to hospital with a suspected heart attack."

Cyril felt *his* heart rate increase. Had his delving into the Smart case increased the stress on the Super? After all, as he'd since found out, he seemed to be the only member of the detective team still around.

"Bloody hell, how is he?" Barton reacted.

"He was taken to Colchester General and he's in Intensive Care. It's serious. He'd arrived at the golf course in Maldon early this morning when he collapsed. Apparently, it was only good fortune that a doctor was on the scene at the time."

"I'm really sorry to hear that, sir," Cyril said.

"I've got to go up to Colchester shortly to see the Assistant Chief Constable but I suspect that this'll mean we'll all have to pick up some other duties. I'll be acting up in the Superintendent's role as well as overseeing my own. John, can you help me out on some of my own work? And Cyril, I'd like you to step up to assist John."

"Of course," Barton said. "But is this likely to become permanent, sir?"

"Truthfully … I don't know. But Mr Viney was due to retire in about six weeks' time. I can't see him returning to work, so I would assume that at some point there will be a formal interview process to go through. For now though, we just need to fulfil the roles."

Cyril had to voice the thought that had burst into his mind. "On Wednesday …" he began.

"Cyril," Barton warned.

"No, if you have a question, Cyril, I'd like to hear it," Sanderson said.

"It was just that on Wednesday, Mr Viney seemed keen for us to wrap up the Harrison case. I was just wondering if recent findings were putting a strain on him?"

"I think we need to keep the two events separate, Cyril," Sanderson responded.

"With all of us spreading ourselves more thinly, do you think we might need another body at DC level … on a temporary basis, say?" Cyril suggested.

"You're thinking of young Woodbridge?"

Cyril nodded.

"He did well on his course, I believe," Sanderson replied. "I'll have a word with his Inspector.

"Now, you two need to dig a bit deeper into Harrison's background and find out as much as you can about the man. The key to what happened to him may well be somewhere in his past." Sanderson stood up. "So, I'm sure you'll want to get stuck in."

Cyril and Barton stood to leave.

"Oh," Barton paused at the door. "Is this general knowledge? Do we tell the rest of the team?"

"I'm sure the rest of the team will want to be kept informed."

Cyril closed the door behind them.

As they made their way back to the CID room, Barton looked to Cyril. "That's a bit of a shock," he said. "I did think for a minute there you were going to mention being warned off your historical case."

"Trust me with some tact," Cyril replied.

Back in the CID room, the place was empty.

"Just a thought ..." Cyril said, "What personal belongings did we find on Harrison?"

"Not much but I brought them back from the PM on Monday in an envelope. I'll fetch it. It's in my office."

Barton returned with a brown paper bag containing the personal possessions found on Harrison's body and emptied it onto Cyril's desk. There was a grubby handkerchief, a set of door keys, twenty-seven pence in coins and a wallet. Cyril opened the wallet and found three one pound notes, and a variety of scraps of paper. The man obviously made notes for certain subjects. One listed grocery items whilst another seemed to be some race horse names with courses checked against them.

"Do we know if he's a regular at the local bookies?" Cyril wondered.

"If nobody has already, make sure someone follows that up."

"And what's this?" Cyril unfolded a piece of paper with what appeared to be a telephone number and a name. "*Gloria*. Interesting," he said, passing it to Barton.

The DI studied it for a second. "I thought the word was he didn't have any lady friends?"

"Not according to Mrs White in the flat below, at least she hadn't seen anyone visiting the flat."

"Mind you, it could be a bloke." Barton grinned as Cyril looked bewildered. "You know like the character they call Gloria in that TV comedy, *It Ain't Half Hot, Mum*."

"Soon find out." Cyril lifted the handset on his desk phone and dialled the number. "Engaged," he said.

"Don't waste too much time on that, get on to the GPO and see if you can get a name and address."

# 29

Cyril joined the team of detectives on Harrison's street and detailed Walker to check on the bookmaker's to see if Harrison was known there. In the meantime, he decided to call on Mrs White once again. Previously, she'd struck him as someone who would notice things. Perhaps she might need a little coaxing.

"Ah, Sergeant Claydon," she greeted, opening the door on the security chain. "I see several of your colleagues around the street this morning. Have there been developments?"

"Could I come in for a minute?" Cyril left her question unanswered.

"Of course." She closed the door, unhooked the chain and reopened it to allow Cyril to enter. "Shall I put the kettle on?"

"Good idea, Mrs White." Cyril followed her down the hall to the kitchen where he'd sat and chatted before.

The woman fussed around filling the kettle, switching it on, pulling mugs and plates from a cupboard and producing some bourbon biscuits from another. "A special treat," she said, placing them on the kitchen table.

"No need to go to any trouble." Cyril sat in the same chair he'd occupied previously.

"No trouble, Sergeant. You helped me out last time you were here. I'd never have been able to get up on the steps to change that hall lightbulb."

The kettle clicked off and she added the water to the teabags in the mugs. "Now, we'll let those brew a minute and you can ask me whatever it is you've come to ask."

Cyril smiled at the woman's candid attitude. "Well, I was just wondering if I could ask you to think about anything out of the ordinary that you might have noticed over the past few weeks. I know you said Mr Harrison didn't appear to have many visitors but ... well, sometimes the most insignificant incidents can provide vital information."

"I can't think of anything," She finished off the tea and added milk from the fridge. "I mean, the postie is a regular visitor, the binmen, of course." She turned and brought the mugs to the table and sat down. "Last time you were here I mentioned that man with the big car that called."

Cyril nodded. That was on his list.

"Oh, unless ..." the woman paused in thought.

"Go on," Cyril encouraged.

"I'm trying to think exactly when it was but ..." she paused for a second in concentration. "It must have been a couple of weeks ago, maybe a bit longer, but we seemed to have trouble with the electricity supply in this block."

Cyril took a sip of his tea.

"Please sergeant, help yourself to a bourbon, they're my favourites."

Cyril picked a biscuit up off the plate. "I quite like them too," he said. "But ... electricity ...?"

"Oh yes. It started with some problems with the lights. They seemed to go bright then dim then back again, several times in the evenings for a few nights. Anyway, I mentioned it to Mrs Weaver next door and she said she'd had similar problems. Well, I reported it to the council and they sent an electrician round. He was a nice young man. He was here for a few days in the flats trying to solve the problem."

"And did he?"

"It took a little while but, yes he did. He was in the other three flats too. Now let me get this straight ... He thought originally it might have been a problem with the supply coming from outside but eventually discovered it was a problem with the boards, is that right? Apparently faulty parts when these properties were rewired about five years ago. I don't know, something like that, I think he said."

"So, did this electrician sort out the problem?"

"He seemed to, as it hasn't played up since."

"So this electrician would have seen Mr Harrison?"

"Definitely. He would have had to have access to all the flats to check they were safe and carry out the repairs. At least, that's what he told me."

# 30
## Sunday 19th February 1978

After a quick catch up with the team going over everything that the Saturday enquiries had produced, Barton informed them of the latest news from the hospital. Detective Chief Superintendent Viney was stable but critical in the Intensive Care Unit. The news had still shocked them. With tasks allocated and detectives cross-checking the new statements that were taken yesterday, Barton called Cyril to his office.

"What's the real position regarding Mr Viney?" Cyril asked, once the door was closed.

"That's as much as I know," Barton responded. "Martin was off to see his wife this morning but word is, apart from family, there are no visitors allowed yet." The DI sat down at his desk and produced a Peter Stuyvesant cigarette from the packet lying there. "I'll let you know if I hear any more." He lit up and puffed out smoke. "But you'll be pleased to learn that I've persuaded the Inspector to release young Woodbridge to us from tomorrow."

"That's good," Cyril said.

"Get him to work with you for the most part. I don't want him picking up any bad habits from the Flower Pot Men."

Cyril smiled at the reference to Bill and Ben aka DCs Walker and Miller. "You're thinking of Miller in particular, I assume."

Barton nodded and tapped his cigarette in the ashtray on his desk. "I've requested Harrison's bank statements just to make sure he wasn't in financial difficulties, but it sounds like his gambling was just a bit of harmless fun." The DI looked frustrated. "He doesn't seem to have had any suspect visitors that our enquiries have discovered. We must be missing something, Cyril."

Cyril began to count on his fingers. "The only visiting characters we know of are this mystery man with the big car, the electrician who was in all four flats and the nurses who tended to Harrison. Actually, that reminds me, I still need to speak to Sister Nelson, the one who stood in for Sister Gallagher that last week."

"You need to speak to that nurse as soon as you can, bearing in mind the findings of the PM." Barton took another drag. "Remind me again about this bloke with a big car."

Cyril reprised the story Mrs White had related about the caller Harrison had about a month ago, driving a car with a figure on the bonnet, possibly a Jaguar, with a number plate that reminded her of her late husband, Harold. "I've tried a few options on the number but nothing so far. I'll pick that up tomorrow with the DVLC in Swansea."

Barton stubbed out his cigarette. "All right, Cyril, there doesn't seem a lot you can do until tomorrow, so bugger off and let the troops work through the paperwork."

Before he left the station, Cyril gave Cathy a quick call. He proposed a run out that afternoon but Cathy thought the forecast iffy and Simon was studying for exams later in the week. "But why don't you come over for some supper this evening," she had suggested. And so he arranged to call round about seven o'clock.

On the drive home, the rain had started so Cyril was not disappointed he and Cathy weren't out and about. By the time he pulled up outside his house, the rain had become heavy. He dashed inside. Shrugging off his coat in the hallway, he was surprised when the doorbell rang. He opened the door to see Doris sheltering under an umbrella.

"Doris, come in. I've only just got in."

"Yes, I saw you," she said as she shook the umbrella and folded it up before leaving it behind the front door.

"Tea?" Cyril offered, making his way to the kitchen.

"Lovely, thanks." She followed him up the hallway. "I called round earlier but there was no answer. I expect you're busy with that case you're working on."

Cyril filled the kettle and switched it on. "Strange one, Doris. Man found dead on the stairs to his flat but it seems he might not be who everyone thought he was."

"And what about Elsie Smart? Have you found anything out about that?" Doris sat at the kitchen table.

"To be honest, I've not had a lot of time to work on that this week. Our Chief Super was taken into hospital with a heart attack yesterday."

"Oh, I'm sorry to hear that." She seemed preoccupied. "Oddly enough, that's what I called round to see you about."

"You're not thinking of having a heart attack, are you?" Cyril chuckled.

"No." she smiled grimly. "No, but I am going into hospital."

"Oh, I'm sorry to hear that too, Doris. It's nothing too serious, I hope. I mean you don't have to tell me if ..."

"Cyril. I would hardly come round to tell you something like that and not say what it is. No, I'm going in to Colchester on Tuesday for an operation. I've been having trouble for some time with a hernia."

Cyril looked concerned. "I feel awful. There you were looking after me the other week."

She waved her hand "You were ill."

"All the same ..." The kettle clicked off and he poured water into two mugs with teabags.

"It's just I wondered if you'd keep an eye on the house while I'm gone," Doris continued.

"Of course I will. I'll bring you some grapes too."

"Don't you dare. I don't like grapes."

Cyril laughed and the mood lightened.

# 31
## Monday 20th February 1978

Sam Woodbridge was introduced to the rest of the team that morning by DI Barton. Following a quick update on the weekend's progress, the officers settled down to continue checking through the latest statements taken. Harrison had indeed been a regular in the local bookmakers. Nothing excessive and he'd made a little and lost a little over the period of time he'd been a customer.

Cyril had chased the GPO regarding his number query and they came back to him with the name of *D Somerville* and an address in the Great Clacton area of the town. He thanked the caller, replaced the receiver and thought for a moment. Seizing the initiative, He picked up the phone once more and dialled the number. It was answered on the fourth ring.

*"Hello?"* the female voice replied.

Cyril tried to form an image of the woman. "Er ... is that Gloria?" he hesitated.

*"Who is this?"*

He decided to take the risk. "Someone gave me your number."

*"Who was that?"*

"Trevor, Trevor Harrison."

*"Who?"*

He was taken off guard for a moment but decided to take a gamble. "Sorry, I mean Graham, Graham Woods."

Gloria's tone softened. *"Oh, the naughty boy."*

"I was wondering if I could come and see you?"

*"Would you want the same treatment as Graham?"*

Cyril smiled into the handset. "Possibly not."

*"Well there are a full range of services available, and it's ten pounds for an hour."*

"That sounds fine, Gloria. Whereabouts are you, by the way?"

She gave him the same address the GPO contact had. *"When were you looking to visit?"*

"Sometime today would be good."

*"How about twelve?"*

He checked his watch. "Okay, I'll see you then."

*"Oh, and the name?"*

He hesitated again. "Er, Cyril," he said.

"Look forward to it, Cyril," she responded with a hint of flirtatiousness.

He replaced the receiver, puffed out his cheeks then grinned to himself. Close call with the names but exactly as he suspected. And he'd bet that's where Harrison obtained the mysterious marks on his backside.

He stood and approached the desk where Sam Woodbridge had been allocated.

"What are you up to, Sam?"

Woodbridge put some sheets of paper down. "Just cross-checking the door-to-door reports."

"I'd like you to come with me at …" he glanced at his watch, "… in about an hour."

"Sure."

"In the meantime, something else for you to puzzle …" Cyril then told Sam of Mrs White's statement regarding a visitor to Harrison, driving a big car with a mascot on the bonnet and a number plate reminding her of her late husband, Harold. What could he come up with as possibilities?

The rain had eased slightly as Cyril drew to a halt outside the Victorian semi-detached house the address turned out to be. The wind, however, seemed as strong as ever as he and Woodbridge stepped out of the car and made for the front door. A small front garden behind a privet hedge gave the house some kerb appeal and a bit of seclusion. Woodbridge stood to one side as Cyril rang the doorbell.

The door opened slightly and a blonde head appeared, peering around it. A wide smile formed on her face as she looked him up and down.

"Cyril?" she questioned.

He nodded.

"Come in, come in," she said. "It's really wild out there."

She hid behind the door, opening it wider to allow him in.

As he stepped inside, Woodbridge followed close behind.

"Here, what's all this?" she panicked. "I'm not into threesomes. You never said ..."

Cyril cut her short by opening his warrant card. Woodbridge did the same, his eyes staring at the woman for a moment before he closed the door.

Her arms wrapped around the flimsy negligee in an attempt to cover her modesty.

"Please don't be alarmed," said Cyril. "We're not interested in any activities you might be carrying out on the premises. We just need to ask you a few questions."

"I need to ... Let me get changed." She scurried off down the hallway and up the stairs.

Woodbridge stood open-mouthed watching the rear view.

The woman appeared to be in her forties with what Cyril would describe as a full-bodied physique.

Cyril put his hand up to Woodbridge's chin to close his mouth. "I'll get you some therapy, Sam," he said, a broad grin on his face. "Just as soon as we finish here."

A few minutes later, the woman reappeared in pyjamas under a dressing gown of a sort that Woodbridge's granny might wear.

"In here," she said sharply, opening the door to a living room with a small dining table at one end. She sat at one of the four chairs surrounding it, pulling out a packet of cigarettes and a lighter from the dressing gown pocket and placing them on the table in front of her.

Cyril took the hint and sat opposite, Woodbridge following suit.

"Can I just ask," Cyril began, "Gloria, it's not …?"

She shook her head. "It's Denise. Denise Somerville." She looked down at her hands clasped tightly together on the table.

"Ah, the D Somerville registered to the phone. Is it Mrs?"

"Technically, yes. He pissed off four years ago." She raised her head, a determined expression on her face. "I had to do something to keep this house on."

"We're not here to judge, Denise." Cyril's voice softened. "I'd like to ask you about the man you seem to know as Graham Woods."

"So that's why you mentioned him on the phone. I don't know. I haven't seen him for a couple of weeks."

"Well I'm sorry to have to tell you but you won't be seeing him again. He was found dead in his flat a week past Saturday."

She looked shocked. "How? I mean … if you're here, is it suspicious?"

"Before we proceed any further, can you tell me if you recognise this man?" Cyril produced the wedding photo that Bob Hewitt had lent him and passed it across the table.

She picked it up and studied it for a second before putting back down. "He's a lot younger but that's Graham."

Cyril glanced at Woodbridge then continued, "What can you tell me about him?"

She pulled a cigarette from the packet and lit it before answering. "Well …" She exhaled smoke. "It's a bit embarrassing." She looked towards Woodbridge.

"I can assure you Denise, whatever you tell us, we've probably heard it all before."

"Not both of you," she said under her breath. "He's been coming here for about a year now, I suppose.

Strange, but he's never wanted to do anything … you know, physical to me." She nervously flicked ash into the tray on the table.

"So what sort of things did you get up to?"

"He liked me to dress in a certain way. Short dresses or skirts, stockings and suspenders. He also liked to talk." Another draw on her cigarette. "I think I was a bit of therapy for him." She hesitated a moment. "He also liked me to spank him. He said he'd been bad and needed to be punished."

"Did he ever expand on that?"

She looked down onto the table nervously tapping her cigarette on the side of the ashtray. "He used to say he'd done some bad things … years ago." She looked back up at Cyril. "I thought he was referring to the war. He told me he was in the Tank Regiment."

"Did he ever say what these 'bad things' might be?"

She shook her head. "No. He just said he'd done wrong and needed to pay for it."

"And you used to spank him."

She stubbed out her cigarette with some force. "Yes. It seemed to be what did it for him. You know, turned him on. He'd tell me he'd done some awful things. I'd tell him to take his clothes off and lie on the bed. Then he'd ask me to do it. Seemed easy money."

"So when was the last time he visited?"

She thought for a moment. "It must have been the week before last. Yes, it was the Monday, so two weeks ago today. So … what happened to him?"

"We're still investigating but he was found dead at home about ten days ago."

"So later the same week he came here."

"So it would seem," Cyril said. "On that last occasion, did he ever expand on what he'd done wrong?"

She shook her head. "No, not really. All he ever said was that it was all a long time ago and no one had ever found out it was him."

Cyril and Woodbridge got back into the car and set off for the station.

"I never knew that sort of thing existed in Clacton," Woodbridge finally said.

"It's in every town, Sam … if you look for it. Anyway, remember to treat that visit in confidence. I dread to think what your mum would think if she knew you were being dragged off to visit some woman of ill-repute." Cyril paused a second then burst out laughing. "Your face …" he said.

Woodbridge was silent for a while, then said, "But that last comment. How did she phrase it? 'It was all a long time ago and no one had ever found out it was him.' That was significant, wasn't it?"

"I think it could be. We need to find out a lot more about our Mr Harrison or Woods."

They were silent for a while before Woodbridge spoke. "Oh, by the way, I've had a few thoughts on that number plate you've been pondering."

"And?"

"I think the ones that would make the most sense would be HAR 301D or 801D."

"Well, when we get back, can you make enquiries with the DVLC in Swansea?"

"Sure."

Back at the station, Cyril reported their encounter to Barton.

Barton gave a laugh. "So one mystery solved then; he liked his arse tanned."

"Not quite how I'd put it but yes," Cyril agreed. "I think she was an education for Sam in some ways too."

Later that afternoon, Woodbridge approached Cyril at his desk. "I think I have something, skip," he said.

Cyril put down the statement he was reading. "What's that, Sam?"

"One of the registration checks came back with a blue Jaguar 4.2 saloon, registration number HAR 801D, registered keeper a Harold Peter Wray at an address in Hitchin in Hertfordshire."

Cyril's face broke into a broad smile. "Good work, Sam. Let's take this to the DI."

Barton seemed to have the weight of the world on his shoulders when they entered his office but his mood lightened at the news. "That's another line of enquiry to follow," he said. "What about that other nurse who visited our man?"

"I phoned the surgery but she's off today, on a course apparently, so I'll call again in the morning and make arrangements to see her," Cyril answered.

Barton nodded. "I tell you what, leave those details of Wray with me and I'll follow that up myself tomorrow. I need to get out for a while. Bloody paperwork the DCI has to contend with ..." he indicated the pile of files on his desk. "A trip out to Hitchin might be just the thing."

Woodbridge handed the slip of paper to Barton, turned and made for the door.

"Thanks, Sam," Cyril said, "I just want a word with the DI."

When Woodbridge had gone, Cyril sat down opposite Barton. "I just wondered if I could have an hour or two off tomorrow morning?" he said.

Barton rubbed his face with both hands. "God, Cyril, you're not off digging into that old case of yours, are you?"

"Not at all. We're too busy on this one. No, it's just my old neighbour, Doris. You remember Doris?"

Barton groaned. "As if I could forget."

"Well, she's off into hospital for an operation tomorrow morning and I said I'd take her in. She doesn't have any other relatives."

"Go on," Barton responded. "I must be going soft in my old age."

# 32
## Tuesday 21st February 1978

Doris had a small case at her feet when she opened the door to Cyril. Coat and hat on, she was ready to go. The nervous expression on her face, however, belied the calm exterior.

"All set?" he enquired, as he reached for her case.

She looked round the hallway before closing the front door and locking it. "As I'll ever be." She followed him down the path to his car.

"It'll be fine, Doris," he reassured her as they set off for Colchester.

"Thanks, Cyril. And I really appreciate you taking the time to drive me in."

"Well you looked out for me the other week. It's what we do."

He managed to find a parking space outside the Essex County Hospital, walked round and opened the door for her. "I haven't got any change to give you a tip," she quipped.

On previous occasions, Cyril would have headed down to the basement where the mortuary was situated. But this morning, he carried her case up to the first floor where she would report for all her pre-op checks. A nurse met them as they stepped onto the ward.

She turned to him. "You get yourself off now," she said. "I'll be fine."

"We'll look after your mother now," the nurse said, prompting Doris to giggle.

"He's not my son, he's my toy boy," she said with a mischievous grin.

"I'll call and see how you're doing later," he said, a smile playing on his face. Inwardly, he thought Doris's light-hearted remarks concealed her anxiety.

As he made his way to the stairs, a familiar face approached.

"Mrs Viney?" he greeted.

Initially distracted, the woman looked up at him.

"DS Cyril Claydon," he announced.

"Of course," the woman said. "I thought I recognised your face, Cyril. Roy has mentioned you a few times."

He could see the concern etched on her face. "How is he?" he asked.

"Not good. I'm worried but he's in the best place."

"We're all thinking of him."

"Thanks. And thank your colleagues too."

As he turned to leave, she thought of something else. "Oh Cyril, can I ask you something?"

He turned back to face her.

"Has something happened at work? Something to make Roy anxious?"

He took a step towards her. "How do you mean?"

"It's just I noticed recently … he seemed distracted … preoccupied."

He puffed out his cheeks. "To be honest, he was his usual self to me the last time I saw him but that must have been … oh, a couple of weeks ago now."

She looked thoughtful. "It was around that time that Roy changed. You notice these things as a wife. He's seemed worried these past few weeks when I think back. Was there anything that might have prompted that?"

Cyril felt the adrenaline pump into his system. "I can't think of anything particular. There again, I'm not dealing with your husband on a day-to-day basis. In his role I'm not sure what pressures he gets from above."

"I'm sorry, I shouldn't be asking you."

"Not a problem, Mrs Viney."

She held out a hand. "Mary," she said. "Call me Mary."

He shook her hand.

"I must get back to him," she said. "I only went for a coffee."

"Don't forget to look after yourself too, Mary." He thought the woman looked strained. "He'll need your support when he gets out."

"Yes." She paused a moment. "Bye, Cyril," she said, before turning away and heading for the Intensive Care Unit.

He produced his pipe and tobacco as he walked back to his car. Lighting up, he sat in the driver's seat, deep in thought. Could it have been his searching for information on the Smart case that had somehow caused Viney's heart attack? Did it put him under strain? But why? Was he involved more deeply than some of Cyril's findings suggest?

He sat for some time, window half down, smoking his pipe, turning things over in his mind. Viney was definitely one of the detectives sent to the bus garage to interview the crews. Did he also take a statement from Molly Pearson, the elderly clippie? According to Barney Cameron, she'd made a statement at the police station. Did she make that statement to Viney? If so, why is there no sign of it in the files? Maybe it got misplaced. Maybe Barton was right - sometimes it happens. But then why the change in Viney's demeanour, according to his wife, from around the time he discovered Cathy copying the files?

When Cyril arrived back in the CID office, he discovered a message on his desk to call Edith Garland. Before he would call her, he had another call on his list to make, that of the nurse who'd stood in for Sister Gallagher on that last visit to Harrison.

Once he'd spoken to the surgery and arranged to meet the nurse later that afternoon, Woodbridge approached him.

"I've got a bit of information for you, skip," he said.

"Alright, Sam. Where's the DI, by the way? Did he go to Hertfordshire?"

"I don't think so. Last I saw he was with Mr Sanderson heading out in the DCI's car."

Cyril raised his eyebrows. "Probably off to Colchester for some meeting or other. Such is life for the higher ranks." He broke into a broad grin. "Fancy a brew?"

In the canteen, the pair sat at a table with mugs of tea in front of them, Cyril preparing to light his pipe. "So what have you got, Sam?"

"Last week you gave me a name. Well I've done some digging around and I've come up with this." Woodbridge passed over a piece of paper. "Not the easiest of searches with women," he said. "The surnames change. Anyway, she married in 1931 and we found the marriage certificate and from that, her maiden name."

Cyril put his unlit pipe down in the ashtray and read. "So we have a date of birth of 25th March 1906, so she'd have been …"

"Forty in 1947," Woodbridge completed.

"Sounds about right. And do we know if she's still with us and possibly where?"

"That's phase two. I've got my sister on it at the rates office."

"Good man, Sam." Cyril picked up his pipe, struck a match and puffed it into life. "How's it going with your new colleagues?"

Woodbridge wrinkled his nose. "Okay, I suppose."

Cyril smiled. "Anything you say to me is in strictest confidence."

Woodbridge took a sip of tea before he responded in low tones. "Well, Ben Miller's a bit of a dinosaur but I like Bill Walker."

Cyril nodded. "You're probably right. Bill shows a lot of promise but I worry that Ben's influence will stifle that."

"You'd be surprised. I think Bill has him sussed."

Cyril spotted George Kidby enter the canteen and raised a hand.

"Have you heard any news about Doris yet?" Woodbridge asked.

"Ah, I'll make a call later this afternoon."

A minute later, Kidby approached the pair, a mug of tea in his hand. “Mind if I join you lads?” he asked.

Cyril indicated a spare seat.

“Terrible news about the Chief Super,” Kidby said as he sat down. “Anybody heard an update?”

“Still in ITU in a serious condition, I believe,” Cyril answered, not keen to mention that he’d spoken to Mary Viney that morning.

“Who’d have thought it, eh?”

Cyril glanced at Woodbridge. “The thing is, he began, “I can’t help wondering if … you know, it might have been brought on by me digging around.”

Kidby also looked over to Woodbridge.

“Don’t worry, George, Sam knows what I’ve been looking at but, officially, he has no idea.”

Kidby was reassured. “What makes you think that, Cyril?”

“Apparently, it was around the same time I was warned off, you know when he would have discovered what I’d been doing, that he began to show signs of stress.”

“How can you know that?” Kidby persisted.

“I just do.”

Kidby leaned in closer. “Well if he did stress about it, it can only be that he knows more than he’s let on in the past. Guilty conscience,” he added with a knowing look.

After a moment, Cyril stood up. “Well, we best get on,” he said.

# 33

Cyril decided he would conduct the interview with Sister Pat Nelson on his own. He thought the challenge of having to keep DC Miller from being distracted would be too much. He'd arranged to speak to her that afternoon when she should be back from her rounds.

His judgement was confirmed when the attractive woman in the nurse uniform showed him into a small room she used as a base at the surgery. She appeared to be in her thirties with dark hair neatly swept up in a bun and just a hint of make-up.

"Please sit down, Sergeant." She indicated a chair by the side of a desk with a few files and basic stationery items on top. Also on the desk and close to hand where he sat were a blood pressure machine and a stethoscope.

Cyril sat and took out his notebook.

"So how can I help?" She sat down behind the desk and smiled at him as she laid her bag on the floor beside her.

"As I'm sure you know and as I explained to your colleague, Sister Gallagher last week, we're making enquiries about one of the patients here, Mr Trevor Harrison, who was found dead in his flat a week past Saturday."

Sister Nelson looked down at her desk briefly before facing Cyril. "Yes, I had heard. Dreadful," she said, a serious look on her face.

"I understand you visited Mr Harrison in the week before he died while you were covering for Sister Gallagher?"

"That's correct. On ..." she paused as she bent over, put a hand into her nurse bag and retrieved a diary onto the desk. Opening it, she flicked over a few pages then said, "… on Thursday, the ninth. I called in in the morning about ten, usual obs., that's observations; BP, heart rate, that sort of thing, then dressed his leg ulcers."

"And how was Mr Harrison? I mean, was there any concern for his health?"

"Well, he wasn't the fittest man for his age; he had a heart condition, diabetes and then, over the last few weeks he'd developed leg ulcers, which is probably a not uncommon complication of his diabetes."

"Was that the first time you'd visited Mr Harrison?"

"Yes, and the only time. I was covering for Sister Gallagher. I'd read his notes, obviously."

"And what was his general condition … in your medical opinion? I mean, did he seem anxious or have any particular questions for you?"

"No, not really. As I said, it was the only time I'd seen him, so I'd got nothing to compare things with."

"And did you examine him at all?"

"I sounded his chest, listened to his heart and took his blood pressure."

"So you'd have rolled up his sleeve for that?"

A look of alarm briefly passed over Sister Nelson's face. "Well, yes, obviously."

"Were there any signs of bruising?"

She now looked bewildered. "No, not that I could see. Is there a particular reason you're asking?"

Cyril ignored the question. "And you would have no reason to examine the rest of his body?"

"Only his legs. He dropped his trousers whilst I examined and dressed his ulcers."

"And you wouldn't have seen his buttocks?"

She gave a nervous laugh. "Why would I have seen that part of his anatomy? Is this a serious line of enquiry?"

"Sorry, Sister, I have to ask. You see, when he was discovered, he had some suspicious bruising on his arms and some unusual marks on his buttocks."

"Well I can assure you, Sergeant, there were no such signs when I saw him on Thursday morning and I certainly didn't see his buttocks."

Cyril brought the conversation to a close. "Thanks for your time, Sister. You've been very helpful." Although what exact help that might be, he wasn't sure at the moment.

When he left the surgery, he decided to go straight home rather than back to the station. He needed to make a call in private to find out how Doris had fared. If he could he would call in and visit her before that evening. He also needed to contact Edith Garland to find out what she might have for him.

He was relieved to be told that all had gone as expected with Doris's operation and she was in recovery. He should be able to call in and see her after seven but only for ten minutes. He asked the nurse on the ward who'd answered the phone to let her know he'd rung.

Later, when he called into the hospital and saw her in the bed, she still seemed a bit drowsy. "How are you feeling?" he asked.

"A bit sore," she answered.

"I won't keep you. The nurse said only ten minutes. I brought you these." He produced some flowers. "Thought they might cheer you up."

"Thank you, Cyril," she said. "They're lovely."

He grinned. "I decided against the grapes."

She gave a laugh. "What have you been up to? Any more on your mystery death, or young Elsie?"

"Not too sure, Doris but I might have more on Elsie's case this evening. I'm off to talk to someone about it."

# 34

Edith Garland had arranged to meet Cyril at her mother's bungalow on the outskirts of Colchester, not far from the hospital. Edith explained that Alice Bowman had moved there after Edith's father had died eight years previously. She wanted to be nearer to her and her next sister down, who is married and lives nearby. Edith's other sister lives in Canada and her brother is in Scotland.

"So four of you growing up in the East End," Cyril had commented when Edith told him her mother had agreed to talk to him. "And with all the bombing, it must have been a real hardship for your mother."

"She was strong," Edith replied. "Most were in those days. You just got on with things."

Cyril parked the car by the kerb, opened the wicket gate and walked up the path to the front door of the low bungalow on a street with many similar properties. As he approached the front door, the muffled sounds of a television drifted out. When he rang the doorbell, the noise ceased as the set was obviously switched off. Old school, he thought, polite manners.

After a few seconds, Edith opened the door, a smile on her face. "Cyril," she said. "Punctual as always."

He threw a quick glance to his wristwatch. "Comes with the discipline, I'm afraid."

"Come in. Mum's been looking forward to meeting you." Edith indicated the door to her left which was slightly ajar.

In contrast to the bitter chill outside, the sitting room was sweltering, the gas fire glowing.

"Mum feels the cold these days," Edith explained, as Cyril shrugged out of his overcoat. "Mum, this is Cyril," she said.

Alice Bowman was sitting on one side of a two-seater settee, dressed in a plaid skirt, blouse and cardigan. She wore glasses and a walking stick was to hand leaning against the armrest. Her hair had been permed and she studied Cyril as he stood in front of her. “Are you the policeman?” she asked.

“That’s right, Mrs Bowman, Detective Sergeant Cyril Claydon.”

“Tea Cyril?” Edith offered.

“Lovely thanks.”

“Sit yourself down and I’ll sort it,” Edith said, as she walked out into the kitchen.

Cyril sat in a comfortable armchair facing the settee at an angle.

“I remember your name now,” Alice said. “John mentioned you a few times. He was my son-in-law, you know.”

“I do, Mrs Bowman. He was a good officer.”

“Call me Alice.”

“Thank you, Alice and, please, call me Cyril.” He looked around the room. A dresser unit stood against the wall behind the settee where various items of porcelain were displayed, and also a number of family photographs.

Alice brought his attention back. “Edith tells me you’re looking into the murder of Elsie Smart, Cyril?”

“It’s unofficial at the moment. It was something my next-door neighbour mentioned to me that got me interested. Before then, I’d never heard of the case. I only moved to the area in 1951.”

“Poor girl. She was only sixteen.” Alice appeared to look into the distance for a second. “And they never found out who did it.”

“So I understand.”

Edith returned with a tray containing tea pot, milk and sugar and three cups and saucers. She placed it on a pine coffee table in front of the settee and began to arrange the crockery. She spoke to her mother as she did so, “I was telling Cyril that the Elsie Smart case reminded me of Gladys back in the East End.”

"I remember you telling me about Elsie when you worked in Clacton. I know you were upset about it when you heard some of the details."

"So what exactly happened with this, Gladys, you say?" Cyril asked.

"Tragic family really," Alice began. "Mr Taylor worked in the docks, like my Bert. Unfortunately, Mr Taylor developed TB and died before the war, 1936, if I remember rightly. And then, poor Margaret, that was Gladys's mother, she was knocked down and killed by a bus crossing the Mile End Road in 1940. That left Gladys to look after her brother, Alfie; he was only thirteen at the time."

Edith passed a cup of tea to Alice.

"Thank you, dear," she said before continuing her story. "But before that, Gladys had married Tommy Vaughan just before war broke out, so she was actually Gladys Vaughan, but we still referred to her as Taylor. And then her Tommy, who had joined the Merchant Navy, perished on a ship that was part of a North Atlantic Convoy sunk by a German U-boat the following year. However, she was pregnant by then and gave birth to Patricia in February 1940. Tommy never saw his daughter."

"That is sad," he agreed as he took the offered tea from Edith.

"It was the last night of the blitz, May 10$^{th}$ 1941, I'll never forget that," Alice resumed. "We didn't know it then but the Germans changed tack after that. One last show before they turned their attention to the east."

He was impressed by Alice Bowman's knowledge of the events.

"The following morning, it was chaos. We'd spent the night down in the tube station at Mile End. But we all got up and tried to go about our business as normal. We weren't going to let Hitler grind us down." A defiant expression appeared on her face.

"What of Gladys Vaughan, or Taylor?"

"It was Alfie who found her. God, I felt for the boy. She was in an outside toilet of a bombed out house on the next street from ours."

"And what had happened to her?"

"Apparently, she'd been strangled. Constable Turner told me. He was our local bobby." Alice lowered her voice as if Edith shouldn't hear. "She'd also been … you know."

"She'd had sex, Cyril," Edith clarified, as Alice turned her head away.

He did know what the old lady meant.

"Although it wasn't clear if it was willingly," Edith went on.

"And no one has ever been charged for this?"

"Not as far as I know," Alice replied.

"And Constable Turner?"

"Oh, he's been dead a long time. He was in his fifties then."

"So what specifically made you think this was similar to the circumstances surrounding the death of Elsie Smart?"

Edith took up the conversation. "She was strangled by a stocking, wasn't that right, mum?"

Alice looked from Edith to Cyril. "Except I know for a fact that Gladys didn't possess a pair," she said.

"How was that, mum?"

Alice looked sternly at her daughter. "Because we couldn't afford them. We used to use gravy browning and paint the seam line up the back of our legs with an eyebrow pencil."

Cyril knew of that trick. "What were the theories back then? I mean, did they have any suspects?" He drained his cup and nodded affirmation as Edith lifted the teapot to pour another.

"Well there was the bloke she was seen talking to in the Arms the night she was murdered," Alice answered as she indicated a top up for her tea too. "She used to do a few shifts a week for Mr Chapman. Mrs Chapman reckoned Gladys was chatting to this soldier fella who was back for a few days to be with his mum 'cos his dad had died. Old Frank Hargreaves reckoned that an' all."

He was amused by the fact that Alice's East End accent seemed stronger now she'd relaxed. "Frank Hargreaves?"

"A neighbour who used to frequent the Arms."

"Who was this soldier?"

"Dotty Woods son, Graham." Alice made a face. "Never liked him, Always thought he was a bit ... you know, weird."

That familiar feeling grew in Cyril's stomach. "In what way?"

"Put it this way, I wouldn't have wanted Edith, or any of my daughters left alone with him," Alice said.

"Was he spoken to by the police, do you know?"

"He disappeared pretty quickly. His mother said he'd gone to Liverpool to rejoin his unit. Nobody ever saw him again. Word was he was killed in action, Egypt, I think."

He drained his tea once more and thought for a moment.

"More tea?" Edith offered.

"No thanks, Edith, I'm awash." Cyril leaned over towards his overcoat. From an inside pocket, he pulled out an envelope. "I wonder if you might have a look at this photograph, Alice?" He produced the picture discovered in Harrison's flat of the group of soldiers. "Do you recognise anyone on there?"

Alice took the photo from Cyril and changed her glasses.

He watched as she studied the snap. Then her eyes widened. "That's him! That's Graham Woods," she said, stabbing at one of the men.

"Which one?"

"Here, this one." She pointed to the unsmiling figure third from the left. The one Cyril knew was next to the one marked up as Trevor Harrison on the reverse.

Alice passed the photo to Edith who nodded her agreement to her mother's identification. "That's the weirdo."

"Thanks for that, both of you. Now can I ask you to look at another photo?" He produced the wedding picture he'd borrowed from Bob Hewitt.

Again, Alice studied the picture. She looked up at Cyril, a surprised expression on her face. "Are you telling me he's still alive? He didn't die in the war?"

"You're sure this is him?"

Edith took hold of the wedding photo. "He's ten years or so older but that certainly looks like the Graham Woods I knew from the Mile End," she said.

"So," Alice said, wistfully, "Alfie was right … what he told me."

# 35
## Tuesday 8$^{th}$ May 1945

This was the day, forever etched in history as VE Day; Victory in Europe. The Second World War would rage on for another three months or so whilst fighting continued in the Far East. But this was a day to celebrate.

Alfie Taylor had mixed feelings. His grandfather, Gramps, Stan Tanner, had not lived to see it. He had suffered a heart attack last year and died at the age of sixty-eight. His grandmother, Dolly, was still relatively fit and healthy at the age of sixty-six. He'd been heartbroken, as was she. His Gramps had taken him under his wing and treated him like his own son. He'd learned so much from him. When he'd left school three years ago now, Stan had fixed him up with an electrical apprenticeship where he'd worked for over forty years. Alfie had really taken to it and was now capable of carrying out some work on his own. He'd also inherited Stan's toolbox, and that meant everything to him.

At school, his best mate was Richard Howells, known as Richie, who, like Alfie, was engaged on an apprenticeship course, only he was learning the plumbing trade. Once this war ended, they thought they could have a bright future working together.

The day before, when news came through that Germany's unconditional surrender had been accepted by General Eisenhower, celebrations had broken out in Clacton and many other towns all over the country. The BBC had interrupted programmes to announce that the following day, May 8$^{th}$, would be a national holiday. And so the big celebration would be in London today. Alfie wanted to be part of it. He needed to be part of it, remembering the Nazi battering he'd witnessed in the East End when he was younger.

Richie and he decided to get the train from Clacton into Liverpool Street and make their way to Trafalgar Square or Buckingham Palace.

"I don't think that's a good idea, Alfie," Dolly had said, when he'd told her what they'd planned. "It'll be crowded and dangerous."

"I'll be alright, Gran. Richie is going too," he'd told her. "I'm a big boy now, you know."

She could see that his mind was made up. "Well I'll do you some sandwiches, for the journey."

"It'll be okay, I'm sure we can buy something."

"You don't need to be spending your money wastefully." She'd passed a pack-up to Alfie and, with a warning not to get involved drinking, waved the two lads off as they made their way to the train station.

In their compartment, other people had the same idea as the two friends and excited chatter broke out as soon as the guard's whistle sounded and the train began to move. A soldier in uniform and a woman they assumed was his wife, both in their forties, told them they were making for St Paul's Cathedral.

"Well, it's a symbol," the woman said. "Standin' proud and untouched after all those Huns could throw at us."

More people crowded onto the train as it made its way to London. Colchester saw a large influx and by the time it left Chelmsford it was standing room only. By then, the pair had eaten the butties that Dolly had insisted they take with them.

"Where do you think we should head first, Alfie?" Richie wondered as they were swept down the platform at Liverpool Street station by the throng.

"Shall we try Trafalgar Square? I reckon that'll be where a lot of people will go."

Two tube journeys later, the friends emerged into the fresh air at Charing Cross station and onto The Strand before they began to make their way the short distance in the direction of the square itself. The place was heaving and their first encounter was with a couple of Scottish soldiers dressed in kilts.

"Here, sonny," one of them said. "Ha' a wee nip." An opened half bottle of whisky was thrust into Alfie's face.

"I'm okay, thanks," he replied.

"Cumawn," the soldier persisted. "We're aw free now."

Alfie didn't like spirits but his grandfather had demonstrated how to appear to drink without actually doing so. He took the offered bottle and put it to his lips, head held upwards, lips pursed closed, half turning away as he did so, before pulling it away and handing it back to the soldier.

"Slainte, son," he said, taking another swig himself, before hurrying after his companion.

Alfie looked at Richie and smiled.

"Did you drink that?" Richie asked.

"Did I hell. I don't like it. I just let him think I did. Come on let's go."

The pair set off again in the direction of Trafalgar Square. They could see Nelson's column but all around was a sea of humanity, hugging, dancing, groups arm in arm, all in a jovial mood. Alfie and Richie were kissed three times, all by middle-aged women. Finally, Alfie caught sight of the fountains, which were turned off, but he could see revellers jumping in and out of the water. The pals were grabbed by other women and danced around as men played war-time favourites on accordions, trumpets and even a trombone.

Just after one o'clock, Alfie and Richie found a pub in a side street not far from the square. They were thirsty and decided they'd have some beer. Alfie had turned eighteen back in February and Richie was four months his senior but looked older than his years. They struggled their way through a mass of bodies, soldiers, sailors and airmen, to the bar and ordered beers. The hubbub of noise made it difficult but the barmaid understood what they wanted. In the other bar to the side, a pianist was rattling out *'Roll Out The Barrel'* to full accompaniment by the crowd. As the barmaid poured the drinks, Alfie's attention was suddenly caught by a loud outburst of laughter from the other bar. When he looked over, he froze. One of the group of soldiers standing there sharing a joke was familiar to him. But it couldn't be; he'd been told he was dead. As he stared at the man, their eyes locked. A slight look of recognition briefly passed over the man's face before he looked away. Richie had paid for their drinks and was standing with Alfie's glass in his hand, puzzled as to why his friend was paying no attention to the offered drink.

"Here," Richie said, "I thought you were looking forward to this?"

Alfie ignored him and began to struggle his way through to the other bar.

Richie took a swig from each glass and attempted to follow him.

Alfie made it to the other bar and looked round in vain for the man who'd attracted his attention. The group of soldiers who'd been with him were still at the bar, glasses in hand in a high state of hilarity. He tapped one of them on the arm. "Excuse me," he said, "Your mate who was just with you…"

The man looked down at Alfie. "Who was that then, sonny?"

"The other soldier who was laughing with you."

The man looked round the bar before turning back to Alfie. "Do you mean the tall bloke, Trevor?"

"Trevor?" Alfie looked confused.

"Yeah," the soldier said. "Here, Frank, where's Trevor disappeared to?"

One of his colleagues looked around the bar then shrugged. "Dunno, Bill. P'r'aps he's gone for a piss."

Richie finally caught up with his friend. "Don't you want this mate?"

Again Alfie ignored him and made his way through the crowd towards the Gents.

Richie rolled his eyes and downed one of the glasses in one, placing the empty glass on the bar before attempting to follow.

As he was about to enter the Gents, a soldier came rushing out, almost knocking the glass from his hand. “Oi! Watch out, mister.”

“And you can piss off too,” the soldier said, as he rushed for the door.

Thinking it would be safer, Richie drank the second beer as well. As he was looking round for somewhere to put that empty glass, Alfie staggered out of the Gents holding his jaw.

“Alfie, what the hell’s happened?”

“Bashtard,” was all Alfie said.

An elderly man sitting at a table with a group of men and women got up. “’ere, sit down a minute, son, he said. “Did ‘e just belt yer?” He helped Richie sit Alfie down.

Alfie looked pale.

“What’s going on?” Richie asked.

“Give me a minute,” Alfie said.

“Here.” One of the men at the table held out a glass with some brown liquid in it. “Finish this. It’ll do you good. It’s brandy,” he explained.

Richie nodded a thanks, took the glass and held it out for his friend.

Initially, Alfie shook his head but Richie persuaded him it was medicinal. Reluctantly, Alfie swallowed it and grimaced. After a few minutes, Alfie got to his feet, thanked the man and began to make his way to the door, Richie following.

Outside, Richie asked him, “Do you want to tell me what that was all about?”

Alfie was quiet for a moment. “It was just someone I thought I knew, but I must have been mistaken.” He looked at Richie. “I want to go down the Mile End Road and see if there’s anybody there I know. There’s bound to be a street party. You can come if you want.”

“Are you sure you’re alright, Alfie?”

“I’m not in the mood for all this crowd now. I want to be with people I know. Come on.” With that, he strode off towards the tube station.

From Charing Cross, they got a tube direct to Mile End station. On the journey, Richie tried several times to get Alfie to talk about what had happened in the pub toilets, to no avail. All his friend would say was that he'd mistaken the soldier for someone else.

Climbing the stairs at Mile End underground station brought back traumatic memories for Alfie. He thought back to that last big raid in 1941 when his sister never appeared; the Home Guard who thwarted his attempt to get back out onto the street to search for her. He was absolutely right to do so. Alfie would have been killed if he'd sneaked past. The nearby explosion clouded them all in dust. Then, of course, when the all-clear sounded and he finally managed to leave, and after his shift in Cunningham's bakery, he'd made the grim discovery. He had nightmares for a long time after it.

Finally, they emerged onto the street and headed in the direction of where he used to live. When he turned the corner onto his old street, his heart lifted when he saw the long table down the middle of the street leading to the pub where Gladys once pulled pints. Bunting hung across the road, children ran up and down and a few familiar faces were seated, cups of tea or beer in front of them along with sandwiches, cakes and all manner of goodies that hadn't been available when he last set foot here.

"Alfie? Alfie Taylor?" came a familiar voice.

He looked round to see the familiar form of his old neighbour beaming at him, arms open wide.

# 36

Cyril looked at Mrs Bowman for a second before asking, "How do you mean, Alice?"

"It was VE Day," she began. "We had organised a street party. When I say 'we' I mean all the residents in the street. Some had baked, and Mr Cunningham, the baker had produced all sorts of good fayre. Mr Chapman at the Arms was selling drinks at half price."

"I remember the day well. We were based in Norfolk at the time."

"Alfie just turned up out of the blue. I hadn't seen him since the day he left after the tragedy. He and little Patricia had gone to stay with his grandparents, Dolly and Stan in Clacton."

"Clacton?"

"Yes. They were the only living relatives they had. I mean, I'd have looked after them if they hadn't been around. It would have been a struggle but we'd have managed. It's what we did then. We'd exchanged a few letters over the years. I tried to keep him up to date with all the news from the street but, you know how these things go, the gaps in between get longer. Anyway, I was surprised and delighted to see him. He'd grown, obviously; he was fourteen when he left and he was now eighteen."

"That's right. He left in 1941, didn't he?"

Mrs Bowman nodded. "He turned up with a friend of his, can't remember his name now. They'd got the train up from Clacton to join in the festivities in town but it had gone wrong, so Alfie came down to where he was familiar with, I suppose."

Cyril leaned forward. "What had gone wrong?"

"That's the strange thing. We'd heard a few months after Gladys was found that Graham Woods had been killed. It finished his mum off. I think she died about a month after she got the news. Anyway, Alfie reckoned he'd been in a pub near Trafalgar Square when he spotted a man who looked like Woods."

"What made him think it was him?"

"Apart from the fact that it had only been about four years since he'd last seen him, it was his birthmark. The man had his sleeves rolled up exposing his elbows. I remembered this too. He had a distinctive dark brown oval-shaped birth mark just below his left elbow."

"Oh yes I remember that as well, Mum." Edith had been listening intently to her mother recounting the story. "He had a distinctive mark on his arm."

"And what did young Alfie do?" Cyril asked.

"Him and his mate joined in with us for food and drinks and then he left about ... ooh, it must have been seven o'clock. I did offer them a bed for the night but Alfie said he'd need to get back otherwise his gran would worry. I never saw him again."

On the drive home, Cyril had plenty to ponder. There was no doubt that the man who called himself Harrison was actually Graham Woods. There was the oval birth mark for final confirmation. But had Woods been responsible for what happened to Gladys Vaughan? That would certainly be a strong motive for swapping identities. He needed to speak to Barton next morning.

# 37
## Wednesday 22nd February 1978

"Anybody seen the DI?" Cyril asked as he closed the door, having checked Barton's office.

"Not sure, Sarge, but he set off early this morning," Bill Walker responded.

"Might have gone to Hitchin, skip," Woodbridge added.

"Thanks, lads." Cyril made his way out of the CID room to DCI Sanderson's office. The man was sitting behind his desk writing on a pad and studying a number of files. Cyril knocked and was beckoned inside.

"Ah, Cyril, how are things?" Sanderson asked. "Nothing but bloody reports to do here ... and meetings, of course."

"That's the drawback of high office, sir."

"So what can I do for you?" The DCI was still writing on his pad.

"Trevor Harrison."

Sanderson put down his pen and invited him to sit down. "Go on."

"A little while ago, you said to us that the key to this whole enquiry may well lie in the man's past."

"What have you discovered, Cyril?"

"As we suspected, Trevor Harrison is really Graham Woods. The identities had been swapped, I think during the war."

Sanderson looked amazed. "But why? What would prompt that?"

"That's what I need to dig into a bit more."

"So how did you find this out?"

"You remember John Garland?"

"Of course. Sad loss a few years ago with cancer."

"I know. Well, I've been speaking to Edith, his widow, and her mum, Alice Bowman." He recounted the conversation from the previous evening.

When Cyril had finished, Sanderson sat back in his chair. "What do you propose now?"

Cyril stroked his thin moustache before responding. "I need to make some enquiries with the Met. Not sure if they'd have any records still remaining from the war years but I need to try."

"Keep me informed. And when Dick gets back, I think we'll need to review where we are."

When Cyril left the DCI's office, he headed back to his own desk. He made a call to the Met's record office. As he thought, the man at the other end told him it may take some time to locate anything they might have. But something else occurred to him since last night's conversations, and that would involve another phone call and, hopefully, a trip out.

The light rain that had greeted Cyril on his way into the station first thing that morning had now turned much heavier as he drove to Walton-on-the-Naze.

As on his previous visit to The Laurels Care Home, his ring on the bell was answered by Ivy Holcombe, the manageress.

"Hello again, Mr Claydon," she greeted. "Good to see you. Beatty is looking forward to your visit."

"Thank you, Ivy," he said, stepping inside out of the rain.

"Let me take your coat."

She hung his overcoat on the peg in the hallway and led him through to the rear lounge as before. Beatty Palmer looked up and smiled as the pair entered.

"What have you got on the go today, Beatty?" he asked, approaching the table where she sat.

"Bit of a difficult one, Cyril. Wild animals."

He looked down at the jig saw puzzle that she'd started. It was circular and she'd obviously not long begun it as the perimeter and a few other pieces were the only ones she had positioned so far.

Ivy Holcombe had left and Cyril sat down opposite the elderly lady. He looked around the room to see that there were a few more bodies than when he was here last time. Four were seated around a table playing cards, one gent sat in an armchair reading a paper and another lady was sitting near the fire knitting. It all seemed homely and safe. And then there were the views across the backwaters. Unfortunately, today, the visibility was not as good as it could have been.

"Oh, I remembered that girl's name," Beatty said, bringing his attention back inside.

"Oh yes?"

"Yes. It was Dorothy Hamilton. Like I said, she seemed a little bit older than Elsie, and Marjorie. And a bit more brazen too."

"Thanks for remembering Dorothy's surname, Beatty but it's her male friend I'd like you to think about."

She screwed her face up. "Him? He was weird. It wouldn't surprise me if he'd done something awful."

Cyril pulled an envelope from his pocket and from it withdrew the photo Bob Hewitt had given him. "Can you have a look at this photograph for me?"

Beatty lifted her handbag from the side of her chair, pulled out a pair of reading glasses and slipped them on. Taking the photo from Cyril she suddenly opened her eyes wide. "Good God," she said. "That's him. Where did you get this?"

Cyril felt satisfied his hunch had proved correct. But the full implications might be more difficult to realise. "It's from another case we've been working on," he told her.

She turned the picture over as if checking for clues on the reverse. It was blank. "He's a little bit older here than I remember but this was pretty much how he looked when he came into the shop." She handed the photograph back. "*Has* he done something awful?"

"I can't really say too much at the moment, Beatty, but I can tell you, you've been a great help."

On the drive back to Clacton, Cyril turned his thoughts over in his mind. Could this man, now identified as Woods, somehow be responsible for not only what happened to Gladys Vaughan in 1941 but also Elsie Smart in 1947? Had he come to the attention of the investigation team then? If so, why was he not interviewed? More to the point, why was that investigation wound up? What does DCS Viney really know? And would that explain Viney's desire to draw a line under the Harrison unexplained death enquiry now?

# 38

In another car, driving west towards Hertfordshire, DI Barton was turning *his* thoughts over in his mind. He was on his way to Hitchin where Harold Wray owned a printing business. The previous evening, Barton had spoken to the man on the telephone and arranged to meet him at his place of work to ask a few 'routine' questions. The man was puzzled but Barton kept the purpose circumspect as he preferred to read the man's reactions face to face.

As he drove, his mind was buzzing. What was the reason behind Harrison's apparent dual identity? It was interesting he'd used the name Graham Woods when arranging to meet the accommodating Gloria. He smiled to himself as he thought of the effect that encounter might have had on young Woodbridge. But who *was* Graham Woods and what had happened to him? Was Trevor Harrison really Graham Woods, as identified by that old soldier snapshot? Harrison certainly had cause to change identity after his prison sentence, but why before that? Then again, who also knew that Harrison was really Woods? As Sanderson had said, the key to this whole enquiry may well lie in the man's past.

The heavy rain made it a difficult journey and so it was just before eleven that morning when Barton pulled the Rover to a halt outside the premises of Wray Printing. Parked in a prominent position was a light blue Jaguar 4.2 litre saloon with the registration mark that had brought Wray to their attention. Barton stepped out and stretched his back and shoulders. Immediately his mind wandered to the lovely Donna and her massaging skills. A smile passed over his face at the thought of finally returning home that evening and persuading her to relieve his tensions.

He locked the car and headed for the reception. An attractive woman in her early thirties looked up and smiled at him from behind the desk. “Good morning. How can I help?” she asked.

A few minutes later, Barton was sitting in a small office opposite a tall man in his mid-thirties, suit jacket on the back of his chair and a tie loosened from his white shirt with the top button undone. The woman from reception had brought in a pot of coffee, two mugs and all the ancillaries and placed them on her boss’s desk.

“So how can I help you, Inspector?” Wray asked, as he poured coffee into the mugs.

“We’re making enquiries into the death of a man in Clacton, Mr Wray.”

Wray looked up at the DI, his expression leaving Barton in no doubt he would have something to tell him. “Oh, and what makes you think I can help with that?”

Barton flicked open his notebook. “We have a witness who tells us you may have visited the man around …” He ran a finger down the notebook page. “… the second or third week in January.”

“Can you tell me who is this man I’m supposed to have visited?”

“We believe him to be Trevor Harrison. You were seen approaching his flat and later leaving before driving away.” Barton stared hard at the man. “In that car parked outside, registration number HAR 801D.”

Wray looked down at his coffee on the desk. After a brief pause he looked back up. “I did call to see him. But he was perfectly fine when I left.”

“The witness said you looked …” The DI flicked through the pages of his notebook once again. “Upset and angry were the words they used to describe you when you left.”

“Well … what can I say?” Wray looked deflated before sitting up straight again. “When did this man die?”

“We think sometime around 9$^{th}$ or 10$^{th}$ February.”

"Well there you are then. You said yourself I was seen around 2nd or 3rd week in January. I had nothing to do with his death.

"Mr Wray, I never said you did. But for the record, can you confirm your movements for the 9th and 10th of February? Perhaps check your diary." Barton indicated the large book on the man's desk.

"No need, Inspector." The man stood, walked over and opened the door then called to the woman on the reception desk. "Amanda, can you come in a moment."

When Amanda walked in, Wray introduced her. "My wife, Inspector."

Barton nodded. "Mrs Wray," he acknowledged.

The man continued, "Now, February 9th Anything of note?"

She smiled at him. "Of course. My birthday."

"And what did we do this year?"

"We went out for a meal at that new Italian place in town."

"And afterwards?"

"We went home."

"All night?" Barton asked.

"Well not all night," she said, looking at him, "but in the morning too. Oh, I see what you mean." She coloured slightly. "Yes, we were together all night. We had a lie in and Jim, my dad, opened up for us."

"Thanks, darling," Wray said, as the phone in reception began to ring.

"Excuse me," she said. "I have to get that."

Barton smiled at the disappearing Amanda before turning his attention back to the man. "Thank you, Mr Wray. Just one more point, what was your connection with Trevor Harrison and why did you visit him?"

Wray smiled nervously. "Look, this isn't easy. If you want to know the full story, there are some things you need to understand ..."

* * *

## 24th August 1977

I was dreading this visit. My mum, Celia, was in the coronary care unit of St Bartholomew's Hospital. Other hospitals were nearer but she'd been treated long-term at Barts. The nurse had called me at work and suggested I come in straight away. I'd caught the first train south and hoped I would be in time. Somehow, I felt this would be the last time I would see her. She'd been a good mum; it couldn't have been easy bringing me up during the war. Her parents, my grandparents had been very supportive but there was always a stigma. I never knew my father, Mum hadn't told me who he was, only that he was a soldier.

She had suffered failing health for the past five years or so; heart failure, and there was nothing that could be done to deter the inevitable outcome. She was still a young woman; only fifty-nine. She'd worked for all the time that I could remember in a GPO telephone exchange until they closed it down but afterwards in other capacities until she'd no longer been able to carry on.

Walking onto the ward, the sister approached me. "Mr Wray, I'm afraid your mother is deteriorating. We've done as much as we can to make her comfortable. We've also moved her into a side room which we felt would give more privacy." She led the way into the small room. "You're welcome to stay as long as you want."

I nodded and thanked the sister who left and closed the door. Looking down at the shape in the bed I barely recognised my mum. Her hair seemed to have greyed even more in the week or so since I'd last seen her and a mask delivering oxygen covered most of her face. Monitors behind told the story of her current state of health.

As I sat down in the chair beside the bed and took hold of her hand, she turned her head towards me and opened her eyes. Slowly, she raised her other hand and lifted the mask. "Harry," she said in a voice that was barely above a whisper.

"Mum," I said. "How are you?"

Her face creased into a smile. "I'm sure you know." She put the mask back over her face for a second and took a couple of breaths before lifting it clear again. "I need to tell you something before it's too late, son."

I squeezed her hand, careful to avoid any additional discomfort due to the cannula. "Don't worry, Mum, there's plenty of time." I knew that wasn't the case but I wanted to reassure her.

"You know that's not true." Again another gasp of oxygen between speaking. "I want you to look in my handbag. It's in there." She waved her hand in the general direction of the bedside cabinet.

I looked down at the unit next to my chair and released her hand while I opened the door and pulled out her familiar black handbag.

"There are a couple of envelopes in the front," she said. "Look in the brown one."

I saw the envelope and pulled it out.

"Open it."

Inside was a photograph. I slipped it out and looked at the group of soldiers in battle fatigues posing for the camera. "Is this what I think it is?" I asked.

Mum nodded.

"Which one?"

"Fourth from the left." Another breath of oxygen. "Next to misery guts." She gave a chuckle.

It had been some time since I'd heard Mum give anything resembling a laugh. But I was studying the face of the man that smiled out at me. The thought sped through my mind that, finally, this is him; this is my dad.

"What …" I struggled to keep tears from forming. "What was his name?"

"Trevor," she answered. "Trevor Harrison."

"And what … happened?"

"His tank, it was destroyed. I think … all of them."

I wiped my eyes with the back of my hand and just sat there for a minute looking at the man I'd never known but had been desperate to find out about for as long as I could remember. Finally, I turned the picture over and saw that someone had written the tank regiment details and the names of all those in the photo. I stared at the name, Trevor Harrison.

"We met at a dance," she said, bringing my thoughts back to the hospital room. "It was 1940. A dance hall down by the Elephant and Castle. He was a good looking man."

"I can see that."

"You look like him."

Again, I wiped my hand across my cheek.

"Although we only knew each other for a few days, it was love, you know. They were different times then. With all that was going on, you never knew if you'd wake up tomorrow. I believed we would see each other again … but it wasn't to be."

"How did you hear about … you know?"

She closed her eyes for a moment. "He used to write. I kept his letters in the other envelope in my bag."

I bent down to open her bag again but she stopped me.

"Later, Harry," she said. "When I'm not here."

I sat up again.

"I'd heard nothing from Trevor for some months," she carried on. "I was increasingly worried." She brought the mask back over her face for a few breaths before continuing, "And then I came across some other army blokes … a little later, home on leave. They were tank lads too. They knew of the regiment and told me about a battle that the boys were involved in. How they were all wiped out."

That did it. I finally succumbed and brought my handkerchief out of my trouser pocket, reluctantly letting go of Mum's hand.

She waited until I'd composed myself. "Anyway," she continued, "I found out you were on the way. And that was a blessing. I'll always be grateful to Mum and Dad, your grandparents, for their support. They could have turned me out like some girls I knew at the time."

"I loved them too," I said.

"You were always something to remind me of him, and I'm so proud of you, Harry."

That was the final straw for me. I burst into floods of tears.

Mum let me get it all out. "Come on, come on, no sadness," she finally said. "I've had a good life and you've turned out to be everything I could have wanted."

I spent the rest of the day by Mum's bedside. Just before nine o'clock that evening, she slipped away peacefully, holding hands with me.

Later, when I took Mum's possessions home, I opened the other envelope with five letters from my dad. It took me about a week to get through them. It was difficult, reading the words of love and the unsaid fears he had. I could see he really loved her. The sad part was that he knew nothing of my existence.

In the weeks that followed, I contacted various regimental associations to find out as much as I could about the regiment my father was in and the actual unit he was attached to. Finally, I discovered that a soldier by the name of Trevor Harrison had survived an attack at Tobruk, albeit injured. After treatment, he had gone on to join another group to serve out the rest of the war.

At the first hint that my father could have survived, I began searching. What had happened to the man? Why had he not sought out my mum? Had he had some head injury that meant his memory from before the attack had been wiped? You hear of these things. Quite quickly, I learned of three men with the name, Trevor Harrison, still living in the south of England. One of those was the man living in Clacton.

* * *

Harry Wray opened a drawer in his desk and produced a photograph; another copy of the same photograph Barton had found in Harrison's flat.

"I thought I'd found him." He looked at Barton, eyes moist. "Can you imagine what I felt like, ringing the doorbell, expecting to see the man that was my dad."

"Can I see that picture?" Barton asked.

Wray turned it round and passed it over the desk.

Barton recognised it and pulled the same one from the envelope he had in his inside jacket pocket. "We found the same photo in the man's flat." He turned the picture over that Wray had given him. "But you found another man." He turned the picture back over again and pointed to the taller soldier. "This man here"

Tears began to roll down Wray's cheeks. He nodded. "Yes. Misery guts."

"I'm sorry?"

Wray waved a hand. "Oh, nothing. It's just something Mum said." He wiped a hand over his face. "The man you pointed to ... he answered the door. I recognised him straight away, because I'd studied that photograph every day since Mum gave it to me. I'd have recognised any of them."

"So when he answered the door, what happened then?"

"I was stunned. After a moment, I regained my composure."

* * *

## Thursday 19th January 1978

"Yes," the man said, "What do you want?"

The man was about six feet tall with uncombed thinning grey hair, dressed in an open necked shirt and trousers which showed signs of food stains and were supported by braces.

"Mr Harrison?" I struggled to say, "Trevor Harrison?"

"Depends who's asking."

"My name is Wray and I'd like to talk to you about the Tank Regiment."

"No idea what you're talking about," he said, making to close the door.

I'd already put my foot on the threshold. "We need to talk."

"Excuse me!" he exclaimed.

He struggled to close the door but I forced it open then stood inside before closing it behind me. I held my hands out, palms up. "Honestly, I just need to talk to you."

He seemed to weigh up the situation for a few seconds. "Okay then," he finally said. "You've got five minutes."

"Can we sit down?" I asked. "I've come a long way."

After another pause, he set off up the stairs.

I followed and eventually, we arrived at a sitting room where the man sat in an easy chair. I remained standing.

"I'll come straight to the point, Mr Harrison ... or should I say, Woods?"

The man grew agitated. "What are you talking about? And who exactly are you anyway?"

"You were in the Tank Regiment during the war."

"So what if I was; what's it got to do with you?"

I produced the photograph from my coat pocket. "I was given this recently," I said.

The man squinted. "What's that supposed to be?"

I had no doubt he knew exactly what it was. "A photograph of a group of soldiers from the Tank Regiment, taken in 1941."

"If you say so."

"One of those soldiers is you."

"I can't say that it is."

"Oh, trust me, it is. The only thing is, Mr Harrison, you aren't really Trevor Harrison are you?"

The man rose to his feet and I thought he was going to attack me. As he lunged forward I stumbled backwards into a table where a glass bowl toppled to the floor. I managed to grab both of his arms and threw him backwards into the chair. He was still quite strong but I only used just enough force to stop him from injuring me.

I must have winded him because he just sat there breathing heavily.

"The thing is, you're noted on the back as being Graham Woods. Trevor Harrison is the man on your right. You might be thirty-five or so years older, but that's definitely you, isn't it?"

"What do you want? And what's it got to do with you anyway?"

I could feel the anger rising. I took a step towards the old man sitting in the chair. "What's it got to do with me? I'll tell you what it's got to do with me. I only found out last August that Trevor Harrison, the real Trevor Harrison, was my father. My mother only told me on her death bed. I thought the man who was my father died in 1941, only to learn, he wasn't dead. He's alive and well and living in Clacton." I leaned in closer to the man, my fists on the arms of his chair. "Only when I knock on his door, I find the Trevor Harrison who opens it is not who he claims to be. So right now, I want some answers."

The man seemed to deflate. It was a minute or so before he spoke, all the while I could see the inner turmoil in him. "You say your father died in 1941. How do you know that?"

I stood up. "I have a contact in Army Records. He told me about the tank being hit by enemy shellfire. All bar one - Trevor Harrison - perished. Except that's not quite true, is it?"

The man leaned forward, arms on his knees, looking to the floor. "I should have been in it. I should have died that day. But we were advancing through an area where there'd been reports of enemy positions. One of the other lads who would normally have carried out the scouting operation wasn't feeling too clever. I also needed a pee, so I volunteered to go. I'd only got about thirty yards in front when we were hit. I must have been knocked unconscious because when I came to, it was a helluva mess. I felt what seemed like water running down my face but when I wiped it away, I saw it was blood."

"Tell me about the real Trevor Harrison."

"He was my mate. We were all mates, looked out for each other. You had to." He looked up at me. "What did you say your mother's name was?"

"I didn't. But she was Celia Wray from Walworth in London."

"Trevor was from there. His parents had died before the war, so he had no one back home." He thought a moment. "But I do remember him mentioning a Celia. He said he'd met this lovely girl in a dance hall in Elephant and Castle the last time he was on leave. He showed me a picture once. I think he'd had a letter from her too. But this was just before it happened."

I turned away and rubbed my face with both hands. So this was it; my father really had perished in 1941. I began to pace the room in an attempt to quell my anger. "So why change identities with my dad?" There, I'd referred to him as 'dad' out loud for the first time.

Again, the man looked to the floor. Finally, he spoke. "It had been difficult for me. I'd had one or two issues in my past life and I thought it was an opportunity to make a fresh start, clear the slate, so to speak."

I paused in my pacing and faced him. "What 'slate'? What had Graham Woods – because you really are Graham Woods, aren't you? What had Graham Woods done that warranted swapping identities?"

"People were after me. Back in the East End. It doesn't matter now."

"But why Trevor Harrison? Why choose him?"

"As far as I knew he had no living relatives. No one to identify him. No one to miss him."

"But that wasn't true was it? My mum missed him."

I know, I'm sorry, I didn't mean ... But when I went back to the tank, I looked to see if any of the lads had somehow survived but it was pretty obvious they were all gone. Trev's body had been blown out of the tank. His head had gone but his dog tags were just there on his chest. So I took mine off and swapped them with his. It was just instinctive, I suppose. Before I could think any more about it there were a group of soldiers coming from behind and, I think I just collapsed again because the next thing I knew I was in a bed in a field hospital."

I was stunned; stunned and angry. The only sliver of consolation was that Mum did know the truth before she died. Those tank lads she'd spoken to were correct, except for one thing. They weren't all wiped out. One survived. The arsehole sitting in front of me now.

"You disgust me," I said. "You acted with complete dishonour. You've brought your fellow soldiers into disrepute. You're an apology for a man. I wished you had died with the rest of your so-called mates. Only now, I hope you rot in Hell forever, when your time comes. And I hope that's not too soon because I want you to think long and hard about what you've done and suffer for it."

I turned and walked out of the room, down the stairs and away from him as quickly as I could.

* * *

Barton listened intently to Harry Wray's narration. The events of the past few months had clearly affected the man. "You said your mother had letters from Mr Harrison. I don't want to impose on any personal matters but I wondered if there were any clues as to why Woods would feel the need to take on his identity?"

Wray opened the desk drawer once again and produced another, fatter envelope. "You're welcome to take a look," he said, "But I can't let you have them." He passed the envelope over the desk.

Barton took it and pulled the aged letters from inside.

"I got the impression my father … sorry, it still seems strange to say that … I got the impression, he thought Woods was weird. And he seemed to think he was worse after he'd had some compassionate leave when his dad died in 1941. They were on training exercises back in Dorset at the time, just before they were posted to North Africa.

"Anyway, see for yourself."

"Thanks." Barton began reading the correspondence.

"I'll get us some more coffee." Wray stood up and gathered the mugs and coffee pot and headed out of the office.

Fifteen minutes later, with fresh drinks in front of them, Barton had finished reading. "I see what you mean," he said. "Thank you for letting me read these. They're personal and I can see how difficult it must have been for you." He also thought it gave him grounds to research Graham Woods' time in East London before his father had died. How he would do that will be a challenge, he thought. But Sanderson's words echoed in his mind again and he was sure that the key to this whole enquiry *will* lie in the man's past.

# 39
## Thursday 23rd February 1978

As DCI Sanderson walked into the CID room, a hush descended on the assembled detectives. The team had been called in for an eight o'clock briefing. Before that, Cyril and Barton had met with Sanderson in his office to consider what had been discovered the day before.

Sanderson addressed the team. "We've suspected for some time that the man known as Trevor Harrison who was found dead in his flat on 11th of this month we believe to be Graham Woods. Dick will take us through the interview he conducted with Harold Wray, who visited Woods on 19th January which, I think, details certain relevant events that occurred during the last war. Over to you."

A few officers reacted to mention of World War Two.

Barton stepped up and revealed the details Harry Wray had given him based on his conversation with the man. A full statement had been taken. As he concluded his report, he introduced Cyril. "DS Claydon will now detail what he's discovered about this man and some more suspicions regarding his past."

Cyril began by telling of the chance remark by his neighbour about the unsolved murder of Elsie Smart in 1947 and giving a few brief details of the case.

Bill Walker interrupted. "Sorry, Sarge, are we now saying this crime from 1947 is being officially re-investigated?"

Sanderson jumped in. "At this point, we're merely exploring possibilities. This is not an official investigation but Cyril, you'll be continuing to review matters."

So there we have it, Cyril thought. He'd been given a bit of a free rein, for now, to carry on digging into the circumstances surrounding Elsie Smart's murder. But reading between the lines, he could only do that, provided there were no ripples of embarrassment and nothing that could bring the force into disrepute.

There were some rumbles of surprise and confusion amongst the assembly.

"If I can just carry on ..." Cyril brought the meeting back to order before proceeding to outline the facts as he had discovered them and relating his conversations with Miss Palmer, Elsie's manager where she had worked. He also outlined what he and Woodbridge had learned from the woman known as 'Gloria' and the comments Harrison (although he had used the name Woods to her) had made during their encounters about having 'done some bad things in the past.'

After Cyril had finished his account, Sanderson stood to summarise what had been discussed. "So, we have some work to do," he concluded.

Focusing on individuals, he walked round the room, coming first to Cyril. "I'd like you to follow up on your enquiries with the Met to see what details of the murder of Gladys Vaughan may still exist." On to Walker and Woodbridge. "Bill, you and Sam need to establish where our man has lived under the name of Harrison since he was de-mobbed, where he worked etcetera. We know he served a prison sentence for sexual assault in the 50s."

He paused for a moment before addressing Miller. "We also need to check the story the man told Wray. Did this actually happen in 1941? Could there be an opportunity for identities to be switched? Ben, I'd like you and Dick to follow that line."

Barton took up the mantle. "So, as well as delving into the man's past, which might give us some motives, we also need to track down this electrician who worked at the flats in the weeks leading up to Woods death. Did he see anything, did he speak to our man and did the man say anything of significance to him."

"I could follow that up, sir," Woodbridge offered.

"Okay then," Sanderson finalised. "There's plenty to do. Let's get on with it. Cyril, a word."

Cyril followed Sanderson into Barton's office with the DI joining them. Barton closed the door.

"Just to clarify, Cyril, because I said you should continue to review the Smart case, that doesn't mean we have a full-scale reinvestigation. You only need to investigate whether there could be any possibility of Woods being around the area at the time." He held up a hand. "I know you have the testimony of the manageress, but this is thirty-one years on and she is in her eighties."

Cyril already had some thoughts as to how he would take this forward without Sanderson's knowledge. "Understood," he said.

"Now, I need to try and have a word with Mr Viney. I wouldn't want him to hear about all this before I can speak to him."

"Is that wise, sir?" Barton wondered. "He is still in ITU."

Sanderson looked as if he had the weight of the world on his shoulders at that moment. "Let me worry about that, Dick." With that, he opened the door and left the office.

"Christ, this has exploded into something else, hasn't it?" Barton thought out loud.

Cyril decided to keep his council. "I'll give the Met another call," he said, before leaving the DI alone in his office.

Woodbridge approached Cyril as he returned to his desk. In low tones, he spoke. "Do you want me to come round to yours at some point, skip? Have another look through the information we have?"

"Keep your distance from that, Sam," Cyril warned. "Just in case this throws up something embarrassing."

"For whom?"

"Just let me make a call," Cyril said, ignoring Woodbridge's question.

His enquiry to the Met officer was inconclusive. He was still searching various locations for any archives with reference to the Gladys Vaughan case. Cyril gave him the name Alice Bowman had mentioned; Constable Turner, in his fifties at the time and presumably based in the Mile End Road district. His contact promised to keep searching and get back to him as soon as possible.

At lunchtime, Cyril saw George Kidby putting on his coat and heading out of the rear door. “Ah George,” he said. “Where are you off to?”

“Thought I’d just get a sandwich next door. Me and the missus are off out for an Indian tonight, so I’ve been told not to have a canteen lunch.” He gave a chuckle.

“Next door?” Cyril thumbed towards the pub.

“Want to join me?”

“You’ve twisted my arm.”

With a pint each and a cheese and tomato sandwich for Kidby and ham and cheese for Cyril, they sat in a quiet corner of The Medena.

“Bit of activity upstairs this morning?” Kidby said, taking a bite of his sandwich.

“Some interesting information has come to light about that bloke John discovered in his flat the other week,” Cyril responded.

“So I hear.”

Cyril didn’t want to expand any further. “I wanted to ask you something, George.”

“Fire away.”

“You knew Albert Burns ...” Cyril took a sip of beer.

“He was DCI when I was a PC, so in that respect I knew him, but we were never in the same gang, so to speak.”

“How old was he when he died?”

Kidby looked to the wall as he trawled his memory for a second or two. “Let’s see ... he wasn’t an old man. I don’t think he was sixty. I told you he married money. Henrietta Chrichton, daughter of Julian Chrichton who had some big pile over Tiptree way. Well her old man died ... it must have been the year before Elsie Smart, so 1946. Henrietta inherited, so Albert was effectively loaded.”

Cyril ate his sandwich, amused by Kidby's history lesson.

"Albert retired in '52. I'm sure of that, because it was just after the old King died. So he was probably fifty-five then and I think he had about four years after that, so he probably passed around 1956."

"So he'd have been around fifty in 1947," Cyril mused.

"Sounds about right."

"And his bit on the side being around forty would fit in."

"Are you referring to the name I gave you?"

Cyril nodded.

"I would think so, lucky bugger." Kidby took a swig of his pint. "I was talking to somebody the other day and he reminded me she used to have a boarding house somewhere in town; one of those big Victorian properties. Her mother died and left it to her just before war broke out. Her mother had rented out rooms and she continued with that afterwards."

"Spare rooms handy for a clandestine meeting," Cyril contemplated.

"Exactly. And not too far from here either."

Before he left for the evening, Cyril phoned the hospital and was told that Doris was comfortable and would be spending the next two or three days recovering from her operation.

As he put the key in the lock and opened his front door, he had an overwhelming sense of melancholy. Here he was walking into an empty house that only a few years before had seemed full of life. His wife, obviously, had passed nearly five years ago, but then Charlie, his beloved companion, the Golden Labrador had left him last year too. All that remained was the slight mound in the back garden where Cyril had buried him. And now, nobody next door for the time being. He wondered how much longer Doris would be his neighbour. She was now seventy-seven after all.

He sighed as he closed the door, took off his overcoat and walked up the hallway to the kitchen. He didn't feel hungry, the sandwich in the pub with George had put him on. He looked at the cupboard where he'd stored the notes and copied files from the 1947 murder enquiry for a few seconds before walking over, opening the doors and pulling out the sheets. He spread Sam's work over the kitchen table and was just about to assess it all when the doorbell rang.

"Sam, I thought I said you should keep your distance on this," Cyril addressed his colleague.

Woodbridge was taken aback slightly. "Sorry, skip, it's just I thought I'd call round on my way home and see how you're doing. I got the impression you were a bit down this afternoon."

Cyril instantly realised he'd mistaken the situation. "No, I'm sorry, Sam. Come in. It's good of you to call." He opened the door wider to let him in.

They walked into the kitchen and Woodbridge saw the sheets of paper covering the table. "I can see why you'd think my arrival was connected." He nodded towards the table. "Spotted anything significant?"

"Only just got it all out." Cyril gave him a look. "But there was something I wanted to check."

"What's that then?"

Cyril began to sift through the photocopied files. "It's related to something Alice Bowman said to me on Tuesday night ... Ah, yes, here it is." He laid a sheet of paper flat on the table and quickly read through it.

Woodbridge stared at him fascinated, waiting to hear what he would reveal.

"Alice said that Gladys didn't possess a pair of stockings. In the war, they used gravy browning and painted the seam line up the back of their legs with an eyebrow pencil."

Woodbridge looked bemused.

"It's what they did back then during the war. Money was tight and non-essentials like silk stockings were rare, until the Americans came in.

"But here, listen, Mrs Smart was asked about the stocking that was pulled around Elsie's neck and she said, ‘I find that very strange as Elsie didn’t possess a pair. We couldn’t afford luxuries like that.’” He looked up at him. “And that would make sense, Sam. We still had rationing back then. I don’t think rationing fully ended until the mid-fifties.”

“I can’t imagine that,” Woodbridge said. “But weren’t stockings found in Harrison’s flat?”

“Exactly. Plus, if I remember rightly, some odd ones that seemed quite old fashioned.”

“I wonder if they still have that in the exhibits collection in the archive,” Sam thought.

# 40
## Friday 24th February 1978

"Skip," Woodbridge acknowledged as Cyril entered the CID room that morning.

Walker and Miller were at their desks sifting through paperwork. He glanced into Barton's office and saw it was empty. "The DI not around this morning?" he asked.

"Not seen him, Sarge," Walker responded.

"Any progress on previous addresses for our man, Bill?"

Walker leaned back in his chair, juggling a pencil between his fingers. "Seems he was at his current address since January 1976. Before that, he was in a flat on Penfold Road, here in town. We think he'd been at that address since at least 1965 but we're still working on that,"

"That's right, skip," Woodbridge added. "We also believe he came here when he was released from prison in 1959."

"Well, keep at it, lads," he said and sat down at his desk. He'd only been there for a minute or so before his phone rang.

"DS Claydon," he answered.

*"Cyril, I've got someone from the Met for you,"* George Kidby said.

"I'm expecting that, George, thanks."

After several clicks, Cyril heard a voice. *"Sergeant Claydon?"*

"Speaking."

*"DC Jones. I think I've got something for you."*

Over the course of the conversation, DC Jones told him he'd located some files in their store. A few statements had survived plus, interestingly enough,

Gladys Vaughan's clothes, including the stocking wrapped around her neck.

"I don't suppose we could have the stocking sent out to us?" Cyril asked.

*"You suppose right, DS Claydon. My guv'nor won't allow it. But, you're welcome to come up here and inspect the items,"* Jones responded.

"I'll get back to you on that. And thank you, DC Jones." With that Cyril ended the call and went in search of DCI Sanderson.

The DCI was in his office along the corridor. When Cyril knocked on his door, he was beckoned in.

"Cyril, what news?" Sanderson asked.

He related the information DC Walker had told him before telling him that he'd had a call from DC Jones at the Met. "So with your permission, sir," he concluded, "I'd like to take the stockings found in Harrison's flat up to London to compare with the one found around Gladys Vaughan's neck."

"You really think there is the possibility of a match?"

"It has to be worth a trip."

Sanderson thought for a moment. "Okay, Cyril, arrange for that."

When Cyril returned to his desk in the CID office, Woodbridge approached. "I've got something else for you, skip," he said in quiet tones.

"Go on."

He placed a note on Cyril's desk. "Reggie Smart works for a company called Martello Engineering here in town. Not sure if you still wanted to speak to him."

Cyril looked at the piece of paper with the name and telephone number written on. "That's great, Sam, thanks," he said. "I've just got to call the Met back." He told Woodbridge of the latest developments and that he'd need to take an evidence bag up to London to compare items.

Having spoken once again to DC Jones, Cyril had arranged to travel to London and meet up on Monday. In the meantime, he made a call to Martello Engineering.

* * *

Martello Engineering's yard was situated near the gas holders off Old Road in town. Cyril's call to their office earlier had confirmed that Reginald Smart was still employed with them as a senior mechanical engineer.

Cyril and Sam Woodbridge stepped out of the car and made their way to the office door.

"Can I help you, gents?" A young man who looked to be in his late twenties approached.

"We're looking for Mr Reginald Smart," Cyril replied.

"Reggie? He's in the back office." The man passed them by and headed out into the yard.

Cyril and Woodbridge followed the directions given and knocked on a door to the rear, marked *'Design Office'*.

A tall man in shirt sleeves, probably in his thirties opened the door. "Yeah, can I help you?" he asked.

"We're looking for Reginald Smart," Cyril responded.

The man turned to look behind him. "Reggie, two gentlemen to see you."

Over the man's shoulder, Cyril could see another man leaning over a drawing board. He looked up and removed his glasses when Cyril and Woodbridge walked in.

"You want to see me?" he said.

"Reginald Smart?" Cyril asked once more.

A puzzled expression appeared on the man's face. He looked to be around the age that he knew Smart to be; fifty. Thinning dark hair brylcreemed over his scalp reinforced his impression.

"Yes," the man cautiously confirmed.

"I'm DS Claydon and this is DC Woodbridge, Clacton CID. We'd like a word, if you don't mind, Mr Smart," he said, before quickly adding, "It's nothing to worry about."

Smart stood up straight. "Sure." He put his drawing pen down.

"I want to get some fags," his colleague said, grabbing a jacket from the back of a nearby chair.

"Okay, Colin," Smart acknowledged before waiting until the other man had departed. "So, how can I help?"

"I'm sorry if this may cause upset, Mr Smart, but I wanted to talk to you about your sister."

"Elsie?" The man's brows furrowed. "Why? After all this time ... I mean, have there been developments?"

"We're just having another look at things and wondered if we could talk to you about what happened back in 1947."

He sat down on a stool behind the drawing board. "What do you want to know?"

"If you could take me through the events as you remember them. To start with, what was Elsie like?"

"She was a young sixteen year old, if you get what I mean; innocent really. She'd left school around the May the year before and got herself a nice little job in a shoe shop. She was never any trouble to Mum."

"What about friends?"

"She had two fairly close girlfriends, Marjorie who was quite shy, I suppose." He paused and smirked. "And then there was Dorothy. She was a bit more forward. I'm sure she used to try and lead me on a bit. I was nineteen then and working. She was real jail bait, if you get my drift."

"So she was a bit of a tease?"

His expression grew serious as he reconsidered. "No, I suppose that's a bit unkind, but she was certainly more of a character."

"Did any of Elsie's friends have boyfriends?"

"Not that I knew of. There again, they were hardly likely to confide in me, were they?"

"But you never heard any talk of that."

"No."

"What about the night it happened?"

"The night she was murdered you mean?"

"Take me through it."

Smart paused a moment as if gathering his thoughts. "Well I got home about six. I worked near the railway station then. I got the bus back and Mum was wondering if I'd seen Elsie, but, of course, I hadn't.

"The snow was really bad but she should have been able to get a bus from town. I'd managed. Well, it would be about ten and she still hadn't appeared, so Dad went to the call box at the top of the road and phoned the police. It was the early hours of the next morning when some big wig detective turned up and broke the news that a body had been found. Dad went off with him but Mum seemed to know that it would be Els."

"Presumably, you had to give a statement?"

"Yes. The main man took mine and Dad's. I think some younger detective took Mum's and Eddie's."

"Could you think of anything else that wasn't reported at the time?"

He shook his head. "No, I can't think. But I'll tell you this, we were pissed off when it appeared that the enquiry had been shelved. It killed Dad; died of a broken heart eight years later. And Mum was never the same again." He looked hard at Cyril. "So is this a new investigation then?"

"We're just looking at the files again but nothing new so far. Thanks for your time, Mr Smart." As the detectives turned to leave, Cyril had a thought. "Oh, by the way, is your younger brother still around?"

"Eddie? Yes, he's a plasterer; works for himself. You'll find him on a few sites around and about, but you'll also find him in Yellow Pages."

"Thanks." Cyril made for the door.

It was Smart's turn to think of something else. "You're not involved in this sudden death the other week I saw in the paper, are you?"

"Which sudden death would that be?"

"Trevor Harrison, found dead in his flat."

Cyril felt the adrenaline course through his veins. "Why do you ask?"

"I knew him. Oddly enough, he worked for us. No doubt you'll know he did time. I gave him a job when he came out. I thought he deserved a break. He was a good worker. He retired from us about five years ago."

Cyril and Woodbridge exchanged glances. “So you knew Mr Harrison?” Cyril asked.

“Yeah. Worked here for us for about twenty years.”

# 41
## Monday 27th February 1978

The weather had been kind on Saturday and Cyril put in a whole shift on his allotment preparing some ground for his potato crop. Frank Scowcroft also put in an appearance for a couple of hours and they'd shared the flask of tea Cyril had brought with him. They chatted about what was happening in the world for a bit before Frank asked if he was still interested in Elsie Smart's murder. Cyril was fairly circumspect and the conversation moved on to what Frank was growing from seed this year. Being on the allotment was an ideal opportunity for Cyril to relax and just let his mind wander.

With Ipswich playing up at Newcastle, Sam Woodbridge meanwhile had decided to watch Colchester United play Carlisle at Layer Road. It meant he was also leaving the investigation alone for a little while.

Sunday had brought an invite from Cathy to join her and Simon for lunch and again, he'd made an effort not to talk about the various investigations and suspicions. Instead, the conversation came round to holidays. It had never crossed Cyril's mind about having some time away together but when the subject was brought up, he found himself open to the idea. Cathy suggested they might look at a trip away in the summer, possibly by coach to Devon or Cornwall. She said she would call in at a couple of travel agents on Monday lunchtime and pick up some brochures.

Earlier this morning Cyril had called in at Jackson Road and collected the evidence bag containing the stockings found in Harrison's flat. They were in a brief case he carried with him to the railway station where he boarded the train for Liverpool Street.

DC Jones had arranged to meet him at a now-closed police station in the East End where storage facilities for archived files and evidence had been set up. This was where Jones had tracked down the information on the Gladys Vaughan murder.

Rod Jones turned out to be a young officer in his mid-twenties with jet black hair and around five feet ten inches tall. He greeted Cyril warmly and unlocked the front door to the old station.

"This was where PC Joe Turner was based back in the war," Jones informed him as he switched on a light and closed the door behind them. "If these walls could talk, eh?" He looked around the foyer and the old front desk.

"It does make you wonder," Cyril agreed.

The young detective led the way through a set of doors, down a corridor to a room at the rear. He unlocked the door. "Apparently all the old cases were archived in here in 1950 when the station was earmarked for closure."

"You did well to find it," Cyril said.

Switching on the light, rows of shelves holding an assortment of boxes were illuminated. A table sat in the middle of the room. Jones walked half way down the left hand side and pulled a box from a shelf at head height, turned and placed it on the table. He lifted the lid and Cyril could see a number of old brown files and some large paper bags. Jones pulled up one of the bags and opened it out on to the table. Cyril felt a wave of sadness as he looked on the clothing that had obviously been the victim's. Amongst it all, Jones freed the stocking that had been wrapped around her neck.

Cyril let out a sigh. Even before he opened his briefcase, he was fairly sure it was a match for one of those found in Harrison's flat. He flicked the catches, opened the case and produced the evidence bag he'd brought with him from Clacton. Carefully, he removed the two loose stockings and laid them on the table alongside the one from 1941.

"I think that's fairly conclusive," Cyril said. "This one here and the one from your archive look the same shade and style. They're both Rayon and look to be the same manufacturer."

"I think you're right," Jones agreed, "looking at the seam up the back, the darker heel and toe details and the giggle band."

Cyril smiled at the expression. "I didn't think you youngsters would know that term."

Jones grinned. "My dad used to say, once you got to there you were laughing."

Cyril nodded. "A wise man."

"Does this mean you might have a suspect after all these years?"

Cyril raised his eyebrows. "Unfortunately, these were found in the flat of a deceased man just over two weeks ago."

"So no chance of a conviction then?"

"Sadly, no."

"Do you mind if I look through what files there are here, Rod?" Cyril asked.

"Take your time," the Met man said.

Thirty minutes later, Cyril had made notes in his pocketbook of what he'd found. With the reassurance that nothing would happen to destroy the evidence, he thanked Jones, shook his hand and set off for the tube back to Liverpool Street and the train to Clacton.

* * *

Sam Woodbridge tracked down Alfred Taylor outside the shop on Station Road where he was told he would be working. The rear doors to the white Ford Escort van were open as the electrician rummaged around inside.

"Mr Taylor?" Woodbridge asked.

The man turned around, a tape measure in his hand and a puzzled expression on his face. "That's right."

"I'm DC Woodbridge from Clacton police." Woodbridge held out his warrant.

"Oh? Nothing serious, I hope?"

"We're just making enquiries into an unexplained death here in Clacton a couple of weeks ago."

Taylor closed both van doors and locked them. "Oh, yes, and how can I help."

"I understand you sometimes carry out work for Tendring District Council?"

"From time to time, they call me in, yes."

"I also understand you worked on a group of flats on Cathedral Road recently?"

Taylor clipped the tape measure to his belt, folded his arms and leant against the van. "That's right. A group of four, two on the ground floor and two on the first. There was a distribution fault in the old boards that had been installed when they were rewired a few years ago."

"One of those flats was occupied by a Mr Trevor Harrison. Do you remember him?"

Taylor's brows furrowed as appeared to make an effort to recall. "Old boy, top left flat. I remember. Was it him who's died then?"

Woodbridge nodded. "Unfortunately, yes."

"I'm sorry to hear that but what about him?"

"Did he ever have any conversations with you?"

"Not that I can think of. Only the usual; state of the country, pensions, oh, and he talked about that serial killer up north. Used to get the Daily Mail every morning, as I recall."

Woodbridge was surprised. "He spoke about the Yorkshire Ripper?"

Taylor gave a short laugh. "Only that it was a bit surprising your lot didn't seem to be getting anywhere with it."

"Did he ever speak about himself, what he'd done in his life?"

"No, can't say he did. I think he was in the army in the last lot, though."

"He mentioned that?"

"I think so, but to be honest it didn't have my full attention."

Woodbridge finished writing a note in his book. "And when was the last time you saw Mr Harrison?"

Taylor opened the van's passenger door and picked up an A4 book and flicked over several pages before running a finger down one. "Here, I finished the job on 2nd February."

Woodbridge closed his notebook. "Well thanks for your time, Mr Taylor."

"No problem," Taylor re-locked the van and headed into the shop.

* * *

When Cyril returned to Jackson Road, on his way up to the CID room he met Cathy coming down the stairs. "Ah, you're back," she greeted.

"Just got back from London."

"I've just had a call from Doris."

"Is she okay?"

She held up both hands. "She's fine. She rang me to say they're discharging her this afternoon. She called me because she knew you were busy and didn't need the distraction."

"Does she want me to collect her from the hospital?"

She put an arm on his. "I said I'll do it. I can finish at three and pick her up after that, I'll settle her in, it's no trouble." She continued to walk down the stairs.

"Thanks, Cathy."

As Cyril set off up the stairs, Cathy turned back. "Oh, I'll do something nice for tea for all of us. She'll probably be more settled in her own house so you'll probably find us there."

"What about Simon?"

"He's playing football this afternoon and going to his mate's for food. And one other thing," she said quietly, "Simon's uncle, my brother, has tickets for the Arsenal game on Saturday, so he's staying with him down in Enfield."

Cyril smiled at the implied invitation. "Okay, I'll see you later."

Up in the CID room Cyril sat down at his desk and looked through his messages. He screwed up the one from Cathy, as they'd just spoken but he saw one from DCI Sanderson. He wanted to see him when he came in.

Woodbridge approached his desk. "Successful trip?" he asked.

"I'd say so, Sam."

"The DCI was looking for you earlier."

"I've just seen the note."

"I've spoken to the electrician who did the work at Harrison's flat."

"Did you learn anything?"

"Not really. He'd finished the work by 2nd February. They'd had just general conversations only. Harrison had talked about this Yorkshire Ripper case up north but nothing else of much interest, although he thought he'd mentioned being in the army in the last war."

"Okay, Sam, make sure you write it up and file it."

"I also tracked down Eddie Smart. He's working on a small site just off Frinton Road." He passed him a slip of paper. "Here's the address."

"Good man, thanks." Cyril stood up. "I'd best see the DCI. We'll speak later."

Cyril knocked on Sanderson's door and entered when he heard the "Come," from inside. DI Barton was sitting opposite Sanderson at his desk.

"Ah Cyril, how did you get on?" Sanderson asked.

Cyril outlined the events of the morning.

"So one of these stockings was a match for the one that strangled your woman in 1941?" Barton surmised.

"But what I'm thinking," Cyril mused, "is that the other odd one we found will be a match for the one used on Elsie Smart."

"That's a bit of a leap," Sanderson responded. "We've got no real evidence that Harrison, or Woods I should say, knew the girl. I know you have this Miss Palmer's testimony but it would be good if you had another witness from the time to corroborate."

"What about forensic evidence from the time?" Cyril wondered. "I mean, what we have downstairs in our archive is written statements and reports but what about the victim's clothing? Was any of that kept and where would that be?"

Sanderson scratched his ear. "If they still exist, then I would expect them to be at Headquarters in Chelmsford. Leave it with me, I'll make a call."

"By the way," Cyril said, "How is Mr Viney?"

"I visited him on Saturday. Still in Intensive Care but seems to have improved. He was still connected up to all the equipment."

"Did you mention we were looking into the Elsie Smart case?"

"Not specifically, no, because it's not an official re-investigation. I did mention that our man here might have had some involvement in a 1941 murder, but I didn't want to stress him any more than he already is."

"How's Mrs Viney dealing with it?"

"She's worried as you'd expect but she seems to be coping well enough."

# 42

Cyril parked the car on the road outside a small building site with four new bungalows and three houses at an advanced stage of completion. The roofs were on and windows and doors had been installed. One of the vans parked in what would eventually be one of the front gardens bore the name and logo for *'E Smart Plasterer'*.

Cyril could see signs of activity in one of the bungalows, windows open and the sounds of a transistor radio playing. He made his way to the front door and stepped inside. From a room to the left, he heard someone singing along to a tune he recognised as the breathless style of the Bee Gees. "*Ha, ha, ha, ha, staying' alive*," the man sang.

Cyril opened the door wider and saw the man sweeping a trowel up the wall in time to the song. The dark brown on the wall he was working on had transformed to a pink colour on parts of the ceiling and other walls as it had dried out. The stocky man turned towards him as he detected a presence. "Sorry, mate," he said, "You'll have to see the site manager if you want to look round but I think these have all gone."

Cyril smiled. "I'm not here to view, thanks," he said. "Are you Eddie Smart?"

The man stopped and stepped down off the low trestles he was using to reach the higher points of the wall. "Who wants to know?" He asked that familiar question Cyril had become used to.

Cyril brought out his warrant card. "Nothing to be concerned about Mr Smart. I only want a quick word."

Smart stepped back onto the platform and resumed his work. "If you don't mind, I need to just keep going with this. But what do you want me for anyway?"

"I'm sorry to bring this up but are you the younger brother of Elsie Smart?"

The man stopped mid sweep and turned to face Cyril, stepping down onto the floor once more. "What's happened? Have you got someone for it?"

"I'm just looking into the facts of the case at this point, Mr Smart."

"Eddie. Call me Eddie, everyone else does."

"Thanks, Eddie. I know this might be painful for you but I wondered if you could tell me what you remember from that time?"

Smart looked back to the wall. "Give me two minutes while I just finish this off."

A few minutes later the pair were sitting on some empty crates. Eddie had turned the radio down, lit a cigarette and was puffing nervously.

Slowly, he began, "She was lovely, was Elsie; innocent too. She loved her little job at the shoe shop, enjoyed working for Miss Palmer. That night she didn't come home, Mum and Dad were worried sick. The weather was so bad. Dad had walked to the bus stop so many times. He knew she should have been home by seven at the latest. The buses were running but only as far as Holland, the road over the marshes was blocked. Finally, he went to the call box on the corner about ten and called the police." Eddie stood up, walked to the open window and stared out at the falling drizzle for a few seconds. Flicking his cigarette butt out of the window, he turned to face Cyril.

"It was about one in the morning when the main man arrived. Stocky bloke, big overcoat and trilby. Got out of a big Riley. I was looking out of the bedroom window. The snow had started falling again. I knew it was bad news when I saw him so I ran downstairs." He sat back down on the crate. "They tried to keep me out of the living room where Mum, Dad and Reggie were sitting with a constable. Mum insisted I stay." Eddie was looking all around the room, anywhere but Cyril. "He told us they'd found a body and wanted Dad to go with them to identify it." Tears welled up in the plasterer's eyes. "I knew then I'd never see Elsie again. Mum burst into tears. Reggie struggled, but tears ran down his face as he tried to comfort Mum. I just hugged her."

"What about Elsie's friends? I gather she had a couple of close friends she'd had from school."

"You're talking about Marjorie and Dorothy. They came round the next evening when they'd heard. We had a uniformed copper at the door stopping anyone coming in. But to be honest, with the weather and all, there wasn't a lot of people pestering. Earlier that afternoon, Mrs Swan from next door had come in to see Mum. They'd been friends since before the war. But when Marjorie and Dorothy turned up, the copper tried to stop them but I insisted Mum would want to see them, so he let them in. They just hugged and cried."

"Did you know anything about their friendships; Elsie and the two girls?"

"They'd been friends since first primary class apparently. They used to come round to the house quite regularly. I liked them."

"Was there any indication that Elsie had a boyfriend?"

He gave a slight laugh. "No, not Elsie. I think she had a crush, I suppose you'd call it, on some lad in her class, but she never went out with him, as far as I know. She did used to go to the pictures with Marjorie though."

"What about the other two? Did they have any boyfriends?"

"I wouldn't know. I mean, two sixteen-year-old girls would hardly divulge their secrets to a fourteen-year-old lad, would they?"

"I suppose not."

"But when I thought back on it, Marjorie was very similar to Elsie, innocent like, but Dorothy was a bit forward. She used to flirt a bit with Reggie, my brother. He was nineteen at the time."

"Did Dorothy have a boyfriend?"

"Again, I wouldn't know but I do remember Elsie and Marjorie mentioning something once, but they didn't tell me."

"Presumably, you would have given a statement to the police at the time?"

"Yes, of course."

"I don't suppose you remember who?"

"Not the main man but his sidekick. A young guy with dark hair. I can't remember his name."

"Well, thanks, Eddie. I'm sorry to have brought all this back to the fore."

"Does this mean some new information has come to light?"

"We're just conducting a fresh look at what we've got but nothing concrete so far."

# 43
## Tuesday 28th February 1978

"So let's just recap," Sanderson said to the assembled group. "What have we found out about our Mr Woods?"

Bill Walker outlined what he and Sam Woodbridge had discovered about the man and his addresses from his release from prison until his demise. "We're still investigating where he lived and his occupation before his conviction, but we know he was in Chelmsford when he married."

"His ex-wife should be able to fill you in on that," Barton said.

"Dick, do you want to speak to her again?"

Barton looked concerned. "Can do, sir, but don't forget we have those reports to finish for the ACC. I think that's something that can be done with a quick phone call."

"Right, well perhaps allocate someone for that." Sanderson turned his attention to DC Miller. "Ben, you and Dick were looking into whether his identity could be switched," Sanderson went on. "How did you get on with that?"

"I spoke to someone at the Imperial War Museum and it turns out what Harry Wray was told could very well have happened," Miller reported. "The soldier's identity could have been swapped."

"What about this electrician who was working at the flats before Woods was found?"

"I spoke to him yesterday," Woodbridge responded. "He'd got nothing of any significance to tell us. He'd completed the work by 2nd February which is when he last saw our man. Woods never mentioned anything of any significance to him."

"And Cyril, just give the rest of the team a summary of your findings regarding that 1941 murder in East London."

Cyril reported the events of yesterday and how the stocking found around Gladys Vaughan's neck matched one of the odd ones found in Woods' flat."

"And I'm sorry, Cyril, Chelmsford have no trace of any evidence related to the 1947 murder of Elsie Smart."

"Bugger," Cyril said under his breath.

As the meeting dissolved, Barton spoke to DC Walker and gave him Helen Hunter's phone number. "You might have to leave it until this evening," he said. "She and her husband both work in London."

At the same time, Woodbridge approached Cyril. "I've tracked down the whereabouts of Elsie's friend, Marjorie Duncan," he said quietly, handing Cyril a slip of paper.

"You're getting very good at this." Cyril looked at what was written down. His eyes widened. "Really?"

Woodbridge smiled. "Apparently so."

* * *

"Mrs Phillips, Marjorie Phillips?" Cyril asked.

The small thin woman eyed him suspiciously from around the side of the large front door.

Sam Woodbridge's aunt, Sophie, had come up with the address in Great Holland. He only hoped she'd got it right.

"Are you Marjorie Duncan as was?"

A flash of near panic flashed across the woman's face.

"I'm sorry, perhaps I should explain ... my name is Claydon, Detective Sergeant Claydon from Clacton CID." Cyril held up his warrant card. The expression of panic morphed into fear.

"I ... I don't understand," the woman finally said.

"Perhaps if we could talk inside, Mrs Phillips."

After a moment's hesitation, she opened the door and allowed Cyril to pass into the hallway.

He paused as she closed the door behind them and led the way down the wood panelled corridor to a room at the end.

"We'll be comfortable in here," she said opening the door to a large lounge with wood panelling from skirting to dado. In relief to the dark wood, a pair of glazed doors provided a panoramic outlook over the rear garden. At the end of the lawn, over a brick wall, could be seen the church spire.

"Has your husband served long in this parish?" Cyril asked.

"About five years now. He's actually at a meeting in Chelmsford and I'm not expecting him back until this evening, but it seems it was me you were asking to speak to, Sergeant." Marjorie walked over to a wing-backed armchair by the side of the fireplace and indicated the sofa opposite. "Please, sit down."

Cyril settled himself on the sofa and studied the woman as she sat in the armchair and smoothed down her light grey skirt. He knew she'd be around forty-seven or eight and her dark hair cut short was showing flecks of grey, although he couldn't be sure if there was dye involved. She wore wire-rimmed glasses and pulled a cardigan closer around her.

"Mrs Phillips, or may I call you Marjorie?"

"Please do, Sergeant. I'm intrigued as to why you want to talk to me. Is it something to do with one of our parishioners, because I'm sure my husband would be more able to help you?"

"No, it's nothing your husband can help me with." He paused a moment. "I understand you were at school with a girl by the name of Elsie Smart."

The woman paled, put a hand to her mouth and gasped. "Oh my good Lord," she said. "Poor Elsie." She became flustered and looked earnestly at Cyril. "Have you found out who did that to her?"

"No, not yet. I understand you two were friends; you along with another girl by the name of Dorothy?"

"Oh, Dorothy Hamilton, you mean?" That confirmed what Beatty Palmer had told him. "Well, I always felt closer to Elsie. Dorothy was always a bit ... well, you know."

"No, I don't really know, Marjorie. But I would like to hear what you can tell me about that time."

Marjorie got to her feet, pulling a tissue from the sleeve of her cardigan. "You must think me incredibly rude, Sergeant. You'll have some tea, won't you?"

Before he could give a response, the woman was striding towards the door, dabbing her nose with the tissue, presumably on her way to a kitchen. He got the impression she needed time to adjust to the way the conversation had progressed. He stood, walked over to the French doors and looked out over the garden for a moment before turning back to take in the room. Bookcases ran along one wall, filled with what looked like ecclesiastical and historical tomes. Various framed prints hung on the other walls and a writing desk stood against the wall behind the door. Walking over, he could see a bible open at a page from Matthew with a notepad alongside. Also on the desk were a couple of framed photographs. He picked up one which was obviously Marjorie and the Reverend's wedding pose.

"That was Bill and I over twenty years ago now," Marjorie said, as she returned to the room carrying a tray of tea things. "We met when we were on holiday in Filey, of all places."

As she stood holding the tray, she indicated an occasional table by the side of the chair she'd been sitting in. "If you wouldn't mind, Sergeant."

"Of course." Cyril returned the photograph to the desk then placed the table in front of the chair for Marjorie to put the tea tray down. He waited until she'd poured their drinks and resumed their seats before continuing the conversation.

"So how long had the three of you known each other? You, Elsie and Dorothy?"

"Since primary school; aged five."

He took a sip of his tea before asking his next question. "How would you describe the relationship between all of you?"

Marjorie put her cup down in its saucer on the table. "I suppose Dorothy was what you might call the natural leader, always pushing the boundaries with the teachers, up for adventures, that sort of thing. Elsie, I suppose, was somewhat in awe of her to some extent. She thought Dorothy was daring."

"Daring, how?"

"When she was old enough, she always seemed to be allowed to stay out later than us, or at least that's what she always seemed to say."

"You thought that might not be true?"

"Oh, I'm sure it was. I think she could manipulate her mother quite easily. Her father had died when she was quite young, you see."

"So, you were all coming up for sixteen when the war ended?"

"Fifteen, we were all born in 1930."

Cyril picked up his cup once more. "Tell me about Elsie?"

Marjorie looked over to the glazed doors, a gentle smile on her lips. "She was really nice. She could be quite funny but she was quiet. She liked the cinema. We used to go to the pictures quite a lot, Elsie and me. I remember the last film we saw together, Great Expectations. It was just before ..." Her eyes were moist when she looked back to Cyril. She lifted her glasses and rubbed them with the back of her hand. "Her family was nice too; her mother especially. She'd always make a fuss of me when I went round there – Dorothy too. She had a couple of brothers, one younger, Edward; he was a couple of years younger than us and Reg, he was about three years older. I wasn't too keen on him but Dorothy used to flirt a bit with him. She had a liking for the boys, especially older boys."

"Did Elsie have a boyfriend?"

"There was a boy she was fond of. Billy, Billy Cooper. It wasn't serious. I mean, I don't think they'd gone out together. She told me they'd kissed once. I remember Dorothy making fun of her about it when she found out."

Cyril recalled the note in the PM report. But maybe, although her hymen was broken, it may not necessarily have been due to sexual intercourse.

"More tea, sergeant?" she asked, picking up the teapot.

"Thanks, Marjorie."

Cyril delayed his next question until she had replenished their drinks. "So Elsie was not … experienced in matters of the world?" he asked, taking a sip.

"If you mean had she … done it with a boy, no, I don't think so. I'm sure she would have told me."

"So tell me about Dorothy."

"Some might have said she was a bit precocious but I think that would have been harsh. She'd started wearing make-up before she left school. Not to school, you understand; that wouldn't have been allowed. But out of school she would."

"I understand she had an older man with her sometimes."

"Oh he was a creep. I didn't like him but I think Elsie was impressed. Like I said, Dorothy seemed older than her years. She also had a thing for older men."

"So Elsie would have met this man?"

"Yes. He was with Dorothy when we went to the shoe shop on at least one occasion that I can remember."

"What was his name?"

"I think it was Trevor, or Trev, she used to call him."

"Tell me about what happened after Elsie."

"How do you mean?"

"Well, did you and Dorothy stick together? Was this Trev still around?"

"Things were never the same after Elsie died. We'd all left school and we all had jobs for the first time, so we never spent as much time together afterwards. Dorothy had ended her friendship with Trevor. I never saw him again. She'd moved on to another man, I think. Not as old as Trevor, probably about twenty-one or so. She ended up marrying him, but it didn't last."

"And what happened to Dorothy? Are you still in touch?"

"Oddly enough, I still get a Christmas card from her. She's in Ipswich now. She's been divorced twice and has a couple of children."

"Do you have an address?"

"Just a minute." She left the room and came back a few minutes later holding an address book. She flicked over some pages. "Here we are. She's gone back to Dorothy Hamilton again."

Cyril copied the address into his notebook.

"I assume you were interviewed by detectives at the time."

"Oh yes. A young man took my statement, I recall."

"Oh, one final thing, Marjorie, do you recognise this man?" He produced Bob Hewitt's wedding photo once again.

She instantly recognised the figure, and in a gesture the same as when Cyril had first mentioned Elsie, put her hand to her mouth. "Oh my good lord. That's him. That's Dorothy's Trevor."

# 44
## Wednesday 1st March 1978

Cyril struggled to see through the plate glass window into the Centurion Café. Condensation on the inside combined with rain on the outside made it difficult to see if there were any customers. Pushing the door open revealed an array of yellow formica topped tables and wooden chairs in the main eating area with a counter to the rear and a kitchen behind. It was just after three o'clock and it appeared the lunchtime rush had subsided. Four men in overalls were sitting smoking at one table with dirty crockery and cutlery evidence of a good lunch in front of them. They looked as though they were about to leave. At two other tables groups of young mums with the odd pushchair and a couple of toddlers were sitting smoking and drinking teas and coffees. In a corner, two men in suits were hunched over their drinks engaged in earnest conversation.

The journey to Ipswich had been made more difficult by the heavy rain and an accident involving an articulated lorry on the A12. Cyril approached the counter where a woman who looked to be in her fifties with dirty blonde hair dressed in a green overall busied herself drying plates. She turned around when she saw him approach in the mirrored wall. "Yes, darlin', what can I get you?"

"Er, just a tea for now," he replied.

The woman looked disappointed. "If you take a seat, I'll bring it over."

He noticed her name badge; *Dorothy*. "Actually," he said, "Are you Dorothy Hamilton?"

She looked at him quizzically. "Who wants to know?"

He discretely showed his warrant.

She raised her eyebrows. “I’ll still bring your tea over. Take a seat in that far corner.”

Cyril made his way to where she’d indicated which was as far away from the other customers as he could get.

The four workmen rose from their seats, two of them collecting their dirty dishes and taking them over to the counter.

“Thanks, lads,” Dorothy said. “See you later.”

As they made their way out the door, three of the young women stood and began putting on their coats.

Cyril glanced at his watch and thought they might be getting ready to collect their older offspring from a nearby primary school.

Finally, Dorothy made her way over to him, carrying a teacup and saucer and a milk jug. Sugar was in a bowl on the table. She eyed him warily as she set them down in front of him.

“What’s this all about?” she asked quietly.

“I understand you knew Elsie Smart.”

The woman blanched. “Give me a minute.”

Cyril watched her return to the counter and walk into the kitchen. “I’m just havin’ a break, Flo,” she said to an unseen woman.

“No bother, Dot,” came the reply.

When she came back, she’d pulled a packet of cigarettes from her overall pocket. She sat down opposite Cyril. “Do you mind?” she asked, producing a lighter from the same pocket.

“Be my guest.”

She took a cigarette from its packet lit up and blew smoke to the side. “What about Elsie? Have you re-opened the case?”

Cyril added milk to his tea and began stirring. “Not exactly, Dorothy. Something has come up in a different enquiry and I’m following that line.”

She nervously flicked ash into the tray on the table. “How did you find me?”

"Your old school friend, Marjorie, gave me your address."

"You've been to the flat?"

He nodded. "A neighbour told me you worked here."

"I'll bet it was that nosy cow upstairs. Did she know you were the law?"

He sipped his tea then put the cup back down in its saucer. "I didn't say, only that I was looking for you."

"She would probably have guessed."

"Is that a problem for you?"

Another lungful of smoke before she exhaled her reply. "No, not really." More nervous tapping of the cigarette. "So what makes you think I can help?"

"I believe all three of you, you, Marjorie and Elsie were friends?"

"You obviously know we were. But all this was covered in statements we gave to you lot at the time. Christ, what can we add to that thirty-odd years later?"

"You were asked for statements?"

"Of course."

"Can you remember who you gave them to?"

"Not after all this time, no."

"Can I take you back through all that happened at the time?"

She stubbed her cigarette out in the ashtray. "Look, I finish in half an hour. You got a car?"

"Parked round the corner."

"We can talk more easily when I'm done." She rose from her chair and looked down at the crockery on the table. "If you've finished, I'll take these back."

He began to put his hand in his pocket. "How much do I owe you?"

She picked them up. "On the house," she said and walked back to the counter.

Dorothy finally appeared from the kitchen area wearing a raincoat and holding an umbrella in one hand and a shopping bag in the other. "See you tomorrow, Flo," she said to the still unseen woman.

"Mind how you go, Dot," the woman replied.

Cyril stood and walked over. The last of the other customers had left over fifteen minutes ago. He opened the door for her and saw that the rain had eased.

"This way." He headed along the road towards the side street where he'd parked the Escort. Opening the passenger door, she climbed in. He made his way round to the driver's side. Once he'd closed the door, he turned to look at Dorothy. She was looking straight ahead. From what Marjorie had said, he guessed she'd had a hard life since those days just after the war. Her face was lined and her skin sallow, giving her the appearance of being older than her forty-eight years.

"I know it might be a bit of a shock to have someone mention Elsie after all this time, Dorothy," he finally said.

She turned to face him, a tear escaping from one eye. "She was a lovely innocent girl, you know."

"You knew her well." It was a statement more than a question.

"We'd all been friends since our first primary class. Marjorie was always a bit straight-laced. It didn't surprise me when she ended up marrying a vicar." She gave a weak smile.

"After you left school, what was your relationship like with Elsie?"

"We were still in contact, still friends. I think Marjorie was closer to her than me, they used to go to the pictures together."

"When was the last time you saw Elsie?"

"It must have been a couple of days before it happened. You know we had the big snow then? So we weren't in contact so much. People just went to work and went home, stayed out of it as best we could. Tried to keep warm."

Cyril nodded. "Where did you work?"

"I was working as an office junior in a solicitor's practice in the town. Pretty boring really but it paid a wage. My mum was on her own; Dad had died when I was ten."

"And how did you react when you heard the news?"

She went quiet for a moment, before pulling out her cigarettes. "Do you mind?"

Normally, he didn't like people smoking in the car but on this occasion, he didn't want to obstruct the flow of information. "Sure," he said. "Just open your window a crack."

She wound the window down half way, then lit up. "We were shocked. I couldn't really believe it. Rumours had started to spread the next morning that a woman's body had been found beneath the pier. In the afternoon, the local newspaper had named Elsie." From her coat pocket she pulled out a handkerchief and dabbed her eyes then inhaled some smoke before blowing it out through the window. "I called round to see Marjorie. I think first of all we had a good cry. Then we decided to visit Elsie's parents. We took the bus and all the talk on board was about her. When we got to the house, a uniformed bobby wouldn't let us in but Eddie heard us at the door and told him Mrs Smart would want to see us, so he let us in." Dorothy took another drag on her cigarette and Cyril could see her cheeks were wet.

"Eddie being Elsie's younger brother."

"That's right. He was a nice lad. When we saw Elsie's mum, we just hugged. All three of us, Marjorie, her and me. We were all in tears too." She wiped her eyes with her hanky.

"After Elsie started work in the shoe shop, I understand you used to visit her?"

"That's right. Where I worked wasn't that far from the shop. Miss Palmer was nice. Elsie liked working for her. You probably haven't spoken to her. She'd be quite old by now, or even dead."

"I have and she's hale and hearty."

Dorothy looked surprised then broke into a smile. "That's incredible."

"Can I ask you something you might not want to talk about?"

Her expression changed to one of puzzlement. "What's that?"

"Miss Palmer told me you sometimes visited Elsie with an older man. What can you tell me about that?"

"Ugh, you mean Trev. He was a slimeball really but I didn't work that out until a bit later."

"How do you mean?"

"He was a good bit older than me. I used to be attracted to older men." She took a last drag on her cigarette then expertly flicked the butt out of the window. She turned and looked at Cyril. "Please don't judge me."

He held up a hand. "I wouldn't do that, Dorothy."

She held his gaze for a moment. "I believe you," she said before continuing, "We went to the pictures once or twice or out for a drink."

"What can you tell me about him?"

"He'd been a soldier in the war and after he was demobbed, he came to Clacton for a job. He rented a room in a boarding house in town."

"How old was he?"

"I think he said he was thirty-seven."

"And you were sixteen?"

"Nearly seventeen but … when you say it like that …"

"Was it just pictures and a drink or was there more?"

"Christ, you don't make things easy."

"I'm sorry, I don't mean to upset you but to look into this again, I do need to know as much as I can about Elsie, her friends and her life."

"I think I know what you're asking and, yes, we did have sex on a few occasions."

"Did you introduce Trevor to your friends?"

"Well, yes, he met Marjorie and Elsie."

"You said you only worked out he was a … slimeball a bit later. What happened?"

"I thought he had a bit of an interest in Elsie. It was just how he looked at her at times."

"Was Elsie aware of this? You said she was innocent."

"Not that innocent but yes I think she was flattered slightly. Trev was quite a good looking bloke then."

Cyril took the Hewitt's wedding photo from the envelope he had with him. "Do you recognise anyone on here?"

She looked shocked. "That's the slimeball. That's Trev. How have you got hold of this?"

"That's not so important, Dorothy but do you think this Trevor would have pursued matters … with Elsie, I mean?"

She looked away for a few seconds. When she turned back again, there were more tears in her eyes. "I thought about that at the time and I've thought about it over the years since. I think Trevor could be very manipulative and coercive. He could have approached her on his own. He knew where she worked."

Cyril's stomach lurched. He had that feeling that he was finally uncovering something he didn't expect. After a moment, he asked, "You might not want to answer this but … was there anything … peculiar in what Trevor liked to do, sexually?"

She looked down for a second before answering. "He had this thing … he liked me to wear stockings. I only owned one pair but he brought me some. As we did it … he'd grab the tops and pull them up harder so they'd ladder."

Cyril stroked his moustache then glanced at his watch. "I'll give you a lift back."

"That's okay, the rain's stopped and I could do with the walk."

"One last thing, I thought I'd read the answer in some of the statements from the time, but did Elsie wear stockings?"

"No, she could never afford them."

"Thanks for talking to me Dorothy."

"No problem. I hope you find out who did it." She pulled the door handle, opened the door and climbed out. Before she closed it, she leaned back in. "Oh, and that detective who took our statements – his name was Burns. I just remembered because I've been watching the

Krypton Factor on TV and the presenter is Gordon Burns."

# 45

"You look a bit frustrated, Cyril," George Kidby said as he saw him about to enter Jackson Road station. Kidby had his overcoat on having finished his shift.

"I don't suppose you fancy a pint, George?"

Kidby smiled. "Is the Pope Catholic?"

The pair made their way next door to The Medena. Pints in front of them, they sat down as far away from other punters as they could.

"What's up then, Cyril?" Kidby produced a cigarette packet and pulled one out.

Cyril took his pipe and tobacco pouch from his jacket pocket. "Seems like we've been in here a few times in the past few weeks, George."

Kidby sat patiently, knowing Cyril would speak when he was ready.

Packing the bowl of his pipe, Cyril struck a match and puffed to draw it. Once he was suitably engulfed in smoke he spoke, "You know Mr Viney took exception to me looking through the archive files on Elsie Smart?"

Kidby nodded.

"Well, I believe we have discovered some evidence which could be connected with the case."

"So what's the problem?"

"All that was in the archive room in the folders was written statements and reports."

"And ..."

"There must have been some physical evidence gathered at the time. I mean, there's no sign of her clothing or anything else. I would have expected that to have been retained from the scene."

Kidby held up a finger. "Have you been in the basement?"

"Basement?"

"Yes, there's a basement here which not a lot of people know about. Maybe they stored something there."

"I didn't know that and I've been here for over 25 years. How do you get to it?"

"I can show you when we finish our pints."

Kidby unlocked the door inside a cupboard behind the stairs that Cyril never knew existed. Flicking the light switch illuminated a concrete staircase with cobwebs dangling from the underside of the floor above.

They descended the stairs.

"How did you find this, George?" Cyril asked.

"We used it as an emergency shelter during the war. Afterwards, nothing much happened with it but I do remember seeing old files from way back. It was just a thought that maybe someone stored some stuff later on."

Kidby led the way towards the back of the large room.

"God, this must have been claustrophobic down here during a raid."

"I don't remember too many occasions when that happened," Kidby said.

By now they were standing in front of a row of shelves fixed to the back wall. Cyril blew dust from the first box he came to. *Jess Howlett 1897*, he read. "I don't suppose you remember this one, George?"

"Very good. Try this end," Kidby offered, making his way to the opposite end of the shelves. There, on a lower shelf, stood two boxes that looked a little newer than the rest.

"Here," he said, wiping dust from the side.

Cyril joined him and they read, *Elsie Smart January 30th 1947*.

The pair looked at one another.

"Let's get these out," Cyril said, pulling the first box onto the floor.

Kidby grabbed the other and they lifted the lids on both boxes. One contained more files whilst the one Cyril opened held various bags with what felt like material.

Cyril looked to Kidby, eyes wide. "This is probably what I've been looking for."

He lifted the first bag and looked inside. "As I thought, clothing. We need to get these upstairs."

They put the lids back on and carried the boxes to the stairs.

"Is the DI in?" Cyril asked Woodbridge as he and Kidby carried the two cardboard boxes into the CID room.

"He's in Colchester this afternoon," Woodbridge responded from his desk. "What have you got there?"

"Just open the door for me, Sam." Cyril paused at Barton's office door, one box under his chin.

Fortunately, there was no one else in the CID office to witness the latest developments. "We need to have a close look in here." Cyril placed his box on the meeting table in Barton's office. Kidby followed suit.

"Do you need me, skip?" Woodbridge asked.

Cyril looked to Kidby then back to Woodbridge. "You've looked at lot of the information we have on this case, so I think it would be useful."

"Do you want me in on this, Cyril?" Kidby asked. "I'm willing to stay."

"It could be tricky, George."

"Count me in," The sergeant responded.

"Right, let's have a look at what information we have in these files." Cyril lifted the lid on the first box and pulled out some manila folders.

Woodbridge and Kidby began looking through them as Cyril opened the other box and pulled out some paper envelopes that obviously contained clothing. As he peered into one, Cyril looked over to his colleagues. "I think, first of all," he said, "we need to check this." From inside he pulled out a single ladies stocking and placed it on the desk. "This looks suspiciously like the other lone stocking found in Woods' flat. Let me get that." He stood and left the office returning a few minutes later with the evidence bag he'd taken to London on Monday. From that, he produced the stocking he'd referred to and placed it alongside the other from the box found in the basement.

All three looked at the two items of lingerie on the desk.

"I think I can safely say that's a match," George Kidby said.

"Is the DCI in?" Cyril asked.

"I saw him about an hour ago," Woodbridge confirmed.

Cyril left Barton's office once again.

Woodbridge sifted through some statements

Kidby looked on before finally speaking. "I think you need to go back to your desk, Sam."

Woodbridge looked across at the sergeant.

"I know you've helped Cyril with this but I think, for your career's sake it might be better for now not to be connected with it."

"I know what you're saying, Sarge." Woodbridge stood up. "Skip has been trying to distance me from it too. But listen, when he comes back, make sure he sees this." Woodbridge placed a file on the desk with a statement exposed, then left the office.

A few minutes later, Cyril returned with DCI Sanderson.

In Barton's office with the door closed, Cyril spoke, "George told me about a basement room we have here, sir."

"I never knew we had one," Sanderson said.

"Nor me."

"I only knew because it was used as a shelter in the war," Kidby explained. "I didn't think it was used at all after that but there are some really old files down there."

"And this is where you found the two boxes?"

Cyril nodded.

"All the others in there appear to be from before the war," Kidby offered.

Sanderson looked at the two stockings laid out on the table side by side. "These certainly looked matched. And one was in Elsie Smart's box and the other from Woods flat?"

"That's right. The one on the left from the flat, the other in Elsie's evidence bag," Cyril confirmed.

"Oh, and you might want to see this." Kidby held out the file Sam had identified to Cyril.

He took it and began to read. After a few seconds, he stopped and looked at Kidby, his eyes indicating towards the door where Woodbridge had been busy at his desk when Cyril had returned with the DCI. Kidby gave a small nod.

"I think you need to see this too, sir." Cyril handed the file to Sanderson.

"What is it?"

"Molly Pearson's statement. She was the clippie on the bus the night Elsie was murdered. She clearly states she saw her in a doorway earlier that evening with an older man," Cyril answered. "And look … her statement was taken by DC Viney."

* * *

Woodbridge looked up from his desk when Cyril returned with DCI Sanderson and headed towards Barton's office. Cyril gave him the briefest of nods to acknowledge the fact he'd left the office before he'd returned. They'd closed the door behind them and he busied himself sifting through some statements. About ten minutes later, the phone on his desk began to ring.

Woodbridge was concluding the call when Barton's door opened and Sanderson, Cyril and Kidby emerged.

"You best let me talk to him first," Sanderson said before leaving the CID room with a serious expression on his face.

Cyril rubbed his face with both hands and let out a large breath whilst Kidby shook his head.

"Everything okay?" Woodbridge asked.

"Far from it, I'd say," Cyril said. "But it was a good idea for George to get you out of there before we came back, Sam."

"Did you see that statement I found in the files?"

"That's what finally persuaded the DCI, I think," Cyril said.

"Convinced of it," Kidby agreed.

"Well I might have something else, skip."

Cyril walked over to Woodbridge's desk, Kidby at his shoulder.

"I just got an address for Violet Bridges, that name you asked me to check, for 1947."

"Oh yes."

Woodbridge handed Cyril a slip of paper with the address written on.

Cyril looked at it, furrowed his brows then showed it to Kidby.

"That's about right," the sergeant said. "One of those big Victorian houses on that road."

"Hang on a minute ..." Cyril walked over to his desk and fetched an evidence bag from a drawer. "Good God," he said quietly, before returning to Woodbridge's desk. "I thought it rang a bell. I think more of this is slotting into place." He looked up at Woodbridge. "Have you got a current address for Violet Bridges?"

Woodbridge smiled at him. "I'm hoping my contacts will have that for me tomorrow."

# 46
## Thursday 2nd March 1978

"How was he?" Cyril asked.

They were in Sanderson's office; Cyril, Barton and the DCI.

"He looked exhausted," Sanderson replied. "When I told him we'd found the two boxes of evidence in the basement, he seemed to fold in on himself,"

"The whole sorry story seems to have finally come to light," Barton added.

"Not quite," Cyril said.

Sanderson looked worried. "What do you mean, Cyril?"

"Last night, I found out the address where a certain Violet Bridges lived at the time of Elsie Smart's murder."

Barton and Sanderson exchanged puzzled looks.

"Who's Violet Bridges?" Barton asked.

"According to one of the few officers who remembered that time ..."

"You mean George?" Sanderson interrupted.

Cyril continued without missing a beat, "...the rumours were that DCI Albert Burns was having an affair with Mrs Bridges."

"These things do happen," Barton commented, prompting a sarcastic look from Sanderson.

"Except," Cyril went on, "I remembered where I'd seen the address before."

"And ..."

Cyril took a breath. "The address was the same as that on the box of medals you recovered from Trevor Harrison's, or Woods' flat."

"What?" Sanderson was incredulous.

"Trevor Harrison appears to have been living at Violet Bridges' address when Elsie Smart was murdered. That's where his medals were sent."

"He lived with her?" Sanderson was astonished.

"Not exactly," Cyril explained. "She ran a lodging house and I suspect he rented a room there."

"Do we know if Harrison's name came up in the Smart enquiry?" Barton wondered.

"We still have to check through all the paperwork, but it's a bit of a coincidence. He's living at her address and the senior investigating officer is known to be conducting relations with the landlady."

"We need to explore this, Cyril."

"I'd like to talk to her, if she's still around," Cyril said. "I'm waiting for more information on that."

"Let me guess," Sanderson said, "you've got young Sam assisting you with your enquiries."

Cyril nodded. "He has some sound connections."

Sanderson nodded. "Just keep me up to date."

"Sir."

Woodbridge was at his desk when Cyril returned to the CID room.

"Anything?" Cyril asked him.

Woodbridge nodded. "We're in luck."

Cyril motioned for him to follow to his own desk. "What have you got?" he asked in quiet tones.

Woodbridge began to outline the information he'd discovered. "Violet Bridges was born in 1906 and was left the house when her mother died just before the outbreak of war in 1939. She'd married in 1937 but when he was killed in 1940 she reverted to her maiden name. Later, in 1956, she remarried and became Violet Osborne. She was widowed again in 1971 and is now living in a bungalow in Great Holland."

"Good man, Sam. You got the address?"

Again Woodbridge held up a slip of paper.

"Get your coat. Let's pay the merry widow a visit," Cyril said.

The address they pulled up outside was a spacious detached bungalow in mature gardens. Cyril and Woodbridge stepped out of the car and Cyril locked it. On the driveway to the right hand side stood a new 'R' plate Ford Cortina. Cyril flicked the catch on the wrought iron gate to the path and walked up between the borders to the front door, Woodbridge following.

The ring on the bell was answered by a slim woman of around five feet eight inches with blonde hair recently coiffured and neatly dressed in slacks and a cardigan over a white blouse.

"Mrs Osborne?" Cyril enquired.

The woman looked baffled. "Yes?"

Although he knew she was at least seventy-one, she still looked an attractive woman. "I'm Detective Sergeant Cyril Claydon from Clacton Police." He held up his warrant. "And this is Detective Constable Sam Woodbridge. I wonder if we might have a word?"

Still confused, she opened the door wider. "Of course. Come in."

She led the way to the front sitting room which looked out over the front garden. The carpets were of good quality and the furniture top class.

"Please sit down. How can I help?"

Cyril and Woodbridge seated themselves on the large settee whilst Violet Osborne sat on a comfortable armchair. The hallway and the room appeared to be freshly decorated. A feature stone fireplace was the focal point.

"We're sorry to bother you, Mrs Osborne but can you confirm you once owned a boarding house in Clacton?"

"That's right. It was my parents' before the war. Dad died in 1928 and Mum kept it on until she passed in 1939 and I inherited it then."

"When did you sell the property?"

"In 1956 when I married Charles." She looked down for a second. "Unfortunately he died just over six years ago now."

"Can I show you a photograph and ask if you might recognise this man?" Cyril produced the wedding photograph he'd borrowed from Bob Hewitt. He handed it across.

A look of horror passed over Violet Osborne's face and her hand moved to her mouth. She quickly handed the photograph back. "That was Trevor Harrison," she said. "He seemed pleasant enough at first but he developed a … shall we say … dark side."

Cyril took the photograph and put it back in its envelope and into his coat pocket. "In what way, do you mean, 'dark side'?"

"Hard to explain. I had the ground floor flat. He rented a room on the second floor. But it seemed that every time I opened my door, he would be there … lurking, I suppose. It made me feel uneasy."

"When was he renting from you?"

She thought for a moment. "He came mid-way through 1946 and disappeared suddenly in February 1947." Cyril and Woodbridge glanced at one another. "I remember because it was when we had all that bad snow."

"When you say suddenly, did he leave you owing money?"

"No, he'd paid up. He just didn't give any notice. Cleared out his room at the end of the week he'd paid for and left."

Cyril hesitated for a moment before he spoke again. "Can I ask you about another man I believe you knew around this time?"

"Who was that?"

"Albert Burns."

Violet flustered for a second or two before regaining her composure. "Erm, yes, I did know Mr Burns."

"And you knew he was a Detective Chief Inspector at Clacton?"

"Yes, I knew that."

"I know this is a bit delicate but … can you tell me what your relationship with Mr Burns was?"

Violet looked at Woodbridge for a moment before returning her gaze to Cyril. She seemed to grow in confidence and stiffened in her chair. "We were lovers."

The response hung in the air between them.

"You knew he was married?"

"Of course I did. You're not going to tell me he led me on, are you? Honestly." She broke into a smile.

"How long did you know Mr Burns for?"

"We met just as the war ended and we were … friends, until he sadly passed away in 1955."

"So a long standing relationship then?"

"We were good friends, yes."

"I'm sorry to ask such personal questions … but, where did you meet? By that I mean, did he visit you regularly in your flat at the boarding house?"

"Yes, mostly."

"So it wouldn't be beyond the bounds of possibility that Mr Harrison would know about your liaisons?"

A look of realisation passed across her face. "Ah, now we get to the point. No I don't suppose it would."

"Can you remember, did Mr Burns ever visit Mr Harrison in a, shall we say, professional capacity?"

"I think he did, yes."

"Alone, or did he have a colleague?"

"He had a young detective with him as I recall."

"I don't suppose you'd remember the name of the other detective?"

She thought for a few seconds. "It was something like Vincent, no shorter Vine maybe, something like that."

"Viney?"

"That's it, yes, Viney."

"And when would that be, can you remember?"

"It may have been just before Harrison left."

# 47

"Let's work our way through those statements, Sam," Cyril said as they walked back into the CID room.

Bill Walker approached the pair.

"Yes, Bill," Cyril greeted.

"DI Barton asked me to have another word with Mrs Hunter about her ex-husband's history in Chelmsford," Walker said.

"He'd suggested you give her a call, didn't he?"

"That's right. But I was just thinking … perhaps we might get more information if a female officer talked to her."

Cyril considered this for a second. "What sort of information were you thinking of?"

"Perhaps what sort of relationship they had … before he was charged."

"You might have something there," Cyril considered. "What about Annie? WPC Annie Cauldwell?"

"Do you think she'd be available?"

"Only one way to find out, Bill."

As Walker disappeared to pursue his idea, Cyril and Woodbridge walked over to Barton's office where the evidence boxes were now stored. Cyril checked his watch. They knew the DI himself wasn't expected back until five o'clock. "We've got a good couple of hours before he's back," Cyril said. "Let's check through what we've got."

Cyril took the lid from the box containing mostly paperwork and pulled out the first batch of manila folders. Seated at the meeting desk they worked their way through the statements and notes.

"What are we looking for, skip?" Woodbridge opened the first folder.

"Anything that doesn't look right, Sam. You'll know when you see it."

After about ten minutes, Cyril paused reading and looked across at Woodbridge. "This is interesting," he said.

Woodbridge put his paperwork down. "What's that?"

"It's Dorothy Hamilton's statement. She said she gave it to Burns. And there's his signature at the bottom of the page. She definitely named Harrison as having met Elsie. And here's Marjorie Duncan's statement too. This one taken by DC Viney."

They both continued to sift through more files.

After a short time, Cyril finally said, "Well would you believe it?"

Woodbridge stopped again. "What have you got there?"

"It's a piece of notepaper ..." Cyril flicked back to another folder and studied that. "... and on it, it says, *'Trevor Harrison – suspect. Check alibi.'* And it's in DCI Burns handwriting." He turned over more pages. "Here, look at this ..." He pulled out another file with Burns handwriting stating, *'Harrison – no further action.'*

"How has he arrived at that?" Woodbridge asked.

Cyril opened the file where a typewritten statement had been placed. Cyril began to read. "Hell's bells," he finally said.

"What is it?"

"According to this, Violet Bridges gave a statement to DCI Albert Burns to say that Trevor Harrison arrived at the boarding house at four-thirty on the afternoon of 30$^{th}$ January 1947 and never left again." Cyril looked at Woodbridge. "We need to speak to her again about that evening."

Rain had begun to fall and it was almost dark when Cyril and Woodbridge returned to the smart bungalow in Great Holland. Lamps were lit behind the curtains of the front room to the left of the front door. A surprised expression appeared on the face of Violet Osborne as she opened the door to Cyril's ring on the bell.

"Back again, Sergeant," she said.

"I'm sorry, Mrs Osborne, but something else has come up and we need to ask you a few more questions."

"You'd better come in," she said.

In the lounge, she turned the television off. A gas fire in the feature fireplace was keeping the room warm.

"Please, sit down," she said.

Cyril and Woodbridge sat on the settee they'd sat on just a few hours previously. Violet Osborne perched nervously on her armchair.

"When we spoke earlier, you mentioned DCI Burns visited Mr Harrison in a professional capacity."

"I think he interviewed him, yes."

"Did he ever interview you … in a professional capacity, I mean?"

"Me? Why would he interview me?"

"Can I show you something, Mrs Osborne?" Cyril produced the manila folder from the case he'd brought with him. From that he took a sheet of paper and passed it across.

This time, Violet Osborne picked up a pair of reading glasses that were balanced on the chair arm. As she put them on and began to read, the colour seemed to leave her face. "What is this?" she said and looked over to Cyril.

"We found this statement from you in our files."

"But it … it can't be. I never gave a statement. I had no reason to. I was never asked about this."

"Is that your signature on the bottom?"

"No. I mean it looks similar, but that's not mine. I did not sign any statement. Why would I say that Harrison was in the house? I wouldn't know for sure anyway. They all had keys to the main door so they could come and go as they pleased. I wasn't a dragon landlady studying their every movement."

"I understand, Mrs Osborne. It would appear that this statement had been taken by DCI Burns."

"I know what it looks like but I can categorically say that I never made or signed any such statement."

"Thank you, Mrs Osborne. That's all I need to know." Cyril stood up and Woodbridge did the same. "I'm sorry to have disturbed you again."

# 48
## Friday 3rd March 1978

Both DCI Sanderson and DI Barton were in their respective offices the following morning. Cyril knocked on Barton's door and was waved in.

"I'm not sure I want promotion, Cyril," Barton said, looking up from the mountain of paperwork he was working on.

Cyril gave a wry smile. "What is it they say, promote to the highest level of incompetence."

"If I didn't know you better, I'd say that was an insult. What can I do for you?"

"I think our problems just got a whole lot bigger."

"Oh, God, don't do this to me, Cyril." The DI sounded exasperated.

Cyril related what he'd discovered the previous day, concluding that DCI Burns had possibly fabricated evidence.

Barton ran his hands through his hair. "We need to see Martin with this. I know he visited Roy again last night."

Woodbridge watched as Cyril and Barton emerged from the office, crossed the CID room and headed out into the corridor. He gave a knowing nod to Cyril as he passed.

DCI Sanderson was on the phone when they knocked on his door. Visible through the glazed panel, he waved them in.

"Right, sir," he was saying. "I'll get that completed and sent up to you as soon as possible. Goodbye, sir."

Replacing the receiver, he looked up to see the serious expressions on both his officer's faces. "That was the Assistant Chief Constable," he said, by way of explanation. "I told him DCS Viney has decided to retire on health grounds. He wants me to organise the forms." He sat back in his seat. "So what's up? I can see from your faces something is."

Cyril explained all he had discovered yesterday, the notes in the files from the evidence boxes, his two discussions with Violet Bridges, as was, and the apparently fabricated statement to give Harrison an alibi for the time of Elsie Smart's murder.

When he'd finished, Sanderson leaned forward and dropped his head in both hands. "Good God Almighty."

"The evidence is pointing to DCI Burns involvement in having the investigation closed down prematurely, sir," Cyril concluded.

Sanderson looked up at his officers. "And Roy Viney was involved too, you think?"

Cyril shook his head in a gesture of disbelief. "His name is on so many of the statements, I don't think there's much doubt."

"Okay, Cyril," Sanderson said, "You come with me to the hospital this afternoon. I said I'd take the forms for retirement for Roy to sign. I need to talk to him about this. I'll come and fetch you nearer the time."

Barton stayed in Sanderson's office when Cyril returned to the CID room. As he sat down at his desk, Bill Walker approached. "You got a minute, Sarge?"

"Of course."

"I spoke to WPC Cauldwell as you suggested and she agreed to come with me last evening when we visited Mrs Hunter. I think she had an interesting conversation with her. She said she'd be in the canteen for refs about now, if you want to talk to her."

"Okay, I could do with a tea now anyway before I get involved in anything else."

Cyril and Walker walked into the canteen and purchased their drinks; a coffee for Walker and a tea for Cyril. They found a table and sat down. Cyril brought out his pipe, filled it and lit up as he waited for Annie to come in.

"So how were the Hunters when you called on them again, Bill?"

"It was Mr Hunter who answered the phone. He sounded pissed off to be honest. I got the impression he didn't think we'd be bothering him again."

"Which we wouldn't have done but for what we've since found out."

"Reluctantly, he agreed for us to call round. I really appreciate Annie's input."

"She's a good officer." Cyril looked to the door. "In fact she's here now." He raised a hand in greeting and she acknowledged then motioned she was ordering something from the counter.

Eventually, she joined them at the table.

"Now then, Cyril, I hear you've dug up a right hornet's nest here," she greeted as she sat down, a broad smile on her face. Originally from Newcastle, her Geordie accent had been softened by the twenty-odd years she'd spent in Essex. In her early fifties, married with two teenage boys, she was a very experienced officer.

"I take no pleasure in it, Annie," he said, puffing on his pipe.

She stirred some sugar into her coffee before she began to recount her conversation with Mrs Hunter. "I managed to get her to take me into the kitchen for a chat." She nodded towards Walker. "I left Bill in the sitting room with Mr Hunter,"

"Sounds like a good move," Cyril said.

"Apparently, she met Harrison at a dance in Chelmsford in 1950 where they both lived. He was working at an engineering firm in the town and she was working in a bank. They got married a year later and everything seemed normal to begin with." Annie took a bite of the sausage roll she'd bought along with her coffee. Pastry shavings dropped onto her plate.

"Slowly, over time, he began to introduce some odd practices into their love-making." At this point, Walker coloured and looked away.

"Go on," Cyril encouraged, putting his pipe down in the ashtray.

"Well, he liked her to wear stockings, ones with seams. Anyway, his favourite position was from behind." Annie looked as though she was relishing holding court. "What he used to like to do was to pull on both of them at the top as he was, you know, thrusting. Ruined more pairs than she could remember." Annie laughed before growing serious. "She could cope with that but she began to become uneasy when he suggested they try doing it with a stocking around her neck."

Cyril nodded understandingly.

"When she raised objections, he became abusive. It was a side to him she'd not seen before."

"Was he violent?"

"No, he never hit her but she was afraid of what things might escalate to. That was really the beginning of the end of their relationship. Things began to break down and after four years of marriage she left him. Then when he was arrested for the two charges of sexual assault, she began divorce proceedings."

When Cyril and Walker returned to the CID room, Barton was in his office with the door open. When he caught sight of Cyril, he beckoned him in. "Close the door, Cyril," he said, once he'd stepped inside.

Cyril sat down at the desk opposite the DI.

"This is a right fucking mess." Barton took a cigarette from the packet on his desk and lit up.

"I suppose I'm being blamed for all this," Cyril responded.

Surprisingly, Barton was calm. "Nobody's talking blame, Cyril. I think we're all just shocked at what's been discovered." He inhaled deeply. "I never knew DCI Burns, he was well before my time." He blew out the smoke as he spoke.

"Me too,"

"But some of the older lads, like George Kidby do." Barton turned in his seat and looked to the window. "And DCS Viney doesn't come out of this too well either."

Cyril thought for a moment. "I don't know how much involvement he had, but he was DCI Burns' bag man from all accounts, so the assumption would be he'd have some knowledge. He certainly took statements from some of the witnesses that were found in those two boxes from the basement."

Barton turned back to face Cyril and flicked the end of his cigarette in the ash tray. "So, from what you've found out, it sounds like Harrison, who was really this Woods character, was likely responsible for a murder in the East End in 1941?"

"Gladys Vaughan, yes."

"And most probably responsible for the death of Elsie Smart in 1947?"

"I wouldn't disagree with that," Cyril said.

"Although absolute proof is probably impossible to establish. Besides, we can't prosecute a dead man." Barton stubbed out the cigarette then spoke slowly. "Which leaves us with one last mystery."

Cyril knew exactly what he meant. "Who was responsible for Woods demise, if anyone was?"

Barton nodded. "So what do you think?"

"All we have is a raised potassium level in his blood, which might have been due to his eating bananas. After all, we did find a load of skins in his bin. But there again, there was no banana material found in his stomach contents."

"Or there again, that might have just been a natural phenomena. At the end of the day we might never know and does it really matter."

Cyril felt anger rise in him. "After what happened last year with the unresolved cases of Sharon Williams and Ruby Walker, how can you say it doesn't matter?"

Barton held up a hand. "I know, Cyril. But at the moment, we don't have anything solid to investigate."

Before any further discussion could take place, DCI Sanderson knocked and opened the office door. “Cyril,” he said. “Time to go.”

# 49

"Just let me talk to Roy first," Sanderson said. The DCI was driving them to the hospital in Colchester. "I don't know how he'll be. He's been up and down with this heart problem. But I'll suggest he needs to speak to you. I'm sure he will."

Cyril's thoughts were in turmoil. In his opinion, DCS Viney was as culpable for the failure to investigate Elsie Smart's murder properly as his boss at the time, DCI Burns. What he would say to him, he wasn't exactly sure.

When they walked up to the Intensive Care Unit, Mary Viney was seated in the waiting area outside. She looked up as the pair approached.

"Martin," she greeted. "Good to see you again." She turned to Cyril. "You too, Cyril," she said.

"How is he?" Sanderson asked.

"They're just attending to him now. He's still linked up to the machines."

Finally, a nurse came out through the doors and searched out Mrs Viney. "We've made Mr Viney comfortable," she said. "You can go in now."

Mary looked to Sanderson. "You go in for now, Martin. It'll be a change of face for him."

Sanderson stood and made his way into the unit.

"Have they said anything regarding his long-term health, Mary?" Cyril asked, once Sanderson had left.

"If he takes it easy, takes his medication, things should be okay." The worried look had returned to her face. "You know he's retiring, albeit only a few weeks earlier than planned?"

"Yes. Mr Sanderson said so. I'm sure they'll sort everything out for you both."

"Thanks, Cyril." She gave a weak smile. "You know the support of his colleagues has been so important."

Cyril gave a nod. "It's what we do."

After ten minutes, Sanderson returned to the waiting area. "If it's okay with you, Mary, Roy would like to speak to Cyril."

Mrs Viney looked bewildered. "Sure, okay, if that's what he wants. I'll wait here."

Cyril stood and entered the unit. There were four rooms inside and he walked to the one with Roy Viney's name written on a board on the door.

When he saw Cyril enter, Viney raised his hand. Cyril sat down on the chair by the side of the bed. "How are you doing, sir?" he asked.

"No need for all that 'sir' nonsense, Cyril," Viney said. "And I'm doing okay, considering."

Cyril didn't think he looked as though he was. "That's good."

There was a pause before Viney said, "I suppose you think I'm a bad officer; and a bad man?"

Cyril shook his head and gave a wry smile. "It's not really for me to judge."

Viney sighed. "So what do you know? And what do you suspect?"

He took a breath and adjusted his position in the chair. "Well, the big thing," he began, "is that Harrison wasn't Trevor Harrison. He was born Graham Woods in London's East End."

"Martin told me. We never knew that back then."

"I know that several people made statements to you that raised suspicions of Woods, or Harrison. Having looked through the files we now have, I suspect Woods, was probably responsible for the death of Elsie Smart."

Viney closed his eyes for a second, opened them and responded, "I never thought you'd get to the bottom of it when I found out you were looking at the Elsie Smart files."

Cyril said nothing.

"I feel for her family, of course I do. All this time not knowing. Her mum and dad going to their graves ..."

"That's the really sad part." Cyril ran a hand over his head. "The fact you knew, or at least suspected who was responsible but covered it up."

Viney tried to raise himself up on one elbow. "I didn't cover it up. On my own, I couldn't do anything about it."

Cyril remained composed. "You could have. Wasn't it Churchill who said, 'The only thing necessary for the triumph of evil is for good men to do nothing.'"

"He pinched that. I think it was actually Edmund Burke."

"But you get the sentiment."

Viney relaxed back onto his pillows.

"Harrison, or as we've subsequently discovered was actually Graham Woods was also suspected of committing a similar murder in London's East End in May 1941."

"Christ, we never knew any of that."

"Because you never investigated properly."

Viney became agitated. "Albert Burns was my boss. He was leading the investigation."

Cyril paused a moment. "I've spoken to Violet Bridges, as she was then. She's still alive, you know."

"You have?" Viney closed his eyes for a second. "If anything about his relationship with her had come out, he'd have lost everything; career, marriage …"

"Money," Cyril completed. "But that was no excuse for not pursuing justice."

"Harrison … Woods made it plain to him that he would make public all he knew about his affair. And he seemed to know a lot. He'd seen the comings and goings at her house. That's where he rented a room."

"So that's why Burns fabricated Violet's statement giving him an alibi for the time when Elsie was murdered. Violet says she never gave such a statement and knows nothing about it. And I believe her."

"Albert agreed to it on the condition that Harrison moved on."

"Oh he moved on all right. To Chelmsford where he sexually assaulted at least two women for which he was convicted in 1956. And suspicions were raised that he'd attacked more women."

"We didn't know his true identity then or what would happen. Albert had died the year before that."

Cyril calmly continued, "And then, of course, not long after the investigation was closed down, you were given a helping hand with promotion to DS, in Hertfordshire wasn't it?"

Viney showed a flash of anger. "That had nothing to do with it."

Cyril leaned forward. "Of course not. But a good word from Detective Chief Inspector Albert Burns wouldn't have done any harm. Besides, anybody looking back at the historical events might not agree with you."

Viney was contrite. "Look, I had nothing to do with the decision to close down the investigation. I was distinctly uncomfortable with that."

"So uncomfortable, two boxes of evidence were secreted away."

"Albert went through all of the evidence and sorted out the two boxes you found in the old basement. He instructed me to take those two down there but leave the others you found in the archive."

"And when DI Barton discovered the body of Trevor Harrison in his flat, you recognised the name, which is why you were insistent the case was brought to a swift conclusion."

As Viney remained silent, Cyril leaned back in the chair and took a moment before he went on, "You served in the last war. In my book, you've acted with dishonour and through your actions, and those of DCI Burns, you've brought the force into disrepute. And I can't tolerate that."

"Look, Cyril, I'm truly sorry for what happened back then. They were different times. I couldn't draw attention to what Albert Burns had become involved in, not without ... oh, I don't know. All I want is for Mary to be looked after. If anything happens to me, I'd like her to be taken care of, pension-wise."

"I'm sure Mr Sanderson will organise all the paperwork as best he can. That's not for me to comment on. What happens regarding the ... incompetencies, to use a generous term, of the original investigation, again, that will probably be for others to decide." He stood up.

"You're a good officer, Cyril; and a good man."

He looked down at the man for a second. "Goodbye, sir," he said before turning and taking his leave.

# 50

When Cyril returned home after six that evening, he was surprised to see Cathy waiting outside in her car.

"What are you doing here?" he asked as she got out from the driver's seat.

"I came to see you, you funny man," she said, stepping forward and giving him a hug. "And to see how Doris was doing."

He looked to her living room window where the soft glow of the standard lamp looked warm against the curtains. "How is she?

"She's fine." Cathy looked concerned. "But it's you I'm worried about."

"Me? Why?"

"Come on, I'm going to take you for a drink and maybe something to eat."

"But why?"

"Because I want to. Now just get in."

Cyril glanced at his neighbour's living room window and thought he saw the curtains move. He smiled to himself as he climbed into the passenger side of Cathy's Vauxhall. She sat down in the driver's seat and turned on the ignition.

Fifteen minutes later, they'd pulled to a halt in the car park of The Bricklayers Arms in Little Bentley. Another five and they were seated at a table near a log fire which provided a comfortable atmosphere. Cyril took a sip of his beer and scanned the handful of drinkers seated at the other tables. "I haven't been in here for years. What made you choose this place?"

"I thought we'd get away from anyone who might know us. I think you need a change of scene." Cathy put her gin and tonic to her lips.

"You did, did you?"

"We did."

"Who's 'we'?"

She placed her glass down on the drinks mat before looking up at Cyril. "Well Doris is a bit worried and Sam told me he was concerned about you too."

"Was he now?"

"He reckons you haven't seemed your usual self. And I must admit you've been a bit quiet with me too."

Cyril seemed to focus on anywhere but her. "Sorry Cathy it's just ..."

"It's okay. If you don't want to talk about it ..."

"No, it's not that ..." He put his hand to his head, exhaled, then looked straight at her. "I think you know me well enough to know that I hate loose ends, I hate people escaping justice and I hate fellow officers who don't play by the rules."

Her eyes opened wide. "Wow. That's some statement."

"Sorry, I shouldn't be burdening you with this."

"So if you didn't, who else would you be letting off steam with?"

He gave a wan smile.

"So I'm assuming it's this Elsie Smart situation you've become embroiled in?"

"It's a bit more complicated than that."

Cathy remained silent and let Cyril consider how much he should tell her.

Eventually, he spoke. "Anything I tell you must not be repeated anywhere."

She eyed him with astonishment.

"I'm sorry, I know you're discreet." He proceeded to tell her of his suspicions surrounding DCI Albert Burns' handling of the investigation in 1947 along with Roy Viney as his DC. He also outlined the connections between Woods and the events in London's East End in 1941.

"I'm shocked," she said when he'd finished. "The trouble is, it's all so long ago and your main suspect is dead."

"I know. That's the hard part. Not only has this character escaped justice but Elsie's parents have gone to their graves not knowing who was responsible for their daughter's death."

"And on top of that, the man responsible for allowing this to happen has escaped punishment too," Cathy added.

"But then we have the DCS."

"Mr Viney? I think you need to tread carefully there, Cyril."

"That's what Barton and Sanderson think too." He rubbed his face with both hands.

"Are you thinking of making a formal complaint?"

"At the end of the day, what good will it do? The only one left around who bears any responsibility is DCS Viney, and he's lying in a hospital bed. The truth is, Cathy, I'm becoming more disillusioned with this job every day. I'm not sure I want to carry on."

She reached over and took hold of his hand. "Listen, you need to sleep on this. Talk to other people."

"Like who?"

"Doris. She has a lot of common sense. Then there's Sam."

He gently shook his head. "I can't involve Sam in this anymore. He's just beginning his career."

"He looks up to you. If the police service is to improve, he needs to inherit your standards."

He broke into a broad grin. "I love that you have such a naive clear view of things at times." He drained his pint. "Fancy a Chinese?"

She smiled at him. "Take it back to mine and it's a deal."

# 51
## Sunday 5th March 1978

Cyril had returned home on Sunday morning. On Saturday, he and Cathy had driven out to Dedham, one of their favourite spots, where he'd taken Cathy on their first 'date' about eighteen months ago. He much enjoyed the time spent together and loved the opportunity to clear his mind of all the events of the past few weeks. He was still unsure as to what to do with what he'd discovered. Cathy suggested he speak to Doris, who had a wise head on her shoulders.

"Come in, Cyril," she greeted when she answered his ring on the bell. "Why didn't you just come straight in? You have the key."

"I don't like to be presumptions, Doris," he responded, with a smile on his face, repeating her comments.

"Tea?" she asked, as she made her way to the kitchen.

"Of course. How are you doing, by the way?"

She switched on the kettle and took a couple of mugs from a cupboard. "A few twinges now and again, but that's only to be expected. I'm almost as good as new."

"We'll have to shoot you."

"Only when the time comes," she chuckled. "Anyway, how was your weekend?"

"You saw out the window on Friday night, didn't you?"

She cocked her head and smiled.

Cyril nodded. "It was good. Simon was at his uncle's and went to the football yesterday His uncle had tickets for Arsenal. " He grew serious. "I needed time away to think."

"I thought so. Sit yourself down in the lounge and I'll bring our teas in. There's the Sunday paper in there, if you want to have a look."

Cyril wandered into the front room, picked up the paper and sat down on the sofa but there wasn't much of interest that Sunday. A few minutes later, Doris appeared with two mugs of tea and some buttered toast. "Thought you might be hungry," she said.

"Wonderful." He stood, took hold of his mug and plate and sat back down.

Doris sat in her favourite armchair, her tea and toast on a small side table. "So what's on your mind, Cyril?" she finally asked.

"Oh, it's just ..." He hesitated, a mouth full of toast. "Have you always been sure of what you're doing? Have you ever doubted the path you sometimes take?"

"Sounds like we're into some pretty heavy philosophical stuff here."

"No, not really."

She put her mug down and looked serious for a moment. "I do wonder whether I perhaps shouldn't have mentioned Elsie Smart's name to you. That's what's started all of this."

"I suppose it was. But I'm glad you did." He sipped his tea. "It does make me wonder how many other Elsie Smarts there are out there." He put his mug down and looked earnestly at his neighbour. "It's like when you pointed out to me in the paper you brought round that day about another Yorkshire Ripper victim and I said I thought that at any one time there could probably be two or three serial killers at large in this country that no one yet knows about."

"You think she might have been the victim of a serial killer?"

"Well I suspect she was murdered by someone who had killed before."

"And you're frustrated that people didn't do their jobs properly and that connection wasn't discovered?"

"How do you? …" He had a puzzled expression which melted into one of understanding. "Cathy."

Doris smiled. "She's a lovely woman. Don't be annoyed with her because we talk. Whatever she says goes no further. I hope you can believe that."

He nodded. "I do. And I'm glad you're friends."

"So am I, especially if you'd like to take things further."

"What?"

"Well you know Maureen and I became close. She confided a lot in me. I've already told you she said I should encourage you if you ever found someone else after she'd gone."

Tears began to form in Cyril's eyes at the memories of his late wife. "Cathy isn't the thing that's disturbed me, Doris." He paused as he swallowed the last piece of toast and washed it down with a mouthful of tea. "It's the incompetencies and sheer selfishness of others that's gnawing away at me. I'm not sure if I want to continue in this job anymore."

"You can't walk away, Cyril. You know that. You still have work to do. I'm sure Maureen would say that too."

"You think so?"

"I do." Just then movement through the window caught her eye. "Is that your DI Barton that's just walked up your path?" she asked.

He jumped to his feet and looked out the window. "Where?"

Just then Barton walked a few steps back down Cyril's path and looked up at his upstairs windows.

"Just a minute," Cyril said, before walking into Doris's hallway. He opened the front door. "Looking for me?"

Barton remained where he was on Cyril's path, looking serious. "We need to talk, Cyril."

He made his apologies to Doris, walked back to his own house and led Barton inside.

Once settled in the living room, Barton broke the news. "I'm sorry to have to tell you that Roy Viney died in the early hours of this morning. He'd suffered another heart attack and, despite their best efforts, he didn't survive."

"Christ." Cyril sat down. "Was this anything to do with our visit on Friday? The DCI and myself, I mean?"

"I doubt it. His heart was in a bad way, according to the doctors."

"God, Mary will be devastated. I'm assuming the DCI knows?"

Barton sat down on the sofa. "It was Martin who rang me this morning. We both tried to call you but there was no answer. That's when I decided to call round."

"Thanks. I appreciate that. I suppose it's too early to know what arrangements will be made."

Barton nodded. "I think Martin will be advising Mary and making sure everything is in order for her."

"That's right, he was sorting out his retirement and pension situation. This has thrown all that up in the air." He shook his head. "And on the subject of what we discussed on Friday, that effectively wipes out any point of conducting an examination into the actions of the investigation team in 1947."

"Look, I know this is eating you up, Cyril, but I think it's time to let it go." Barton stood up. "Anyway, I just thought you should know before you come in tomorrow." He broke into a broad grin. "Now, Donna's doing me a nice Sunday lunch."

Cyril got to his feet. "Enjoy, John," he said. "And thanks for letting me know."

# 52
## Monday 6$^{th}$ March 1978

There was a solemn atmosphere in the CID room next morning. DCI Sanderson called the officers to a briefing at eight and told them of the news of Detective Chief Superintendent Viney's demise, although all seemed to know already.

He concluded by saying, "I know you will all miss the DCS but he'd want us to carry on and perform our jobs to the best of our ability. Obviously, you will be informed of any arrangements in due course. Okay, gentlemen, carry on." Before he left the room, he motioned for Cyril to follow him.

As Cyril passed, he saw Ben Miller turn to Bill Walker and heard him quietly say, "None of us had that much to do with him anyway so I'm not sure how much we'll miss him."

Cyril glared at him as he followed DCI Sanderson from the room.

"Sit down a minute, will you," the DCI said when they entered his office. Sanderson walked round his desk and sat in his chair. "Christ, this is the worst news."

"It is for Mary Viney, sir," Cyril responded, "but on the other side of the coin, there's probably not much point pursuing any of what we've discovered in the past few days."

"Not like you to be so cynical, Cyril."

He ignored the jibe. "I just hope it wasn't our discussions with him that brought about his end."

"Mary told me the specialists had said his heart was in a poor condition. They reckon it had gone undiagnosed for years."

"So what do we do now?"

"I can't see there's much more to investigate. Both main players in the 1947 enquiry are no longer with us, the man suspected of murdering Elsie Smart is dead. So, case closed."

"There is one other thing, sir," Cyril said.

"We have no real evidence of foul play in the death of Trevor Harrison, otherwise known as Graham Woods, so I suggest we let that lie too."

"I wasn't actually thinking of that but, I take your point."

"Well just put those files back in the archive then, Cyril and we can get on with our other duties."

He stood and left the DCI's office and headed back to the CID room.

When he arrived, he walked over to Sam Woodbridge who was sitting at his desk. "Come on, Sam," he said.

"Where are we going, skip?"

"I owe Eddie Smart an explanation of what we've discovered. And older brother, Reggie, for that matter," Cyril grabbed his coat from the stand by the door to the CID room as Woodbridge followed in his wake.

On the way to see Eddie Smart, Cyril changed his mind and decided not to visit Reggie. He didn't want to be pressured into revealing who the suspect was. It would do no good to tell him that he'd given the man a job and employed him for about twenty years. That would be like rubbing salt in the wound and he saw nothing to be gained in that.

So Cyril drove to the site where he'd met Eddie the week before. As he pulled up, he could see his van parked on the road. Some workmen were laying paving and a pallet of turf had been delivered too. No doubt, an instant garden would be produced in a few days.

This time, he was directed to one of the houses. As they walked to the door, Woodbridge glanced across at another van he recognised. Once inside, Cyril found Eddie upstairs in a back bedroom, sitting on an upturned crate having a drink of tea from a flask by his feet and the radio on.

"Mr Smart," he said, "Eddie, can I have another word?"

Smart pulled a foil pack from the rucksack he had behind him. "As long as you don't mind me having my breakfast."

Cyril smiled. "Won't keep a working man from his food," he said.

Smart unwrapped the package to reveal some butties then took a bite. "The wife makes these for me. Delicious." He swallowed a mouthful. "So how can I help you now?"

"Actually, I've come to inform you of some recent developments."

"Oh?"

"We think we now know who may have been responsible for your sister's death."

Smart stopped mid bite and looked shocked. "Don't you mean my sister's murder?"

"Apologies, yes."

"So who was it?"

"It's a bit complicated."

"I assume you'll be bringing charges?"

"I'm afraid that won't be possible."

"Why?"

"You see, the suspect is dead."

"What?"

"I'm afraid that after making further enquiries, it would appear that the man we suspect is already dead." Cyril had no intention of providing any further details. He saw no benefit in releasing names or circumstances.

"So that's it. Case closed once again." Smart shook his head in frustration. "It's just like before. Who was the bastard?"

"I'm sorry, I'm not at liberty to provide any more information than that."

Smart stood up. "You can't just walk in here and tell me this and expect me to accept it. When Reggie finds out he'll go ape."

Just then, another man walked into the room. "Hey, Eddie," he said. "Have you seen the site manager?"

"I think he's in number four, Alfie."

As the man turned to leave, Smart spoke to him, "Here, have you heard this? The police here reckon they found who murdered my sister all those years ago but they're ..." He put both hands in the air as if forming speech marks. "... not allowed to tell me who."

"That's ridiculous."

As he turned to leave, Alfie threw a quick glance towards Woodbridge who didn't react.

"So come on, I need a name," Eddie persisted.

"Look, Mr Smart, I can't tell you that. It's only a suspicion and if he was still alive, we'd need more evidence than we've got."

The man visibly sagged and sat back down on the crate.

They heard Taylor leave by the front door. Woodbridge asked the plasterer, "That was Mr Taylor, wasn't it?"

"Alfie, yes. Do you know him?"

Woodbridge looked to Cyril. "Mr Taylor was the electrician who attended those flats on that enquiry you asked me to look into." He was purposely circumspect. "I thought I recognised the van."

A wave of stimulation came over Cyril. "Oh really?" he answered before turning his attention back to Smart. "Which house is he working in?"

"I think he's in bungalow number three now."

"How well do you know him?" Cyril asked.

"Alfie? Yeah, we go way back. Orphaned in the war, he was. Brought up by his grandparents in Holland." Smart was referring to the town rather than the country. "I think it was his grandad that got him into being a sparky. Left their tidy little bungalow to him, they did."

"Has he got any other relatives, do you know?"

"I think it's his niece, although she looks like she could be his younger sister. Nice looking woman. She's a nurse, you know."

Again Cyril had that feeling in the pit of his stomach telling him that he was on to something.

"Anyway, why do you want to know all this?"

"I'm just curious about people really. Anyway, come on, Sam, we need to get on. I'm really sorry I can't disclose any more information but we're satisfied the perpetrator is dead."

They left the room with Eddie Smart shaking his head in disbelief and reaching for his flask to top up his tea.

Back outside, they stood and watched the groundworkers laying slabs in the garden two down from them. "I didn't like keeping what we know back but can you imagine how his older brother would feel, Sam?" Cyril looked around and nodded to a bungalow on the other side. "Number three's over there. Let's go and have a word."

Alfie Taylor was engaged in a second fix operation, wiring up sockets in the kitchen. He looked up and rolled his eyes when Cyril and Woodbridge walked in but continued with his work.

"Mr Taylor, Alfie," Cyril said.

"What do you want with me?"

"I understand from my colleague here that you were called to rectify a fault in some flats on Cathedral Road recently."

"What of it?"

"I believe you came across a Mr Trevor Harrison then?"

"The old boy who died? I told your colleague here all I know. We had some conversations, as you do when you're working in somebody's house, but I finished that job over a month ago."

Woodbridge opened his notebook and flicked through a few pages. "Second of February, you said."

"Yeah, that's right."

"Did you ever see Mr Harrison again after that?"

"No, why should I?"

"Tell me about your niece, Mr Taylor."

Taylor stopped what he was doing, surprised at the change of subject. "My niece? Trish? What about her?"

"Does she live in Clacton?"

"Yeah, why?"

"What does she do?"

He put down his screwdriver. "She's a nurse, why?

"Attached to a practice not far from Cathedral Road?"

"Look, what's all this about? Why are you so interested in Trish?"

"She's Sister Pat Nelson, is she not?"

Taylor stiffened. "What if she is?"

"Just curious, Mr Taylor. Thanks for your time."

Cyril turned and abruptly left with Woodbridge following behind.

Once in the car, Cyril drove them quickly away before pulling in to the side of the road.

"What was all that about, skip?" Woodbridge asked.

"That was a striking coincidence. And I don't believe in coincidences."

Woodbridge was puzzled. "I don't get it."

"Let's get on," Cyril said.

"Where to now?"

"I think we need to speak to the lovely Sister Pat Nelson."

# 53

When the pips sounded, Alfie Taylor pressed the coins into the slot. "Can I speak to Sister Nelson please?" he said. "It's urgent."

*"Who's calling please?"* the receptionist answered.

"Tell her it's her Uncle Alfie. And it's extremely urgent."

*"I'm afraid she's out on her rounds at the moment. We're not expecting her back until after two."*

Taylor glanced at his watch. Ten minutes to eleven. "Thanks," he said and hung up.

"Shit! Shit! Shit!" He thought for a second then came to a decision.

He knew the rough boundaries of her patch and he knew her distinctive orange Hillman Imp. He'd drive around until he spotted it. It was vital he speak to her before the coppers did.

It took him just over half an hour, but finally, he spotted her car parked on a street not far from Cathedral Road where the bastard had lived. Rain had begun to fall and he occasionally switched on the wipers so he could see where Trish would come from. Ten minutes after parking up, she appeared.

He got out of the van and approached her.

She was surprised. "Alfie? What are you doing here? Are you working nearby?"

"We need to talk." He checked his watch and looked up and down the road. "Follow me. I know a quiet pub."

"But I've still got three patients to see."

He grabbed her by both elbows. "This is important."

She could see from his face that something was seriously wrong. Reluctantly, she agreed and followed his van to a back street pub not far from town. He was right, it was a quiet place. There was one other customer at the bar when they entered. He ordered a pint for himself and a lemonade for Trish then took the drinks through to an empty rear lounge. He sat at a table in a corner where he could see anyone entering.

"Okay, Alfie, what's all this subterfuge about?" she eventually asked.

He took a gulp of his pint then answered. "I've had police round where I'm working."

"And?"

"They were asking about Woods, or Harrison, as they called him. They asked me when I last saw him. You know I had another dick ask me all about me working at his flat the other week?"

"You told me."

"Well he was there with this other more senior character." Taylor took a breath. "They asked about you too."

"Me!"

Taylor shushed her. "I only referred to you as 'Trish', but he came back asking if you were Sister Pat Nelson."

"What did this senior detective look like?"

He described Cyril.

"Sounds like the bloke who came to see me a couple of weeks ago."

"What did he ask?"

"About Harrison. I had to admit I visited him standing in for Sister Gallagher. Christ this is worrying. How did he connect me to you? He obviously knew, otherwise why immediately say my full name when you always refer to me as Trish?"

"I don't know but we need to stay calm. As far as we're concerned, I never saw the bastard after I finished the work at the beginning of February and you never saw him after your visit on the morning of the ninth."

"Do you think anyone saw us when we went in that night?"

"Look, it was dark, it was raining, I parked my van well away in another street. You did the same. We passed nobody. Well I certainly didn't. Did you?"

"Not that I noticed."

"Right, well, they won't have anything. We stick to our story. The last time I saw him was February the second. It was only coincidence that I happened to be working in those flats. You saw him only when you were substituting for your colleague on the morning of the ninth."

"If you hadn't noticed that birthmark on his arm and I hadn't seen it when I was taking his bloods ..."

"We wouldn't have discovered the bastard."

"But ... "

"Listen, we were never there on the evening of 9th February, remember that."

"What did you do after I left?"

"As I said I would, I put some banana skins in the bin in the flat and some in the outside bin. And I put some of the insulin syringes and needles below that, well hidden."

"And I took my syringe, needle and vial back to the surgery where I'd taken that vial."

"So don't worry, there's nothing to implicate us."

* * *

## Thursday 9th February 1978

He paused briefly to look behind him checking there was no one about. Satisfied, he dodged up the path between the overgrowing privet hedges that provided cover from any prying eyes. The light rain that had been falling since lunchtime was becoming heavier and darkness had fallen a couple of hours ago. There was a dim light visible through the upstairs front room window curtains. Good, he thought, the bastard's in.

He walked up to the door and pressed the bell. He heard it ring inside. A few seconds later, through the small obscure glass panels in the top of the door, he saw the hall light go on then a shape slowly heading down the stairs towards the door.

"Hello?" an old man's voice said. "Who is it?"

"Council, Mr Harrison," he said. "Electrician. I was here the other week to fix that fault. I just need to do some more testing."

"It's a bit late, isn't it?"

"It's something that needs to be carried out during the hours of darkness."

Reluctantly, the old man opened the door a crack and peered out. "Oh, I remember you," he said.

He lifted his tool box off the ground. "That's right, Mr Harrison."

The door opened to allow him in.

The old man turned and began to climb the stairs. "Where do you need to be?" he asked.

"Meter cupboard at the top of the stairs." He followed him up.

"You know where you're going then," Harrison said before walking down the hallway towards his living room.

Opening the toolbox, he pulled out a couple of bananas. "You don't want one of these, do you?" he asked before the man had disappeared. "I haven't had my tea yet."

Harrison turned. "Oh, a banana. No thanks," he responded. "I can't have them with my heart condition."

He gave a wry smile. "I'll bet you can't," he said to himself.

As arranged, a couple of minutes later, the doorbell rang.

"I'll get that for you, Mr Harrison."

"Who the hell is it now at this time of night," the old man shouted from the living room.

"Don't worry, I'll find out. If they're Jehovah's Witnesses I'll get rid of them."

"Tell them to piss off," Harrison shouted.

He descended the stairs and opened the door to the woman. "Come in," he said. "He's in the living room. Did anybody see you?"

"No, and I've parked around the corner."

"Good. You got everything?"

"Yes." She began to climb the stairs, carrying her bag.

He closed the door and followed her up.

It was when he was called in to investigate an electrical fault at the block of four flats a couple of weeks before, that he'd come across Trevor Harrison. He thought there was something familiar about him, but the name had put him off. However, Harrison had answered the door without a shirt, dressed only in a vest and trousers held up by braces. If he hadn't appeared like that then he might not have had his suspicions. It was his bare left arm, exposing the distinctive oval shaped birth mark that increased his heart rate. After he'd spotted it, he studied the man's face more closely. Nearly thirty-three years may have passed since he last saw him but he was now positive. The man before him may call himself Trevor Harrison but he was sure he was actually Graham Woods.

"I've seen him, Trish," he'd said to her on the phone that night.

"Who?"

"Woods. The bastard that murdered your mother; my big sister."

"But … where?"

"Here in Clacton."

"Are you sure?"

"He has the oval birthmark just below the left elbow. Then I studied his face. He might be thirty years older but it's definitely him."

"God, what are we going to do?"

"I'll think of something. But don't worry, we *will* get him."

Over the course of the next few days, a plan was formulated. And now, here they were in Harrison's flat.

"It's the nurse, Mr Harrison," she shouted as she made her way along the hallway.

"Oh, I wasn't expecting you," Harrison said from the living room.

When she walked in he was pleasantly surprised to see it was the nurse who had visited him that morning; the pretty one. "Is there something wrong?"

"I've had the results of your blood tests I took this morning and we just need to give you a boost." She sat down in the chair opposite his and opened her bag.

The electrician, meanwhile had followed her up the hall and was standing outside the doorway to the room, waiting.

"Now before I do, can I check a few details?"

"How do you mean?"

She removed a card from her bag. "I have here, Trevor Harrison, date of birth 28th June 1907."

"That's right."

The electrician walked into the room. "Except it isn't, is it?"

Harrison looked up, confused. "What? What's it got to do with you? What are you saying?"

"Your real name is Graham Woods, date of birth 27th March 1912. So you're actually only sixty-five and not seventy as you claim."

"No. No. You're crazy."

"Not me, Graham. You see, I remember you. You might be some thirty-three years older than when we last met on VE Day in that pub near Trafalgar Square but I definitely remember you."

"I … I don't remember."

"More convenient to forget, I suppose." The electrician stepped closer. "That was the day you smacked me. In the pub toilets before you ran off."

"I don't know what you're talking about."

The electrician shook his head. "You might try and deny that but what I want to know, what we both want to know is, what happened that last night of the Blitz? You remember that? The 10th and 11th May 1941. You were back in the Mile End Road to see your mother because your father had died."

"No idea what you're on about. Who are you anyway?"

"My name is Taylor. Alfie Taylor. Remember me now?"

Harrison looked down then across to the nurse. "I've no idea what he's on about."

"Stop it! Stop lying." Alfie took another step towards Harrison. "You were with my sister Gladys in the pub. You were seen."

"I've had enough of this ..." The man made to rise but Alfie grabbed him firmly by the upper arms and pushed him back into the chair. The fear was etched on his face. He was obviously an ill man and not strong enough to resist.

"Now, are you going to start telling the truth?"

Harrison looked again at the nurse. "Help me," he said.

"If you roll up your sleeve I'll help you," she said. "I need to give you an injection."

He began to comply, exposing the tell-tale birth mark. "How can you let him say these things?"

She'd produced a syringe from her bag along with a vial. Drawing up some fluid, she ejected any air from the syringe. "Because," she said slowly, "Gladys Vaughan, Alfie's sister was my mother."

Harrison looked shocked. "Patricia? You're little Patricia?"

Alfie leaned over him. "Memory come back has it, Graham?"

Harrison looked from one to the other and back again, opened and closed his mouth several times but never actually spoke.

"So what happened that night?"

He covered his face with both hands and began to sob. "Oh God," he said. "You don't understand."

"Try us," Alfie said.

"We were ... friends."

"Friends?"

"Well, more than that."

Alfie grabbed him by the lapels of his shirt and raised him off the chair.

"It ... it's true," he whimpered. "We'd been friends for a long time."

Patricia put her hand up to Alfie and he dropped him back down onto the chair.

"Glad … she liked older … men," he stuttered. "I was twenty-nine then and she was …"

"Only twenty-one," Alfie interrupted. "I know."

"We got talking one night in the Arms. She'd started working there just before the war when she was eighteen. Well, we just sort of hit it off."

"Are you seriously trying to tell me she liked you?"

"She did. But it wasn't only me; she enjoyed the company of men."

Alfie's anger grew once again. "Are you trying to tell me she was a tart?"

"No. No, that's not what I'm saying. But I did take her out a few times. That was before she met Tommy."

Alfie began pacing the room.

Woods carried on. "I met him once. He seemed alright but then he went away and I remembered her telling me his ship had gone down. She was distraught. There was one time when I was back on leave and we … you know."

Alfie stopped and looked at the man, his fists balled. "I don't believe you, you cretin."

"She was a young woman with needs. She also liked it a bit risky. It was what did it for her. That last time I was home to see my mum after dad died, we met up in the pub. Then the sirens went off. 'You'll need to go to the shelter,' I said to her. 'Why don't we stay out,' she said. 'Don't you think it would be exciting to do it and not know if we'd be blown to bits?' I tell you, at times she was just crazy."

Alfie started pacing again and put both hands to his head as if to tear his hair out.

"She said she knew where there was a place near a bombed out house, so that's where we went." Woods looked at Alfie through wild eyes. "She also liked … other things. She was fascinated by something around her neck. I'd bought a pair of stockings for her but she wouldn't wear them. Instead, she wrapped one around her neck. She wanted me to pull it tight. Then the bombs started dropping. The noise was ... I know that most were a good mile or so away down at the docks, but there were some nearer than that. With the sounds of the planes' engines, the ack ack guns and the explosions, we just got carried away. Then I noticed she wasn't responding, she'd gone limp. And that's when I realised … It was a complete accident. Honest.

"I was panicking. What could I do? We were in the middle of a bloody big bombing raid. It was obvious she was gone. There was nothing to be done."

"And you were hoping that one of those bombs dropped on that shit house where you left her and there would be nothing left to find." Alfie leaned over him, his face inches from his. "But someone did. I found her. Can you imagine what that's been like carrying that image round with me all these years?" Alfie was tapping his head with both hands. "No you bloody can't. You're a fucking coward. You were a coward on VE Day when you ran away from me. Christ you're pathetic." Alfie turned to the nurse. "Trish, do what you need to do."

Patricia held his arm and aimed for a vein. "Hold your arm steady."

"What is this? What are you doing?"

Alfie bent over the man to hold him down.

"Just keep still. I told you your blood results mean you need this injection."

As Alfie held his arm, Patricia found the vein and inserted the needle.

"No! No! I don't trust you!" He struggled but Alfie held him firm.

Slowly, she pushed the plunger and the fluid entered his blood stream. But he struggled and the needle came out. She moved back. "Let him go, Alfie."

Woods looked ashen. "What have you done?" He struggled to get to his feet.

They watched as he staggered to the door then stumble down the hallway. Following him, they watched, mouths open.

"You don't … understand …" he said, grabbing at his shirt, his features contorted in pain. He made to grab the door frame before finally disappearing through the staircase door at the end of the hall. As he fell, they heard him say, “I’m your … dad, Patricia.”

The sounds of a heavy impact on the stairs then silence.

Alfie and Pat looked at one another then rushed to the end of the hall.

* * *

## Monday 6th March 1978

Trish was tearful. “But what he said … that night …”

“He wasn’t your dad.”

“But his blood group; B negative. That’s the same as me and only about two per cent of the population have that.”

“No, he couldn’t be.”

“I think it’s entirely possible.”

Alfie shook his head. “She loved Tommy. She wouldn’t be involved in a shit bag like Woods.”

“Look, as you said, we need to stay calm. It sounds like the police need to speak to me again. You too, probably. So let’s see what happens and, as you say, we stick to our stories. If they try and trick us by saying either of us has changed them, we resist. We don’t believe them.”

“Agreed.”

“Now, I need to get back to complete my rounds.”

# 54
## Tuesday 7th March 1978

The phone rang on Cyril's desk just after nine that morning.

"Hello," he answered.

*"Cyril, I've got two people here to see you,"* George Kidby said.

"Oh yes. Who are they?"

*"An Alfie Taylor and Patricia Nelson."*

"Thanks, George, I'll be down in a bit. Oh, by the way, are the interview rooms free downstairs?"

*"Both clear, yes."*

Yesterday, after they left the site, Cyril and Woodbridge had driven to the surgery where Sister Nelson worked. It had been just after eleven o'clock when they strode into the Surgery reception. About half a dozen patients were seated in the waiting area. A mother and a young baby, four elderly women and a man.

"Can I help," the receptionist had asked.

Cyril discreetly showed his warrant and asked to speak to Sister Nelson.

"A popular lady," she'd said. "Just had someone else on the phone for her. Unfortunately for you, she's out on her rounds. We don't expect her back until after two."

"Okay, nothing too urgent." Cyril produced a card from his wallet. "If you could ask her to call me at Clacton Police Station when she can, I'd appreciate it."

"Sure."

"Oh, by the way, who else was looking for her?"

She looked down at a notepad. "He said he was her Uncle Alfie."

"Thanks." Cyril turned and gave Woodbridge a small smile.

He wasn't surprised they'd come in together; probably rehearsed their stories to word perfection. He looked over and saw Sam Woodbridge at his desk, sifting through some paperwork. He made his way over.

"Busy, Sam?"

"Not especially, no. Why?"

"The EastEnders are downstairs."

Woodbridge looked confused

"Alfie Taylor and Pat Nelson," Cyril clarified. "Come on, let's see if they've got their stories straight."

Downstairs, Cyril greeted the pair. "Mr Taylor if you'd like to accompany DC Woodbridge to Interview Room One, while Mrs Nelson if you would like to follow me."

"I thought you'd want to speak to us together," Taylor said, a slight panic in his voice.

"No," was all Cyril said and ushered the nurse down the corridor.

"This way, Mr Taylor," he heard Woodbridge say.

Room 2 had a high level window and a basic table with three chairs, two on one side and one on the other. Patricia automatically made her way round the table and sat in the chair on its own.

"If you could make yourself as comfortable as you can, I'll be back shortly," Cyril said, before heading back to join Sam in Interview Room 1.

That room was very similar to the one where Patricia Nelson was waiting. Woodbridge had seated himself opposite Taylor. When Cyril walked in, Taylor looked annoyed. "What's going on here?" he said. "We came in this morning because you were asking to speak to Trish."

"All in good time, Mr Taylor." Cyril sat in the vacant chair next to Woodbridge. "Now, first of all, I'd just like to get your statement about when you were last at Mr Harrison's flat."

Woodbridge opened his notebook.

Taylor glanced across at the DC. "I've told you, it was when I finished those electrical works on 2nd of February."

"You never returned at a later date?"

"No."

"Did you recognise Mr Harrison?"

"Recognise him? What do you mean?"

"You knew him from way back, didn't you?"

"I don't follow."

"Do you remember Mrs Bowman?"

Taylor seemed flummoxed for a moment. "What's that got to do with anything?"

"You do remember your old neighbour from when you were growing up?"

"Of course I do. Where's this going?"

"The last time you saw Harrison, I mean before you carried out those electrical repairs, you recognised him then."

"What are you on about?"

"VE Day. Where were you then?"

"I ... I went into London with a mate at the time."

"And did anything unusual happen?"

Taylor smirked and shook his head. "Have you spoken to Mrs Bowman? Is she still around."

"Oh, very much so."

"So she probably told you that I thought I saw a man in a pub in London who reminded me of someone I knew from the east end."

"And did you?"

"I ... I was mistaken."

"Really?"

"It was all so crowded and confusing then. People, service men and women, ordinary people, all celebrating."

"So you didn't think the man you saw was someone you recognised from the east end? A man with a distinctive birthmark just below his left elbow. Someone by the name of Graham Woods?"

Taylor was ashen but tried his best to keep his emotions from showing. "Who?"

"Come on Mr Taylor ..." He leaned in closer and spoke quietly. "Alfie, Graham Woods was the last person seen with your sister, Gladys, on the night she was murdered. And you found her the following morning."

Tears began to well in Taylor's eyes.

"And Trevor Harrison had that same birthmark."

Taylor wiped a hand across his face.

"I'll be back, Alfie. Have a good think about what you might want to tell me."

Cyril stood, left the room and made his way back to Interview Room 2.

"Sorry about that, Mrs Nelson," he said, as he entered the room. "I was just having an interesting conversation with your uncle. I've left him thinking hard." He sat down opposite her. "What I'd like to confirm is when you last saw Mr Harrison."

She was playing with her hands on the desk. "I told you when you came to see me the other week. It was Thursday morning, the 9th February."

"That's right, you said you conducted an examination of Mr Harrison, took bloods, performed observations."

"That's it."

"Which arm did you take bloods from?"

She removed her hands from the desk and sat back in her chair. "What? Er, the left."

"So you would have noticed the birth mark just below his left elbow."

A quick look of recognition passed across her face before her expression became neutral once again. "I don't remember. Is it important?"

"You tell me."

"I'm confused."

Cyril leaned forward. "I don't think your uncle is. You see, he recognised Mr Harrison. Except, he didn't know him under that name, well not until he turned up to carry out some electrical repairs on behalf of the council. *He* recognised the birth mark. He recognised it on VE Day up in London too. And he recognised it again when he was working at Mr Harrison's flat. He recognised him as Graham Woods."

Patricia blanched.

"That name means something to you too, doesn't it?"

"I've no idea what you mean."

"Come on Mrs Nelson, Alfie must have told you about Graham Woods. After all, he was the man who was last seen with your mother before Alfie found her body. He was the man suspected of murdering your mother, Alfie's sister."

"Stop it! Stop it!"

At that moment the room door burst open. DI Barton entered. "DS Claydon, a word."

"Not just now."

"Now!"

"Excuse us a moment," Barton said to the woman.

Reluctantly, Cyril stood and followed Barton out into the corridor, closing the door behind them.

"This stops now."

"But I'm making progress."

"DCI Sanderson wants to see you."

"But ..."

"But nothing. This is from the top."

Grudgingly, Cyril made his way with Barton to the first floor office of the DCI.

Once inside with the door closed, Sanderson spoke. "Cyril, I know you're heavily invested in this case but it stops now."

"But I'm getting somewhere. Alfie Taylor, the electrician who worked at the flats and his niece, Pat Nelson, the nurse who last attended Harrison ..."

Sanderson cut in on him with a firm voice. "This has come from the top. The ACC wants this wrapped up. DI Barton has prepared a report for the coroner. Mr Trevor Harrison died on 9th February 1978." Sanderson held up a hand to stop any interruptions. "Yes, Trevor Harrison; died of natural causes. There were no signs of a break-in or any foul play. That's it, end of. There will be no mention of Graham Woods; he died during the war."

Cyril was incredulous. "What about Alice Bowman and her daughter, Edith's identification?"

"They made no official statement. No, this ends now."

"So, just like Burns and Viney in 1947, we cover it up."

"Look, Cyril, it serves no purpose. All the main players are dead. What is it with all this self-flagellation?"

Cyril turned to Barton. "You found the body. Your nose was telling you something wasn't quite right. We have the raised potassium levels."

"*Slightly* raised potassium levels," Barton clarified.

"Raised all the same," Cyril persisted. "We have those two down there with connections to the victim. They have motive, they have opportunity, she definitely has the means."

Barton shook his head. "All because of one photograph. If he'd thrown it away; if names weren't added to the back."

"If. But it does exist and from what we've found out …"

"Enough!" Sanderson shouted. "We have our orders." He turned to Barton. "John, arrange for those two downstairs to leave."

# 55

Cyril stormed out of the police station and got into his car. Initially, he headed for the seafront. Unusually for early March, the sky was cloudless and the visibility was crystal clear. He wished his thoughts were. In a few weeks' time at the end of the month, the holidaymakers would be back and the front busy. Easter this year is early. He drove past the Butlin's Holiday Camp, the focus of so many of those looking for a break.

Some time later, he found himself pulling into the side of the road by the allotments. He needed time to think and this place always helped him do that. He'd prepared the ground to his own plot a couple of weeks ago, ready for some seed potatoes which he planned to put in over Easter. In the distance he saw a couple of figures working on their land. He sat down on the bench outside the shed where he kept his tools and looked out over the other allotments.

It frustrated him to think that he'd been thwarted by his bosses in solving a serious crime. He was sure Alfie Taylor and Patricia Nelson had contrived to murder Harrison or Woods. He thought they'd probably returned to his flat on the Thursday evening. That was when Mrs White down below had heard what she described as thumping around and raised voices. With Alfie having carried out some work not long before and Pat having visited in her nursing role earlier that morning, it was entirely possible for them to have persuaded the man to let them in. With the connection to Gladys's murder back in 1941 confirmed by the stockings, they would have had a strong motive to have carried out some form of assault on him, leading to his death. On the other hand, he had sympathy with the pair. They both felt that the man had murdered their sister or mother some thirty-seven years ago. A long time to wait for justice, if you could call it that.

He had his eyes closed, deep in thought, when he felt something rest on his knees. He looked down to see a pair of brown eyes looking up at him from a shaggy black dog's face.

"Dusty, come here," came a voice he recognised.

He looked up to see Frank Scowcroft walking towards him. "Sorry about that, Cyril."

"Don't worry Frank." Cyril ruffled the dog's head.

"He obviously likes you."

"They all love this." Cyril rubbed his fingers behind the dog's ears. "I didn't know you had a dog?"

"I don't. This is old Joe Penton's dog, my next door neighbour." Frank sat down on the bench next to Cyril. "He's gone into hospital this week, and to be honest, I don't think he'll come out."

Cyril looked down at the dog, contentedly looking up at him. "He'll be great company for you, Frank."

"I'd love to, Cyril but I'm too old for a dog now. I'm looking for a good home for him."

"He looks like he deserves it. How old is he?"

"He's two; so well trained. It's a shame really."

"How do you mean, a shame?"

"Well if we can't find another home, I'll have to call the RSPCA."

"You can't do that, Frank."

"Well the missus says we can't cope. It's all I can do to keep this place on." He waved a hand in the direction of his own allotment, two down from Cyril's.

"Anyway, how have you gotten on with that little puzzle you mentioned the last time we spoke? Elsie Smart."

Frank's question hit him in the gut. After a moment or two, he answered, "Been a bit busy on other things, Frank. You know how it is."

"Aye, well, I'm sure there's lots of mysteries like hers that are unsolved." He looked at Cyril. "So, what do you reckon to Dusty then? I reckon after losing your Charlie last year, he'd suit you just fine."

"I'm not sure the time is right, Frank. He ruffled the dog's head again and stood. "I best be off. I'll see you later."

"See you, Cyril."

As he reached the gate in the allotment fence, he turned round to see Frank at his plot. Dusty was lying down looking over towards him.

# 56
## Wednesday 8th March 1978

The two men walked into the reception area of Jackson Road Police Station just before midday. The taller of the two strode up to the front desk and confronted the desk sergeant.

"I need to speak to the man in charge."

George Kidby was unruffled. He'd seen it all before. "Which man would that be, sir?"

"Whoever is in charge here." The man prodded the counter with his finger.

The other man who was standing at his shoulder spoke. "Take it easy, Reggie."

Kidby looked to the shorter man then back to the other. "If you could tell me what it's about, I could get the right officer to have a word with you."

"Don't go giving me any of that flannel. I want to hear who you suspect of murdering my sister."

Kidby reacted. "I'm not aware we have any active murder enquiries."

"My sister, Elsie Smart. Your Sergeant Claydon told my brother, Eddie here, you'd solved the case. I want to know who. And don't bring me Sergeant Claydon. I want to speak to the top man."

"If you'd both like to take a seat," Kidby said, "I'll see who's available."

Eddie put a hand on his brother's shoulder and guided him towards the seats the officer had indicated. "Come on," he said, "Let's do as the sergeant suggests."

With a scowl, Reggie turned away reluctantly and sat down next to Eddie.

Kidby made a telephone call and ten minutes later, Barton appeared at the door to the side of the reception desk. "Mr Smart? Reggie, Eddie? If you'd like to follow me."

The pair rose and walked behind the DI down the corridor and into an interview room. "Please, take a seat," he said, "I'll just get another chair."

When he returned a few minutes later, Barton had not only brought another chair but DCI Sanderson followed him into the room.

Reggie took notice of the well-dressed Sanderson. "Are you the top man?"

"I'm Detective Chief Inspector Sanderson and this is my colleague Detective Inspector Barton. Now, the desk sergeant said you wanted to speak to a senior officer about the death of your sister, is that correct?"

"The murder of my sister, you mean. Elsie was murdered on January 30th 1947."

Sanderson held up both hands. "Apologies, Mr Smart, the murder of your sister. Now what is it we can help you with?"

"One of your officers, a DS Claydon, visited my brother, Eddie, and said you'd discovered who was responsible. But you couldn't bring any charges because he was dead."

Sanderson looked to Barton before focussing his attention on Reggie Smart. "Well, I'm not sure DS Claydon was authorised to tell your brother anything, but yes, we do think the perpetrator is deceased."

Reggie looked straight at Sanderson, his eyes moist. "You were also investigating a sudden death the other week too, weren't you?"

"We look into many cases of people who have died suddenly, Mr Smart. That's not to say any of those are connected with my last statement."

"Just tell me the truth. I need to know. Was your suspect Trevor Harrison?"

Sanderson tried to keep his expression neutral. "Like you've probably been told, there's nothing to be served by giving out any further information."

Reggie Smart stood up. “There bloody is! I need a conclusion. And I need to know if it was Harrison.”

Eddie put a hand on his brother’s arm and looked across at the two detectives. “We do need to know if Harrison was responsible. You see, my brother here gave him a break when he came out of prison back in ’59. He worked with him for twenty years.”

Reggie subsided back into his seat, tears now fully formed. “Have I been duped all that time? Has he taken the piss and abused my goodwill?”

Sanderson and Barton exchanged glances before Sanderson spoke. He saw no advantage in prevaricating any further. “We can’t absolutely say that Harrison was responsible for your sister’s murder but we strongly suspect he was.”

Reggie collapsed onto the table, his head on his arms, sobbing.

Eddie stood and put an arm around his older brother, tears rolling down his cheeks. “Thank you,” he said.

“Where the hell is Cyril?” Sanderson asked as he took the stairs up to the CID room. The Smart brothers had been offered words of condolence and shown out.

“I’d take it a bit easy with him, sir,” Barton responded. “He’s taken all this hard.”

“Hard? What was he doing telling them that we’d solved the case but there was nothing further to be done as the suspect was dead. He should have kept his mouth shut. What was it they said in the war about loose lips? Christ!”

Cyril was at his desk when Sanderson spotted him. “Cyril. My office.” With that, he turned and bundled past Barton to make his way down the corridor to his office.

“What’s up now?” Cyril asked Barton as he rose from his seat.

Barton put his finger to his lips and walked out into the hallway. Cyril followed.

In a voice just above a whisper, Barton told him about the Smart brothers’ visit. Before Cyril could protest,

Barton interrupted him. "Look I understand. But Mr Sanderson wants a word. Just keep your cool."

Barton led the way to Sanderson's office. Once inside, Cyril closed the door.

"Just what the hell did you think you were doing DS Claydon?" Sanderson began.

Cyril knew he was upset by the fact he'd addressed him with his title, but he kept calm. "In what way, sir?"

"In the way of telling the Smart brothers we'd solved the murder of their sister but there was nothing further to be done as the suspect was dead."

"I only told Eddie Smart. And I did not mention who our suspect is. I purposely did not tell his brother, Reggie. And I didn't approach him because I knew he'd employed Harrison after his release from prison and had worked with him for twenty years. He would have been devastated."

"Well, this morning, downstairs, he was."

Cyril thought a moment. "Eddie and Alfie Taylor work on the same building site. Eddie's a plasterer and Taylor is an electrician. Taylor came into the room when I was with Eddie. They must have talked afterwards and worked out a probable connection. But I did not mention any name."

"That's not the point. You had no right to tell any of them anything."

"Eddie needed to know."

Sanderson put his hands to his head. "God Cyril, what am I going to do with you?"

"My feelings exactly."

# 57
## Wednesday 12th April 1978

Steady rain was falling as Cyril pulled off Mersea Road and drove through the gates of Colchester Crematorium. There was a large cemetery to the right hand side but he kept left and drove down the lane to the parking area at the end and found a space. As he looked over at the red brick building, mourners from the previous service were extending their condolences to their nearest and dearest. There would be none of those for this one. He'd be surprised if he wasn't the only one attending.

This was in marked contrast to the funeral he'd felt obliged to attend two weeks ago. That was full of pomp and all sorts of hypocritical nonsense that Cyril couldn't stomach. Roy Viney's coffin had been brought here on a horse drawn hearse by two black horses with black plumage. Draped in a force flag with his police cap on top, it had been carried into the chapel by six police constables. Cyril had been told to attend in police uniform and had sat alongside DI Barton towards the rear. DCI Sanderson was towards the front, just behind the family, sitting with the Assistant Chief Constable. Cyril wondered if the ACC was aware of Roy Viney's involvement in the Elsie Smart investigation. He either was, and chose to ignore it, for the sake of the force, or he didn't, in which case, he should have been. But it was the ACC who had ordered the cessation of any further enquiries into the death of Trevor Harrison, as he'd been known, or Graham Woods as they knew he actually was.

Various bigwigs had offered words of condolence and uttered thanks for the service of the man in the coffin. If only half of them knew what he knew, they probably wouldn't have turned up. As it was, the chapel was full to overflowing.

After committal, as they left through the side doors, Cyril offered a hand to Mary Viney and a few words of condolence. After all, he didn't think she knew what her husband had been involved with, and shouldn't be tarred with the same brush.

As he left the widow, he was approached by the ACC. He offered his hand which Cyril felt obliged to take. Cyril recognised the handshake but didn't respond. "I hope you can let things lie, Cyril," he said, almost under his breath. "No good will be served by anything now. I hope you understand." He gave a false smile before quickly turning his attention to another high ranking officer.

Barton came over to him and put a hand on his shoulder. "I know, Cyril, but you can't win."

Cyril looked at him for a second before walking away.

The coroner had released the body and a solicitor acting for the estate had arranged the funeral.

Cyril stepped out of the car and locked it, pulling up the collar of his coat before hurriedly making his way to the chapel entrance. There was a vicar standing waiting for the hearse. He nodded a greeting towards him. "I'll just go in."

"There are two more inside already," the vicar responded.

Cyril was surprised. There again, they may just be a couple of' professional mourners. He'd heard of some elderly women turning up to random funerals. He walked into the chapel.

On the right hand side, half way down two figures were seated, a man and a woman, both wearing heavy coats with the collars turned up. He sat in the last row on the opposite side. But there was something vaguely familiar about the pair. The man, who was seated next to the aisle turned slightly, and that's when he realised who they were.

Some organ music began to play and the coffin was brought in on the shoulders of six pall bearers. It was a short service and fifteen minutes later, Cyril followed the other couple out past the vicar and into the courtyard.

"I thought it was you two," he said.

Alfie Taylor and Patricia Nelson turned to see the detective approach. They both looked down initially.

"I didn't expect to see you here," Cyril said. "Come to pay your respects?"

Taylor sneered. "Huh. We just wanted to make sure the bastard was actually dead."

"I thought you'd already confirmed that at his flat."

Taylor gave a laugh. "Very good. Now if you'll excuse us, we've wasted enough time on this as it is." He put an arm around his niece's shoulder to lead her away.

"I know you did for him." Cyril took a step closer. "But don't worry, I can't prove it, but I do know. I can't say I blame you. After all, he was responsible for Gladys's death."

Patricia threw her head back. "Maybe, maybe not. And just maybe he was my father."

At that they turned and left, leaving Cyril bemused.

# 58
## Saturday 16th April 1978

Bright sunshine broke through the clouds as Cyril drove through the entrance to Clacton's cemetery. Just a few days before he'd attended the funeral of the man known as Trevor Harris. Now, it was time to pay his respects to one of his innocent victims.

Behind him, another car drew to a halt. He looked in the mirror and saw Cathy climb out of the driver's seat. Sitting in the passenger seat was Doris.

He got out of his car and walked round to the other side and opened the passenger door.

"I think this is a lovely idea, Cyril," Beatty Palmer said, as she lifted herself out of the car.

"It's the least I can do," he responded.

A minute later, Cyril and Beatty were joined by Cathy, Doris and an excited black dog on a lead.

"I'll keep hold of Dusty for now," Cathy said.

Cyril looked down at his new friend. "Don't disgrace yourself in here."

The dog looked up at him and wagged his tail.

Doris and Beatty both held bouquets of flowers as they all set off down a few paths until they found the grave they wanted.

*In loving memory of a darling daughter and sister*
*Elsie Smart*
*born 25$^{th}$ June 1930*
*taken too soon 30$^{th}$ January 1947*
*also*
*Joseph Smart*
*died 5$^{th}$ March 1958, aged 58*
*and*
*Dorothy Smart*
*died 8$^{th}$ May 1974, aged 72*
*Reunited*

They stood in silence and read the epitaph. Dusty lay down, his head on his paws; he seemed to know.

In the base of the headstone, two metal flower pots sat in specially formed holes. It was obvious they hadn't been in use for years. "I'll just fill these up," Cyril said and took both pots over to the standpipe that was next to some waste bins.

When he returned, Cathy had given Dusty's lead to Doris and was on her knees separating the blooms. He placed the pots full of water back into the openings and Cathy began to arrange both bunches between them.

Finally, she got to her feet and all of them stood in contemplation.

Cyril wiped away a tear. "I'm sorry we let you down, Elsie," he said quietly. "Joseph, Dorothy, I'm truly sorry we let you down even more. Rest in peace now." He bowed his head.

"Rest in peace," Doris said.

"Yes, rest in peace," Cathy echoed.

"Sleep well, my young friend," Beatty said.

They remained silent for a few minutes more, then the four of them and Dusty turned and headed back to the cars, Doris and Beatty taking each other's arm while Cathy held on to Cyril. He had hold of Dusty's lead.

"I'm glad you found out who was responsible, Cyril," Doris said as they walked.

"Thirty-odd years too late though, Doris."

"They'll know."

"I'm sure they do," Beatty added.

After another quiet spell, Cathy said, "You did a great job, you know."

Cyril stopped and looked at her. "Did I? A pair of murderers got away."

She squeezed his arm. "You can't beat yourself up like that. There was no real proof the man was murdered."

"But I know he was and who did it."

They resumed walking. After a while, Cathy spoke again, "Have you decided what you're going to do? Are you staying or taking retirement?"

He paused again and looked at the dog, who sat down looking up at him with those brown eyes. "What do you think, Dusty?"

The dog cocked his head to one side then the other as if to say, 'I'm still considering it. I'll let you know.'

THE END

*Did you enjoy DISCOVERY?*

*Then please review on Amazon, Goodreads etc.*

*Have you read more in the series?*

*See the next few pages …*

# The Tendring Series

Book 1 DISPOSAL

August 1976 and it seems as though the long hot summer will never end. Early morning at Clacton on the north Essex coast, a light aircraft takes off from the airstrip but struggles for height and crashes into the sea. First on the scene, Sgt Cyril Claydon pulls the pilot's body from the wreckage. But something else catches his eye. A bulky package wrapped in black plastic is on the passenger seat. Returning to investigate, he makes a grim discovery – another body. And so begins a series of events that puts him and others in danger as he is drawn into the investigation, having to work alongside DI 'Dick' Barton, a man with totally alien attitudes.
Can they work together?

Available through Amazon:

http://mybook.to/Disposal

Book 2 DISTRESSED

1977. Clacton-on-Sea on the north Essex coast.
Despite previous friction between them, DS Cyril Claydon can't believe his DI, John 'Dick' Barton, is involved in a murder, despite evidence linking him to the victim and the crime scene. When Barton is the last person to visit his old boss in hospital before he too dies in mysterious circumstances, Cyril and Barton wonder if there is some sort of vendetta going on.
The deepening entanglement of an old crime with suspected rule bending and a new killer on the loose, means Cyril and the team have their work cut out to get to the truth.

Available through Amazon:

http://mybook.to/Distressed

*By the same author ...*

## The Wakefield Series

Book 1 TROPHIES

By the turn of the millennium, memories had dulled. But the discovery of a trophy case at the scene of a murder leads to the realisation that a series of attacks on women over the previous twenty years had gone unconnected. DI Colin Strong is convinced there is also a link with one other notorious unsolved crime. His best friend from schooldays, journalist Bob Souter, has returned to Yorkshire and begins to probe. Working separately and together in an awkward alliance, they seek the answers.

Available through Amazon:

http://mybook.to/Trophies

Book 2 TORMENT

A message left in error on a young woman's answerphone is the catalyst for uncovering some dark deeds. Three young women are missing; luxury cars are being stolen; and just what did happen to two young schoolgirls, missing since the 1980's?

DI Colin Strong and journalist Bob Souter are drawn into murky and dangerous worlds

Available through Amazon:

http://mybook.to/TormentDavidEvans

Book 3 TALISMAN

A man's body found naked and shackled to a frame in a house fire; a body lying undiscovered in a bath for over a year; massive European funding for a controversial construction project. Is there a link between the bodies and the business deal? And what exactly is the Talisman Club?

In the third instalment of the Wakefield series, DI Colin Strong and best friend, journalist Bob Souter must work together to bring the guilty to justice before time runs out.

Available through Amazon:

http://mybook.to/TalismanDavidEvans